REVIEW QUOTES FOR CAPTIVE SCOUNDREL

"One of Blair's early works, this one ranks right up there with the best of them. Written in the true tradition of the Rogues. Justin is yummy. Lots of sexual tension, with one surprise after another."

~ Lee Lee, Amazon

"Another winner by Annette Blair ... a fast paced read. Faith is sent to nurse the Duke of Ainsley, after he suffers what is believed to be fatal injuries. Hired by the duke's brother, Faith is given specific instructions in how to care for the duke, who is in a state of limbo.... Their journey will not be easy as they enter into a cat and mouse game to catch a madman ... and realize the fulfillment of their love."

~ Daisy, Vine Voice, Amazon

"Annette Blair is a master artist in the world of romantic fiction." Linda Lukow, MyShelf "Annette Blair is a master at sweeping you from one emotion to the next with the flip of a page."

~ Sandy M, The Good, the Bad, and the Unread

Captive Scoundrel

KNAVE OF HEARTS, BOOK THREE

by

Annette Blair

COPYRIGHT:

AMISH HISTORICAL ROMANCES

Butterfly Garden

Jacob's Return

A Winter Heart

CONTEMPORARY ROMANCES

Three Days on A Train

Sisters of Spirit

NOTE TO READER

SURPRISINGLY, THERE seems to be several schools of thought as to the length of the Regency Period. Purists say it lasted from 1811 to 1820, at the time George IV ruled as Regent during the well known "madness" of his father. Others say that the Prince Regent's influence lasted beyond 1820, and not until William IV came to the throne, in 1830, did the Regency period finally come to an end. And still others place the Regency at 1811 to 1837, when Queen Victoria succeeded William IV. For this series, I have chosen the broadest Regency timeframe.

DEDICATION

With love to my muse, Ruth Cardello,
And a big thanks to fate,
Because she sat next to me at her first meeting,
And inspired me to kick my career into overdrive
By kicking me into action.
Here's to humor, laughter, zest, and adventure.
Ruthie!

PROLOGUE

England, The Bognor Coast, May 1827

T HE STACCATO OF horse's hooves shattered dawn's silence. Fear clawed at Justin Devereux's soul, rage engulfed him. He wanted to roar his fury to the heaven ... but no one would hear him. Not even God.

"Damn you to hell and back Catherine Devereux!" Slowing his mount as the carriage trail disappeared, Justin took stock of his surroundings. Though he couldn't see it beyond the thicket, he approached the sea, for he could smell the brine and hear the burgeoning murmur of waves in the distance.

Despite his impatience, he urged his horse slowly on, through field madder and budding gorse. Tender-leafed oaks, ironically, augured new beginnings. Would to God it could be so.

Then he saw an old winding trail, its grasses recently trod by carriage and horses. A family of rabbits scattered as he quickened his pace. For the love of God, he thought, let those tracks be left by the coach carrying Beth.

Three years before, kicking and bawling, his daughter, Beth, had taken his heart in her wee hands the moment he gazed upon her. Before her birth, he'd thought his life a living hell. Now, without her, he truly knew what hell was. He would find her, he vowed, or perish in the doing.

Upon clearing the thicket, he froze.

A coach and four stood perilously close to the edge of the cliff, its horses snuffling, ribbons of early-morning fog swirling about them. The chanting, "see, see, see," of rock-pipits along the ledge stepping to the sea imparted a false sense of serenity.

Heart pounding, Justin dismounted to make his way toward the unfamiliar conveyance. Sensing movement, he whipped about and came face to face with Catherine, his wife. More's the pity. His brother stood beside her. "I should have known you would be involved in this, Vincent," Justin said.

Vincent bowed from the waist, his wide smile nearly grotesque on his dissipated features.

Catherine nodded. "We have what you want, do we not, my dear?"

"I have come for my daughter, as was your plan."

"Our daughter."

Justin laughed and knew by Catherine's look that she felt the insult he intended. "Since before her birth, Beth has been mine alone, and you've been more than content with the arrangement," he said. "Never even held her, damn your selfish hide." Fighting an overwhelming urge to wrap his hands around his wife's perfect white throat, Justin flexed his fingers to prove his control.

"Come now, dear brother," Vincent drawled, mocking the endearment. "You cannot remove a child from her mother."

"I can, if she would have it so. When she found she carried, she said bearing a child would ruin her, said she would—"

"Justin!" Catherine blanched and Vincent threw her a startled look.

For a moment Justin was relieved. Beth's conception must have predated intimate relations between them, else Vincent would have known Catherine's feelings. Then it occurred to him that Vincent's shock might stem from the fact that ... "Beth is mine," Justin affirmed. "Where is she?"

"Safe," Catherine said.

The word reassured Justin, likely because he wanted it so, but he didn't trust her and trusted Vincent even less. "She's a babe, Catherine. Do not use her as your pawn. Besides, I'm wise to you. You left a trail a fool could follow. Keeping Beth is not your plan; we both know that. What you want is freedom without the disgrace of divorce. Fine. Give her to me and you shall have the protection of my name. With my title and wealth at your disposal, the ton will forget my defection soon enough. I will take Beth and go away. Forever."

Catherine raised her chin, a gleam of satisfaction in her eyes.

"And you, Vincent, will have your heart's desire," Justin said.

At Catherine's smile, Justin shook his head. "I hate to break this to you, my dear, but you are not Vincent's desire." Studying his brother, Justin continued to address his wife. "His singular goal in life is to remain my heir. And he has as much as attained that by separating us forever. Divorce would do the same, of course, but it would ruin you both."

Vincent nodded his acknowledgment, making Justin want to plant the bastard a facer. Instead he stepped close to Catherine. "Now we will never produce a male heir." He lowered his voice. "Not that I've been inclined in recent years, as you well know."

When Catherine paled, Justin hated himself. Though he was stuck in the mire with them, he would lower himself no further. He sighed. "I want my daughter. Where is she?"

"Safe away from here," Catherine said.

God, how he wanted to believe her. "Where?"

"In the—"

Vincent backhanded Catherine across the face with a growl,

and felled her.

"Bastard!" Justin shouted, packing every bit of his frustration into the punch he dispensed. Justin gazed at Vincent lying in the dirt, before he lifted Catherine and touched her swelling cheek. "A lover who beats you. Fine choice, Cat." He sighed, examining her face. "Tell me where Beth is."

Vincent stood, rage contorting his features. "I'll make you sorry until the day you die."

"I am all atremble," Justin responded dryly, unable to look away from his wife's cut and swollen lip. He once thought he loved this woman. What a fool he'd been. "Where is she, Cat?"

"In the bloody coach," Vincent spat.

Justin jerked with shock and tasted the bitterness of bile in his throat as he raced toward the coach.

"No!" Catherine screamed.

A shot rang out.

The horses reared and bolted.

Gulls shrieked and took flight.

A demonic cry escaped Justin. He lunged and grabbed the coach's bracings, praying for strength, but could not stop the forward surge. The horses' legs scrambled for ground where there was none. Justin dug his heels into the dirt. The cords in his arms knotted and tore.

All was lost. Yet he could not give up.

"BETH!" he screamed as he was dragged over the edge and toward the sea-washed rocks below.

CHAPTER ONE

Killashandra Hall, Lancashire, June 1827

FOR FAITH WICKHAM, sleep would not come. The strange bed was hard, the waves in the distance disturbing.

God help her. What had she gotten herself into?

God help Justin Devereux. He'd had less choice than she. He needed her care and her family needed her wages, so Faith broke her vow never to hold another life in her hands. Sometimes this healing skill seemed more curse than blessing. But she would not fail a second time. Perhaps if she saved a life, she could atone for losing one. Justin Devereux might be more dead than alive now, but she would do all in her power to save him.

A sound opened her eyes. A cry. Then another, louder, longer, brought her to her feet. A seabird in the distance?

It came again. Human. Distressed.

Faith chafed her gown's soft-worn sleeves and stepped into her slippers. She tried the door connecting her room to her patient's and found it locked. She'd meet him tomorrow she'd been told upon her arrival earlier, except he needed her now.

Another cry, one of undeniable pain, sharpened her wits.

Seeing nothing save blackness in the hall, Faith felt her way along the wall, his door further from hers than she thought. Her trembling fingers encountered torn paper and cracked plaster. Skittering and scratching broke the silence. Were her room less fine, she'd think they occupied the attic.

She turned his knob slowly, opened his door, heard the rasp and shush of her slippers as she stepped into the black pitch. Her hiss and cough, as sickroom mustiness assaulted her, caused her to clamp her hand over nose and mouth, to muffle the sound and sever herself from the unpleasant odor.

For a moment she hesitated, then she chided herself for her foolishness, just before the animal-like whimper began— and grew to an ear-splitting demon's lament.

Faith thought her heart could beat no faster nor echo any louder in her brain than a moment before, but now it did exactly that. For his cry had grown as piercing as a knife, as mournful as a clod of dirt breaking against a lowered casket.

Her patient endured more than physical pain; he suffered from an agony of spirit. And in that instant Faith experienced the deepest connection she imagined one person might with another, as if she had seen into his soul. With startling clarity, she knew that her life would be entwined with Justin Devereux's, perhaps until the day he died, and despite the raw fear the knowledge evoked, Faith accepted this as her destiny.

She knew not how long his cry rent the air, but remorse for her idle reflection assailed her. Here she stood, his nurse, and utterly useless to him. She needed the candle in her room. Moving with speed, as the situation warranted, she ran, smack, into an object coming with force from the opposite direction.

"What the bloody hell?" The words added to her surprise as she hit the floor. Catching her breath, she couldn't speak. Not so the owner of the raspy voice muttering a string of curses as he searched on all fours, her patient's lament filling the air.

"Sir, your candle has rolled toward my room," she said rising. "I'll fetch it for you."

"Who the hell ... Ah, here's the holder."

Faith pushed her door open, retrieved his still-burning candle and lit hers with it. She could see him now, picking himself up. An older man, short, barrel-chested and muscular.

"Give it to me, woman, my master needs me." The man grabbed his candle, slammed it into its holder, and ran to Justin Devereux's room. Faith followed, stopping at the foot of the great four-poster to watch the man straddle the figure in the bed and wrestle him into submission. The lament ended on a whimper and the sturdy fellow stood. "He'll do for now. He don't do that often, but he's hurt himself a time or two."

"He seems strong for a sick man."

"Always was strong as a prize bull at market fair. Can't understand why he's no better." The stranger raised his candle for a too-bold scrutiny of her person. "You the new nurse?"

She nodded. "Faith Wickham."

"Harris." He grinned. "B'God, the master would like you. Always did like 'em dark-haired and winsome."

Faith felt an all-too-familiar warmth steal up her neck. "And why should I care what Vincent Devereux likes?"

Harris scowled. "Justin Devereux's master here." He pointed to the bed. "Been with 'im since 'e was no more'n a lad of seventeen, near eighteen years now. I'm all he's got."

"Well, Harris, now he has the both of us."

His lowered brows spoke of suspicion and doubt.

"But isn't *Vincent* Devereux master here?"

"Vincent's the younger brother, and ... Well, it ain't up to the likes of me to judge. But my master is the Duke of Ainsley, will be in my mind till the day he dies. But accordin' to the House 'a Lords,

Vincent's the present duke. Gave him the title."

"He'll have to give it back."

"If you say so, Miss."

She saw that he thought her daft. "You'll see." She raised her candle and gazed at a room from a child's nightmare. Thick-tapestried windows and blood-red velvet bed hangings dominated— as if Justin Devereux was already confined to his coffin.

Two portraits hung above the bed. One, of a handsome devil holding a babe in a long, white gown. The other of a blond goddess. Both would be better placed in the drawing room. Faith doubted the goddess lived here, else she would never let such a likeness go to waste so far from sight. "Who is she?"

"Catherine Devereux. Justin's wife."

"I didn't know he had a wife."

"A witch, that one. Never figured how she snared him. Not in his style. And he hasn't got a wife. Not now. She's dead."

Shocked, saddened, Faith rubbed her arms at the chill ... and realized she faced this stranger in her nightrail. She should leave or ... "Mr. Harris, I'll sit with him if you wish."

"Just Harris. Go back to bed. Ye'll not start till Vincent sets you to it. Go on with you now."

Back in her room, Faith fell asleep wondering if she had the strength to withstand the darkness of spirit that permeated Killashandra Hall.

She approached a huge castle encircled by thick gray mists.

A shrouded figure wove aimlessly among gnarled bracken bearing neither leaves nor flowers, but large menacing thorns.

With foreboding, Faith turned away, casually at first, then with a more determined step. But the robed being steadily followed, an emaciated hand clawing its face and hood, as if trying to clear its vision ... until one skeletal hand stretched toward her in mute, agonized appeal.

That silent plea frightened Faith more than the slow, steady steps plodding in her direction. She began to run.

Gasping, she stopped at the edge of a deep precipice overlooking a jagged cliff, a black whirlpool at its base. Heart hammering, she turned to face her pursuer.

He came close, bearing fear. Neither alive nor dead.

Faith screamed, stepped away from his seeking hand ... and went too far. She was falling. Falling.

Just when she could smell the whirlpool, and feel it filling her nostrils, gentle arms caught her and held her close, saving her from certain death.

Heart calming, Faith warmed, content, safe. Then she looked into the eyes of her savior and the skeletal face of the cloaked figure stared back with black, unseeing orbs. Her fleeting safety in his arms forgotten, she wrestled free and tumbled toward the dark turbulence below.

Panic seized her, hands grabbed her.

Faith fought frantically. She began to scream.

"Wake up, miss. There, there. Are you all right now?"

Faith recognized the abigail who'd accompanied her here to Killashandra. Was it only yesterday? "Oh, Jenny."

"You were dreaming, Miss." Jenny opened the curtains. "The master says 'e'll see you in 'is study soon as you've eaten."

"Good, then I can get on with my duties." After the girl fixed her hair, Faith smoothed her faded, gray percale. A few minutes later, she stood before the duke's door fighting an urge to beg transport home. But remembering Justin Devereux's anguish, her desire to flee vanished. A footman opened the door and bowed for her to enter. "Miss Faith Wickham," he announced.

Vincent Devereux gaped. The nurse bore the beauty of a goddess. Huge, green eyes gazed straight at him, bold as you please. Black curls framed a porcelain face, tumbling to rest against full breasts. He coughed and stood. "Ah, Miss Wickham, from Arundel is it? Come to care for my unfortunate brother and little Beth." He took her hand and brought it to his lips. *A pretty piece*, he thought, *for Justin's final days.* "Welcome. You are gravely needed. Please sit down."

"Thank you, your Grace." She took the straight chair facing his desk. Vincent sat behind it.

How Vincent loved to hear, "your grace," in reference to himself, and about time. Vincent had waited his whole life for this, and he deserved it. It had been difficult to have his brother declared incompetent—Justin's tenants needing care having won it. A new dilemma, however, sat across from him. The dratted nurse. Her abilities in the sickroom were damned near legendary, which was why he could not say no to hiring her. Well if she was so dedicated, dosing Justin would be primary, which he could applaud. It still infuriated him the way Justin's *Scoundrel* friends—school friends, of all things—had other influential big-wigs stipulate that someone be appointed to Justin's care.

But alas, Faith Wickham could be his answer.

He smiled. "The most important task you will execute ..." He coughed, cleared his throat. "Your foremost task is to care for my brother. He had a carriage accident you know; went over a cliff. Catherine, his wife, died. My brother suffered untold damage. Brain fever. Irreversible." He shook his head. "Can't walk or speak. Lies there like a babe." His voice quivered. "We must put food to his mouth, drink to his lips."

Closing his eyes, Vincent touched his brow before allowing himself to continue. "A medicine has been formulated for him. No cost has been spared. It is crucial to his welfare. Miss Wickham, do you attend me? Ah yes, I see that you do. The medicine is to be given without fail each morning and evening at eight. Eight precisely. Should you stray from this for even a few minutes, he could die. It is imperative that you follow this routine for the handsome wages I will pay you. My brother's life is in your hands. I do not need to tell you how much that means to me, Miss Wickham."

"Am I to understand your brother could die at any moment?"

"I didn't say that. Did I say that? Listen carefully now. If given his medicine in the proper dose at the proper times, he may live for years. But he will surely die if you neglect it for even a short time. Obviously, the doctors could not say how long it would take, and we wouldn't want to find out, would we?"

"Certainly not." She seemed to compose herself. "You previously mentioned a little one?"

"Justin's daughter, Beth. You will see to her as well. You will be caring in my stead for my family, as I shall be away."

"How did your brother survive such an accident?"

Vincent looked down to see ink covering his hand. He took a calming breath. "Justin and his wife were thrown from the carriage. Catherine tumbled to the sea below, but Justin landed in an outcropping of bushes." Vincent stared at his hand, detesting the need to recant something so painful. Again.

"Thank God."

He swiped, uselessly, at the ink on his palm. "What?"

"Thank God he was saved."

"He was not saved, Miss Wickham!"

Her chin came up. "I see."

Leave it to Justin to have a champion, even now. "You don't understand. My heart aches to see my brother suffering so."

She nodded. Her eyes glistened. "It does hurt to see someone you love suffer, and no matter how very much you try, you cannot ..." She drew a ragged breath. "You just cannot...."

Vincent experienced an alien stirring, but he shook it off. Deuced uncomfortable. "If you're finished quizzing me...."

The nurse looked up in surprise, ire replacing sorrow. *Good.*

"My niece has a nursemaid ... Sally, I think. You will oversee her work with the child. My brother's man, Harris, will see to his personal needs. The servants will answer directly to you." He rose to pace. "Even the housekeeper, Mrs. Tucker, will defer to your judgment concerning the running of the house."

"But certainly, it is the housekeeper, not the nurse—"

"It is my wish, Miss Wickham," he shouted. "That you bear the responsibility for everything happening in this house. You will answer for every person's actions." He narrowed his eyes. "Every person's errors. This will be done as I wish." He braced his hands on the desk. "If you are not in agreement, you may pack your bags, and your family may forfeit your wages."

The mantle-clock struck the hour.

"It will be as you wish, your grace."

Those had not been the words behind her tight lips. Vincent was gratified she understood. He sat. "Hemsted, my man of affairs, will give you an allowance for household needs. He will be here often; he runs my estates. I leave tomorrow for France. I will return from time to time, though I cannot say when, nor if it will happen with regularity. If you wish to contact me, you may do so through him. If you have no further questions...."

She stood, her beautiful self ramrod-straight, and Vincent smiled inwardly. "Your wages will be sent to your family as Vicar Kendrick requested. The dressmaker will be here this afternoon to measure you. No cost will be spared."

"The dressmaker? But I need no clothes—"

"Yet you will accept them. We must not have anyone thinking I am clutch-fisted or would employ an unworthy to care for—"

"But, I assure you—"

"Miss Wickham!" He walked around her and hovered close enough to smell springtime. "If you do not do as you are told, on your first day, concerning such a simple matter, then I have made an error in hiring you." Silence. At last. "I trust we understand each other?"

Hands fisted tightly, the beauty nodded. "I will endeavor to do my best for those in my care."

Vincent chose a new pen. "See that you do."

When the door closed behind her, Faith knew if she were to respond to the turmoil inside, she would run and never look back.

New clothes? Oh foolish squandering of money—money better spent in Justin's room or the hall. But she *must* do her employer's bidding; too many depended on her.

With dirt-water gray eyes and thin blond hair, Vincent had nothing of the look of his brother. Justin Devereux, near death, looked more imposing than Vincent in his prime. And he hadn't convinced Faith that he cared a jot about his sick brother. His words were correct, but his manner. She shivered. Yes, he faced a difficult situation, yet there was something she could not like about him.

A few minutes later, anxious to meet her young charge, Faith approached the second room connecting hers, that door opposite Justin's. Also dismal, Beth's chamber was as much in contrast to Faith's beautiful room as her father's. And the child ... a tiny, hollow-cheeked toddler with a crown of burnished ringlets, her striking blue eyes filled with fear. When Faith tried to embrace her, the child became frantic, so Faith let her go, and the child ran to hide in the corner.

Faith regarded the nursemaid. "What is wrong with her?"

"She's afraid of everyone. I don't know what to do, Miss."

"We need to teach her to trust, Sally. Tell her stories so she will know your voice." Faith opened the curtains and Beth whimpered and turned away. "Above all, be patient." Faith examined the grim room. "I'll find her something to play with."

Faith endured her fittings; losing her position was not a risk she could take. She chose a few warm things, for it was brisk by the sea, and happily departed.

That evening, Faith found dining with the duke both silent and tense.

She poked at her turbot. "When will I meet your brother?"

"You cannot meet someone who is unconscious. You may begin his care tomorrow. Harris is expecting you at precisely eight."

"What is this medicine I am to give him?"

Her employer choked on his pudding and held a napkin to his mouth until his throat cleared. "What do you mean?"

"What manner of medicine is he being given?"

"Ah." The duke indicated a need to have his wine glass refilled. He sipped it. "The medicine. Yes. The doctor had it specially mixed for Justin, as I believe I told you."

"How long have you been giving it to him?"

"Since the accident."

Faith stopped pretending to eat. "If he hasn't progressed in weeks, I don't see how you can believe the medicine will help."

The duke's wineglass snapped in his hand. Glass shards sprinkled his plate and the goblet's bowl bounced thrice at the foot of an unblinking servant. "Blast, can we talk of *nothing* else?" He signaled for another glass and more wine.

Tense, Faith feared she would snap, if she didn't speak. "Beth's eyes are extraordinary. Whom does she favor?"

Her host almost smiled. "Beth is a fetching thing. I rather think she looks like herself. My brother's eyes are nearly black. Our nurse used to call them demon's eyes. Be glad you shall never be pierced with the likes of his stare." He placed his hand on hers. "Tell me about yourself."

Faith surprised them both by standing. "If you will excuse me, your grace, I am fatigued."

"A toast first," he said. "To success."

A short while later, Faith calmed as she rocked Beth, who'd

sighed in her sleep as they began. Odd this: Awake, Beth fears. Asleep, she trusts. She must have been secure and happy once.

Caring for Beth, teaching her to smile, to trust, became an unexpected but welcome challenge.

Lord, and didn't she have her work cut out for her?

CHAPTER TWO

FAITH'S EXCITEMENT GREW from the moment she heard carriage wheels on gravel. She opened her curtains to watch the crested bottle-green coach amble down the drive. If only in her heart, dawn brightened. Vincent Devereux, on his way to France.

Not fifteen minutes later, down the hall she went, afraid no longer, for what could frighten her now?

In Justin's dismal room, Faith went to the window to gaze at Morecambe Bay, the Irish Sea beyond. Releasing the stiff latch, she pushed the casement out and breathed the salt-sharp air.

As she turned, the rogue in the second portrait called to her. A handsome fellow, she thought, wondering who he was. The babe he held must belong to him, his smile having too much fatherly pride for it not to be so.

She approached her patient. More dead than alive—an apt description. His cheek, fragile and transparent as rice paper, felt cool and waxen to her touch. His skeletal features, sunken cheeks, and skin stretched taut over bones, would make her think him dead, if not for the rise and fall of his chest.

His hand, double the size of hers, had calluses from some long-ago tasks. Here was a man unafraid of hard work. She admired that and suspected he and his brother differed in this way also.

His hair, black, with gray at the temples, badly wanted trimming. She swept it from his brow, letting her hand linger for a moment, then she combed though the thick main, top and sides, until her fingers rested behind his ear, and he sighed.

Prickles assailing her, Faith snatched her hand away. Then she realized his sigh might have been a shiver, so she shut the window and stirred the embers in the fireplace.

Chafing her patient's hands, she encountered his ring. Big for the finger it encircled, someone padded it to keep it from falling off. The smooth emerald stone boasted a miniature crest formed by a thread of liquid gold. She ran her finger over the raised design and recognized it as the coat of arms on the coach door. Then it occurred to her. Who else's portrait would hold pride of place beside Catherine's, but her husband's? Examining Justin's face, it did not seem possible, and yet....

As she suspected, the man in the portrait above wore the same ring. There on canvas, in his full, arrogant glory, hair black as the devil's heart, stood the Justin Devereux who used to be. Here on the bed before her, scarred and fading, lay the Justin Devereux of today. The gilded frame had been engraved two years before, yet her patient looked as if he'd aged twenty.

Faith smoothed his brow and fingered the scar at its edge. "You're strong, Harris said. That's a start. My name is Faith, Justin, and I plan to help you recover."

When the fire blazed, Faith reopened the casement and strode the row of sea-gazing windows opening curtains. Swatting at dust motes, she sneezed and turned back to the bed. To her surprise, her patient had raised an arm to shield his closed eyes.

Light pierced him.

Hell was not flaming light, but icy darkness. Yet light invaded.

Justin contemplated the walls of his tomb. The huge black slabs, thousands of miles high, not so much as a name or date carved in their slick unblemished surfaces, stood straight and tall. Inviolable as ever.

Were it conceivable to scale such smooth, upright surfaces, Justin knew he could never do so. He was too weak. Too dead.

To Faith's shock, her patient trembled and released a sob.

She stroked his brow. "You have nothing to fear. Do you mind if I call you Justin? Mama would scold, but I won't tell, if you don't." She removed his arm from his eyes and placed it beside him. When she let go his hand, he re-sought hers as if he'd lost something precious. His breathing became labored.

The scent of violets and the touch of silk in the blackness of hell. A hand offered in solace. *Where are you?*

For the love of God, help me. I beg for life. Not death.

Faith's patient grasped her trembling fingers. When he calmed, so did her heart. Releasing her breath, she examined his square jaw, aquiline nose and arched brows. "I'll wager you've broken a score of hearts." Crinkle lines radiated from the corners of his eyes. Once upon a time the hawkish-featured Justin Devereux had smiled, and smiled often.

Now the plea in his frenzied grasp alarmed Faith. Despite the warming room, ice needles shot through her. She yearned to run ... yet there was no place she would rather be.

Disconcerted, she shook herself. Her patient needed her and he would need his medicine soon. Again she tried to take her hand from his, but he held tight. In panic, she tugged it free.

A wicked trick, Satan. No hope. No life. Just death. Death is forever.

Faith watched a tear trickle down Justin's cheek and she swallowed the stone in her throat. "Neither alive nor dead," now rang false. Justin Devereux was more alive than anyone imagined.

Then Faith's knees went weak as she looked into those unseeing black orbs. "Justin." Hope died. His stare was blank. He could neither see nor hear her. His hand, which had moved with need a moment before, stilled. He closed his eyes.

How long had he appeared ... alive? A minute? Five?

Faith checked the mantle clock. The time! She ran to the bell-pull and tugged three quick times. She hugged herself as she stared at the door, willing it to open. And when it crashed against the wall, she jumped. "Thank God. Hurry."

White-faced, Harris lifted Justin to a sitting position, put an amber vial to his lips and poured the contents into him.

Justin swallowed, for it was swallow or be drowned. A reflex intact that Faith saw as a good sign. She released her breath. "When I saw the time ... I was told if he didn't take it by—"

"I know, I know. That damnable dog came tearin' at me. Knocked the tray from my hands, broke the vial. Had to fetch another." Harris's hands shook as he replaced the stopper.

"I hope he suffers no ill effects," Faith said.

"He's taken it late a time or two. Gets skittish. In pain. Sicker, you understand, until he gets it."

Faith's question was answered. Justin had responded before. She looked about, hope dimming. "Why has his room been neglected?"

"They're afraid of him below stairs." Harris shook his head in sorrow. "They act as if he's a ghost ... of his old self, more like. But they haven't been made to come and clean. And his high'n'mighty don't so much as set a polished boot in here."

"What about Mrs. Tucker?"

"Can't bring herself to come, because it grieves her to see him. The maids won't do it on their own, blast them." He flushed. "Pardon, Miss."

"Harris, when we're alone, instead of minding your speech, just speak your mind. I'll see that someone comes to clean. Now I need to know everything about our patient's care."

Harris's embarrassment turned to doubt.

"I won't fail him, Harris."

The retainer grunted, an acknowledgment of sorts, Faith guessed. "If you please, I would like to know your routine."

He gave a half-nod. "After his medicine, I bathe and shave him then give him his milk for breakfast. I feed him three times between and again at eight when I give him his evening dose."

"Fine, I'll let you finish." She turned away, then back. "Have the door that leads to my room unlocked. Today, please."

Faith went back to see Beth. When she entered, Beth began to cry, until Faith took a gingerbread man from her pocket, stopping her mid-sob. A lone tear on the brink of falling, Beth popped a finger in her mouth, but she didn't take the offered treat.

Faith pointed to the cookie's raisin trim. "Eyes." She traced the curved row. "Smile." She touched her own lips. "Faith smile." She touched Beth's. "Beth smile?" But Beth's mouth did not turn up at the corners, so Faith set the treat on the bedside table. "You may have the cookie, Beth."

As Faith and Sally talked, Beth took the cookie and nibbled its feet. Faith's heart warmed when Beth pointed to its smile.

Over the next week, Faith improved Justin's care. "Every day, the maids will clean," she told Harris. "And I'll change his bed." She lifted a curl off Justin's forehead and looked at his portrait. "Trim his hair and nails. He's a man who once took pride in his appearance. He is no less a man now."

Harris smiled fondly. "Worried more about his appearance than he did. Laughed at me a time or two. He was ... *is* a good man. Cared for his dependents. Doted on that baby girl."

When the servants finally came to clean, they worked around Justin. But Faith believed the only way he would feel alive would be if he was included in life. So she included him.

"Good morning, Justin. How are you today? You're looking better." She massaged his shoulders. "Did I ever tell you about my family?" She rubbed his arm, his wrist, his fingers. "Andy is the baby. Then there's our Lissa...."

Faith missed her family, but when she stroked Justin's hand, she realized touching him gave her comfort. "I'm not sure if talking to you will make a difference," she said. "But I believe that deep inside you're whole, and I intend to reach you."

Harris came in just then and Faith turned to him. "To lie in bed so long seems inconceivable. Let's sit him in a chair."

Harris stared as if she'd sprouted horns. "He'll fall."

"We'll tie him with strips of cloth and sit him by a window."

Harris nodded, but he muttered all the way out the door.

The day Faith's new clothes arrived, Jenny couldn't hide her excitement, nor Faith her irritation. "It makes no sense. He spends money on clothes for me but not on a doctor for Justin."

Jenny looked up. "A doctor came once. He said there was no hope." But Faith refused to be discouraged.

She established a routine with Beth. Every morning she chose Beth's dress. Every afternoon she brought Beth a gingerbread man and pointed to its smile. Every night she rocked and sang to Beth as she slept. Until one night when Faith was rocking her, humming ... and Beth stiffened and opened her eyes.

Faith faltered. Beth didn't seem frightened, but she was tense, so Faith continued to hum. Beth gazed about, but didn't move much. After a while she raised a tentative hand to touch the broach pinned to Faith's bodice. Then, to Faith's utter surprise, Beth lifted that tiny hand further to trace Faith's lips, as Faith had often done on a cookie's smile.

When Faith smiled, Beth stopped tracing, but didn't remove her fingers, so Faith kissed them. And there was a spark, just a spark, of something other than fear or mistrust on Beth's face. Oh her mouth did not change, but her eyes did. They surely did.

Faith pulled the child close. "Sleep, sweetheart," she whispered. And with a sigh, Beth obeyed.

Faith was still elated the next morning. "Good morning, Justin. You won't believe what Beth did last night."

Justin shuddered as if he'd been startled.

Placing her hand over his heart, Faith wondered why he'd reacted in such a way and why his heart beat so fast. Did she frighten him? Was he in pain? Or was it the mention of Beth?

"Beth misses you, Justin."

He shuddered again. No mistaking it.

"Justin? Is it Beth?"

He whimpered.

Poor Beth. Poor dead baby. Dead baby. Dead baby.

Justin watched in horror as scores of golden-haired baby girls fell toward him.

Their cries split the air tormenting him beyond sanity. They tumbled and plunged. Pitched and lurched. Each of them getting closer, closer to their moment of death.

Horror welled within him.

A scream of anguish tore from Justin, slashing Faith with a keen blade. She pulled him into her arms and held him until his wail of grief ended and his heart against her own calmed.

She held him for a long time, wondering how she could ever hope to heal his tortured soul.

When Harris came in, he read her despair. "You looked exactly so your first morning. I'd think you'd be used to it by now, though God knows, I'm not."

Later, after Harris shaved Justin with the same devotion he put into everything he did for his master, he poured milk into him, the same way he did the medicine.

Harris gave him the milk more often now, but Faith worried

Justin would never get stronger without proper nourishment. "What if we were to give him watered gruel?"

Harris turned to her, brows furrowed, but willing to listen.

"If that works, we could try mushy peas or soft-boiled eggs. Continue to give him milk as often as you do now, but we could try beating a raw egg into it. What say you?"

"You're probably fooling us both with your crazy notions."

Faith touched Harris's arm. "I want him to recover."

Harris nodded. "Aye. So do I."

An hour later, Faith had Justin sitting in a chair by the window while she fed him his first gruel, Harris beside her. "Saw a chair in a London shop window once," Harris said. "A queer thing with a big wheel on each side. Could get him around in a chair like that."

Faith stopped, spoon in the air. "Can you make one? Or go to London and buy one? Soon? Today? Tomorrow?"

"A body could go blind from the sparkle in your eyes right now. My master would have liked that fire, he would."

"Not to encourage your Irish blarney, Harris, but I intend for Justin to have the opportunity to appreciate many things in the years to come. Now about that chair?"

"Get right on't. Holy St. Patrick, he's eaten it all. I been starving 'im."

"You've kept him alive. Now, he's going to get better."

Beth was the one who got better. With curtains for her room and a rocking horse from the attic, she blossomed. She didn't smile, but she offered her hand each morning for her walk, took her cookie each afternoon and waited to be rocked each night.

The better part of every day, Faith spent with Justin. She ate with him, talking all the while. When she ran out of stories, she went to the family library for books to read to him.

Harris fashioned a wheelchair and Faith learned how to get Justin out of bed, into the chair, and back, by herself. Cook created new foods for him to eat.

Time at Killashandra flew.

"You look better. You have flesh on your bones and color in your cheeks. I wish I could see your eyes." She'd seen them once. They were dark and beautiful, not the sightless orbs of her nightmare. And she wanted to see them again.

Why had Justin responded that first morning? Why, when she'd mentioned Beth? She sighed with frustration, for she had only a suspicion that the later he got his medicine, the more alive he became ... which went against every normal precept.

Her suspicion, however, about his meals, reaped benefits. "You have quite an appetite, you know. You're eating soup, stew and even the filling from cook's pasties. We make sure everything's easy to swallow, but I'm beginning to think you'd swallow the spoon, did I leave it there long enough."

Faith realized her life was fuller now, though she missed her family. Curious notion that. She had not been unhappy at home, yet she had such purpose now.

He knew her scent, violets. He craved her touch, silk. He relaxed to the music of her voice. *Soothing angel, touch my hand, cool my brow. Bring me home.*

"I would have liked to know the arrogant Duke of Ainsley. But you would hardly have noticed a country miss like me. The ladies probably swooned if you so much as—"

Faith stopped speaking, for Justin's hand, amazingly, caressed hers. She'd never experienced so intimate a touch. His fingers slid along hers, across the back of her hand, inside her palm. Liquid heat filled her and she sighed.

He sighed at the same moment.

Justin wondered why he could never quite reach the angel. Sometimes hope filled him, hope that he might find his way to her. Then without warning, he would be lost in the cold black pitch once again. Alone.

Let me touch you, silken angel, the way you touch me.

Take my hand. Lead me home.

Faith saw Justin's beautiful dark eyes once again. Fear of frightening or alarming him, or of ending the fragile moment, filled her, but she couldn't remain silent. "How do you feel?" She grazed his cheek with the back of her hand. "Sometimes you seem so close, at others, so far." She blinked to clear her vision. "Do you even know I'm here?" He caressed her hand, yet his eyes held no spark. He was as one blind, and the tears she'd tried to hold back, coursed down her cheeks.

A crash startled her. Harris saw her face. "Oh God, he's dead. I'm late and he's dead. I killed him." Harris fell to the bedside and wept in his sleeve.

"Harris, what are you babbling about?"

"Stable boy got hurt. Had to tend the lad. Missed the eight o'clock dose. It's gone half past. I'm late. You're crying. My master's dead." He wiped his eyes with his sleeve.

"He's not dead, you dear old man," she said helping him to his feet. "Now raise him so I can give him his medicine."

Faith thought Harris would collapse when Justin opened his eyes and looked him full in the face. "Don't drop him! I know you're surprised." She put the vial to Justin's lips. "This isn't the first time. He's opened his eyes before. Tears have coursed down his cheeks. He's grabbed my hand and held tight. I think he's getting better."

The expression on the old man could only be termed fearful. He was afraid to hope.

"Now, mind," Faith cautioned. "This is only the second time. It also happened the first morning I was here." The later Justin got his medicine, the more he responded; it was a paradox. And with it came a warning Faith could not name. "Harris, let's keep his progress to ourselves for now."

Harris accepted each change in Justin's care, but when Faith suggested he be bathed in a tub of hot water everyday, she could tell he was close to calling her mad. "You sure got some strange notions, Missy. But if you say do it, I will."

"And if I tell you to jump in the bay?"

"If you say it will help my master, I'll do it."

His confidence touched her. "After his bath, we'll exercise his legs—move them back and forth at knee and hip. That will make it easier for him to walk later. My grandfather's doctor insisted on this."

A few days later, Justin's doctor finally came, but the horsy-smelling quack said, fresh air, hot baths, good food, were bad for a patient in a coma. Just give him the medicine.

Faith lay in bed that night, her mind in turmoil. The doctor was wrong. Justin was getting stronger, gaining weight. He looked healthy, distinguished, his dark, wavy hair shiny. Oh, how she wanted to see the crinkles in the corners of his dark eyes when he laughed.

Faith rose and donned her dressing gown, frowning all the while. Justin *was* better when his medicine was late. Had she not proved that? The doctor had named Justin's illness a coma. She had never heard the word until today. What did it mean?

In the library, Faith found *A Dictionary of the English Language* by Dr. Samuel Johnson. "Coma, a state of physical torpor. Extreme sluggishness or stagnation of function. A state of profound sleep caused by disease, injury, or poison."

Faith's hand shook as she sat in a massive leather chair. Disease. Justin showed no sign of affliction, though that was not proof against it.

Injury. His wounds from the carriage accident were healed. Faith steepled her fingers, closed her eyes.

Poison. Her grandfather's doctor said to keep his medicine away from the children. Medicine for one could be poison for another. Could Justin's medicine be poisoning him? He likely required a large dose, but what would that be? She wasn't asking that quack. And she couldn't call in a new doctor; the cost would alert ... Vincent—she could no longer call him the duke. He had as much as stolen the title, had he not? With his brother still alive?

And there she had it.

She must face her fears and consider the evidence. Vincent would irrevocably *keep* both title and fortune if Justin died. If the medicine was poison, real poison that *she* gave to Justin while Vincent was out of the country, no one would suspect him of ... Oh, Lord.

Vincent brought a dressmaker to Killashandra before bringing a doctor. Yes, he'd shown more concern over her clothes than he did the comfort and care of his brother and niece, but misplaced priorities did not a murderer make.

Faith heard a noise. Waited. It came again. From above.

Dismissing her fear, she raised her candle. An upper balcony marched along the outer perimeter of the library. A circular staircase, leading to that gloomy level stood in the center.

It came again. A rustle. A swish. Ghost-like.

Faith shook her head and placed her foot on the first stair, and when no goblin flew down to snatch her up, she continued to the top with no worse than a racing heart. Leather chairs faced a fireplace with swords and dueling pistols mounted above.

Something pulled at her skirts. She shrieked, and a cat hissed.

Faith scooped up the feline. "You frightened me, little one. Is this your room?" She gazed about, her fear slipping away like mist at dawn. No answers here, unless ... She petted the cat. "If you could speak, you could tell me what you know. What ails him, pray? Disease, injury, or poison?"

But the ebony feline merely licked her thumb and purred. Faith held that cat for a long time accepting the warmth and companionship it offered, until she reluctantly set it down.

The door to her right, she discovered, opened to the hall to her room, though not at the back where she and her charges were hidden away.

Were they? Hidden? She hadn't considered that.

Back in Justin's room, Faith sat on his bed and took his hand, knowing if he died, so would some fundamental fragment of herself. "Of all my patients," she said. "I lost one. My grandfather. And I came here thinking if I could save you, I could atone." She brushed his hair aside. "Now I want to bring you back for you, and for me. Selfish, I know. Justin, if I stop your medicine, you could die. But is this ... *existence* of yours enough?" She touched his heart, felt the beat she could stop with a wrong decision. Her own accelerated. "Lord, tell me what to do. Please. What right do I have to make such a decision?"

Faith woke the next morning kneeling on the floor, her head on Justin's bed, her hand in his. And she knew what she must do.

She went to his window at dawn yearning to walk beside him to the turbulent sea in the distance. She wanted to hear him laugh or shout, to watch emotion play upon his features—joy or anger, it mattered not. She wanted him to know she existed, that *he* existed.

At eight, she faced Harris. "I need you to go to London."

"You need me here."

"I need you there more. There's no one else I trust. Find out about the doctor who visited last week. Is he known? Is he reliable, well thought of? Has he come into money of late?"

"Miss Faith?"

"Don't ask. Just get some answers. Go to where you purchase the medicine and attempt to find out who makes it, what's in it."

Harris stared at the fire, his hands behind his back. "I should not ask these questions of just anyone, should I?"

"You should be *discreet* in your inquiries."

"I feared as much." He regarded her intently. "When would you be wanting me to go?"

"Tomorrow. Tell everyone you're going for more medicine."

"The doctor who tended the master in London. The one his high-n-mighty discharged, do you want to know about him too?"

"Good Lord. I didn't know he'd dismissed a physician." A good one, she'd warrant. "Find him. Ask him about Justin's condition after the accident. What were his recommendations?" She could think of few reasons a physician would be removed from the care of a sick man. None of them pleased her.

Harris cleared his throat. "I'm glad you came to us."

"Godspeed, Harris."

Early the next morning, Faith stood at her window. Such a simple tableau—Harris riding sedately down the drive—to represent such an extraordinary quest.

An amber glass vial nestled in the palm of her hand. She tested its weight. What evil hid within this innocent vessel? As she watched her only ally in this house become a speck on the horizon, she squeezed the tiny bottle as if she might crush it, and along with it, her apprehension. But when she opened her palm, both remained. Faith dropped the vial into her apron pocket and placed the flat of her hand on the window.

"I pray your faith in me is well-founded, old man. God grant your master may live 'till you return."

CHAPTER THREE

FAITH KNEW THAT everything she'd done thus far had helped Justin. What she planned to do now could very well kill him ... and yet, some irrefutable inner voice said she must try.

At eight o'clock, she sat him by the corner window. His breathing was better, for he was coming around to the kind of sleep that she considered normal. She fetched Beth, Vincent's warning that Justin could die if he didn't get his medicine on time stalking her like the robed being of her nightmare.

For Beth, Faith tried to remain calm. "Here we are," she said as they came into Justin's room. "I have a surprise for you."

Beth wiggled her hand from Faith's and ran about. She stood on tiptoes to examine the washstand and nearly came away with the strop. She looked beneath the massive four-poster and crawled right under. She poked her finger into the warm soft wax at the base of a candle and happily peeled it away. If Justin could see her now.

Both anxious and fearful, Faith sat beside him and took his hand. "Over here, Beth," she called, and Justin shuddered to such a degree that Faith felt his shiver in *her* hand, his grasp growing strong.

Justin struggled to free himself as he lay fettered, ankle and wrist, at the bottom of hell, while miles above him, Vincent tossed Beth over the edge of a cliff.

In horror, he watched his daughter hurtle toward him.

Through the air she tumbled. Falling at a furious pace.

He pulled at his chains. Struggled to get free. To catch Beth. But his shackles held firm.

His baby girl hit the bottom of hell and shattered like a porcelain doll.

Justin's wail pierced the air as he struggled against his bindings.

Before Faith could calm him, Beth's shriek was no less plaintive as she came running. "Poppy!" she cried as she clambered into his lap and threw her arms around his neck. "Poppy," she sobbed. "Poppy."

With a start, Justin lifted his arms—arms that seemed uncertain of their proper place—and wrapped them around his little girl. His hold, tentative at first, grew strong.

"Poppy," Beth said on a soft sigh.

With a cry Justin hugged her tight and drew a deep, shuddering breath. He rubbed his cheek against her hair.

Faith could neither move, nor contain her tears.

A cookie-man's smile paled in comparison to Beth's, the first Faith had ever seen on the child, while she held her small hands to Justin's cheeks. "Poppy?"

He opened his eyes, but as if to clear his vision, he closed and reopened them, his look finally one of awe. Gentling his embrace, he combed palsied fingers through Beth's bronze curls. With a cry, he hugged her so hard, Faith feared he would hurt her. But Beth's smile grew until she giggled.

Joy transported them, until Justin took a sharp, piercing breath and lost all the color in his face. He turned ashen.

Faith's elation fled. Fearing Justin would faint and drop Beth, she supported Beth as she dipped the corner of her apron in a cup of water and held it against the back of his neck.

His color did not improve; his skin felt slick and cool. Faith leaned over and shut the window as she checked the clock. After nine. His medicine had never been this late. They'd entered a new realm. A dark, frightening forest of deadly possibilities.

For all Justin was weak as a kitten, he'd not lost hold of his daughter. Neither had Beth lost hold of him. They wouldn't be willing to part any time soon.

Faith swallowed her regret. "I need to give your Papa his medicine, Beth." She tried to take the child, but Beth shook her head in refusal and held her father tight.

Faith tugged. "Come along now and let Poppy rest. You may see him again later." Justin's weakness, it seemed, did not extend to his arms.

"I don't wish for you to have found each other only to be parted again," Faith said. "Oh, if you could only understand. If we delay much longer, you might lose each other forever."

For whatever reason, Justin loosened his hold and Beth came quietly, but at the door, she turned with a sorrow too keen to be borne. "Poppy?"

If this was *not* the first step in Justin's recovery, Faith feared it might destroy them both. Beth could become more fearful. Justin could fall into a speedier decline.

Faith considered the possibility that by keeping Justin sedated, his medicine might be allowing him to live longer. What had she done? Her guilt trebled when she shut the door to Beth's room a few minutes later. Faith had promised another outing soon and left Beth crying in the arms of her confused nurse. What a dangerous game she played. A game whose loss others would suffer.

Back in Justin's room, Faith approached him, his medicine in her trembling hand ... and she stopped.

This was not the first time he seemed to watch her. It was,

however, the first time he gazed in this particular way. Where his eyes, previous to this moment, stared blankly, they now held a spark of awareness.

Faith took the vial of medicine from her apron pocket. "You cannot know how distressed I am to give this to you," she said.

His Angel was beautiful. He had never seen her so clearly.

He knew her soothing touch. Her violet scent. Her sweet voice. But her beauty—this he did not know.

Faith lifted the vial to Justin's lips ... and he turned his head. Her heart, that aching core that had been tugged and cajoled, crushed and swollen, accelerated and arrested—all during her time at Killashandra—beat a new thundering rhythm.

Lowering herself into the chair beside him, Faith watched her patient's hard profile until he turned to face her. She could almost believe he looked, and yes, saw, into her eyes.

Into his hand, open on the chair's arm, she placed her own. He curled dry parchment fingers around it. Gentle. Caressing.

Warmth invaded her to her soul. "Justin," she whispered. "Listen to me. You must take your medicine so you will live. I cannot allow death to win."

His posture suddenly alert, he raised his chin.

In the event he understood, Faith unstopped the vial and raised it. Again, he turned away. Implacable. Stubborn. Headstrong.

How dare she judge his character by the tilt of his head, the set of his shoulders. And yet ... his refusal to take his medicine was the most hopeful, most distressing improvement—if improvement it was—she had seen thus far.

Faith began to laugh. Her laughter accelerated until it could only be termed excessive, part and parcel of what Grandmama used to call, "a fit of madness."

She was hysterical. And she knew it. But she could no more stop her tears than she could make Justin swallow his medicine. And she was not certain she wished to do either.

With no choice left, Faith bent her head, wrapped her arms about herself and allowed her sobs free reign. She would feel better at any moment now.

Just another minute. Soon.

She attempted a breath. A deeper one. She began to calm.

A butterfly touch in her hair alerted her. She looked up, and a sob, the last remnant of her temporary flight from reality, escaped her.

Justin bent forward, morning light illuminating the angular planes of his face, his no-longer unseeing eyes more night-sky blue than black. Did he sense her fear, her excitement? Did the sound of her heart's quickened pace beat as loud in his ears as it did in hers?

For the love of God, he looked ... worried.

She raised her hand to her hair and encountered his stroking fingers. "Oh." She couldn't pry her gaze from his.

His gentle but trembling hand palmed a slow path down her neck and along her spine. Finally, yet too soon, it came to rest at the small of her back, and warmth pooled there. Exerting a slight pressure, he urged her toward him.

Heart hammering with as much wonder as worry, Faith allowed Justin to tuck her face into his neck. Marveling at her sense of destiny—her cheek against his, his scent enveloping her—she wondered when melancholy ended and elation began.

They stayed that way for a span of time that might have been moments or hours; Faith didn't care which. Oddly, in Justin's arms, his heart beating against hers, she felt protected and cherished.

A rusty voice near her ear asked, "Are you ill?"

Startled, Faith jumped and smacked the top of her head against his chin. She looked up, not certain who she expected to see, and there sat Justin—more alive than dead—rubbing his jaw.

"Oh! No, sir. I am not ill, you are. I expect you think you have awakened in a mad house." Faith rubbed the top of her head, then thought better of it and gave over to rubbing his chin. "Did I hurt you? Oh dear, what a foolish question. Surely, you have suffered worse. Well, but perhaps you do not remember."

With furrowed brows, he touched his stomach and grimaced. "Some demon has taken possession of my insides. Death, I think, had me in its clutches." He paled further. "Death." His eyes turned to flint. "Beth." He looked straight through Faith. "I have to kill my brother." What little color he had regained, drained entirely away.

Faith believed hers did also, so stricken was she by his savage statement. Did the brothers hate each other so much?

Justin was as close to passing out as ... "You must allow me to give you your medicine."

He was too weak to argue. She brought the vial to his lips and to her relief he swallowed. But only once. Then he pressed his lips together and pushed her arm aside. "Enough! Evil crawls into me when I drink that." He closed his eyes. "No more."

Before long, he slept.

The entire episode might have been her imagination, so peacefully did Justin rest now. So normally.

She sighed. Normal.

But relief died as quickly as it was born, for the depth of his sleep worried her. She wanted him to rest, yet she wanted the security of knowing he could wake. Grimacing inwardly at her fickle self, Faith sought sanity, and decided to accept the event of his awakening for the miracle it was. From the time Justin should have taken his medicine, until the time she finally gave it to him, more than an hour had passed. And not only did he *not* die, he woke. And he *spoke* to her.

Glory be. Though she trembled over what might have been—what might yet be—she felt giddy. She had played God, and she didn't know whether to pray for forgiveness or shout for joy. Smoothing her skirt, Faith denied her urge to stand and dance across the room.

Justin had spoken to her.

Lord, she wished Harris was here. She needed to tell someone. Anyone. Everyone.

She'd like to throw open the casement and shout, "Justin is awake. He is awake and getting well!" But no. She was not certain he *would* get well. Nor did she know who to trust at Killashandra. For both reasons, she must keep this incredible knowledge to herself.

Such a wonderful burden to carry.

Faith answered the knock at the hall door and took his breakfast tray from a maid. But for the girl, she would have forgotten his meal entirely. After setting it beside him, she placed his napkin on his chest and proceeded to spoon creamed eggs into his mouth.

He choked on the first mouthful.

Lord, had her interference upset the delicate balance of his progress? She tried getting him to sip milk to clear his throat.

He opened his eyes and pushed the glass away, spilling milk on both of them. "What the devil? What are you about, feeding a man while he sleeps?"

The glass slipped from her fingers and hit the floor. The imperious tone had clearly belonged to the Duke of Ainsley.

"If I did not feed you while you slept, Sir, I would have no need to feed you at all, for you would be quite dead by now."

His anger turned to smoke, confusion taking its place. "What?" He looked about, brows furrowed. "What is this place?"

"We are at Killashandra."

His bewilderment called up her compassion. "Killashandra is your home by the sea. Do you not remember? You've been ill, your grace. Several months ago, you were in a carriage accident and nearly died." Your grace, indeed. How foolish to be so formal, yet however close she felt to him, *he* had no knowledge of their relationship. Yet calling him Justin seemed too intimate. Oh bother, she'd sort it out later.

"I know Killashandra. But I find myself ... over-set."

"With good cause," Faith granted. "Do you remember what I told you?"

Justin closed his eyes. "Yes," he whispered. "You are ... Your name is Faith, and you're here to care for me. I've been ill. Isn't Harris here?"

Faith had neither mentioned her name, nor Harris, this morning. Now she worried about what else he might remember. Had he, even in sleep, sensed her infatuation? Lord, if ever there were a time for her to establish herself as his nurse, this would be the time.

"Yes. My name is Faith Wickham. Harris is in London at the moment, but he has been here since the accident."

Her patient watched her as she spoke, nodding in apparent understanding. He pointed to the vial on the table. "That poison is evil. I feel worse, not better, since you gave it to me."

Faith shuddered inwardly. How odd that he should name it so. If only he knew her suspicions. But until certainty replaced doubt, she must keep her own counsel. However, he did seem better since taking a bit of it.

She looked at her hands and cleared her throat. "I think you should know, I have been told that if you do not take that medicine twice a day, at eight o'clock in the morning and evening, you could die. That you will die if I delay giving it to you for even a few moments ... I have been told," she repeated. "But I have given it to you late several times, and today I waited nearly an hour. You took no more than a sip of it even then, and you are still doing quite well."

Justin's eyes widened; incredulity etched his features. "Do you mean to say you experimented to see if I would die?"

Faith shot from her chair. "Of course not! Well. Not precisely. What a provoking thing to say."

His ill-chosen, if astute, remark agitated Faith more than she would like to admit. She stepped away, then back, and resettled Justin's lap rug, wondering how to make him understand. The closer she stood to him and the steadier he watched her, the greater care she gave to each detail as she smoothed his dressing gown's lapels and cuffed its sleeves.

After an interminable time, unable to bear his scrutiny a moment longer, she took his breakfast tray to a table by the hall door and rearranged the items to be taken away later. If only she could avoid the eyes boring into her back.

Bracing herself, she turned to him once more, to be arrested mid-stride with a look of blatant distrust.

Faith raised her chin and stood before him. "If anything, you ungrateful man, I wanted to see if you would live!"

He regarded her steadily for several uncomfortable beats while her assertion echoed in the silence. "Tell me more," he said.

His sincerity disarmed her. Taking a relieved breath, she sat facing him and placed her hands primly in her lap. "You only responded, ever, when the medicine wore off. I felt a strong obligation, a moral one, if you will, to do everything in my power, no matter how frightening—and it was frightening, make no mistake—to see you recover.

"I sent Harris away just this morning, because if I had been wrong—and, oh, God, I still worry I have been—I didn't want him involved. I am determined, you see, to bear the responsibility for this decision as my own.

"As the results," Justin said, with acerbity. "Will be mine to bear."

Faith ignored his tone. "Harris would blame himself, if something went wrong. He cares for you like a lion does its cub."

"Ah."

The arrogant duke looked humbled. And well he should be. Feeling on level ground again, Faith reached for his hand, then, flushing, she re-adjusted his lap-robe instead.

Wishing to consign the rogue before her to the devil, Faith reminded herself that he needed to know everything, no matter his hostility. If he *had* been poisoned, he had a right to his animosity, after all.

She took another breath. "From the day I arrived, you were more dead than alive, yet I saw a spark of life when your medicine was delayed. Suppose, I thought, the medicine was having the opposite effect? It seemed to, and I needed to know why, because you had been asleep for weeks, robbed of life in all but fact, which you must agree is in no way normal. You were not living, though you were alive. Do you understand?"

A look akin to respect transformed him. And with regard in his eyes, he looked more striking. And *she* must keep track of her thoughts. "It's important that you understand why I did what I did. The first time you responded, surprised me. But the second time, when I told you how well Beth was doing—"

An invisible blow slammed him and he cried out as his head hit the back of his chair.

Shaken, Faith stood. "Are you all right?"

With a sudden palsy, her weak patient could not seem to answer. "Don't die on me now! Here, you need your medicine—"

"Damn it! No more medicine!"

His firm, albeit rusty, shout sat her down again.

"'Twas the mention of my daughter," he whispered. "Beth died in that carriage ... accident."

Faith once thought she understood the word, *haunted*, but she had not imagined its despair. "Justin, Beth—"

"Stop!" He covered his eyes with an arm, as if to protect himself from a blow. "I cannot think of her ... gone."

For the first time since he woke, Faith took Justin into her arms. "I'm so sorry," she said, seared by his agony. "I would take your pain as my own, if I could." Why did Justin remember simple things like her name and Harris having been here, Faith wondered, but he did not remember holding Beth just this morning? How could he be so certain that his daughter had died?

Would telling him be too great a shock?

As much as she feared harming him further, Faith knew she must tell Justin that his daughter lived.

And she would. As soon as she stopped shaking.

CHAPTER FOUR

FAITH RUBBED JUSTIN'S back to calm him and to put off that moment when she might risk his progress by revealing what he most needed to hear. That Beth lived. His stubbled chin abraded her cheek. And she realized she was as late shaving him as dosing him this morning ... or had it gone past noon by now?

His confusion might be caused by his illness or his need for medicine. Perhaps she should make him take it ... as if she could. "I wish to God I knew what to do," she whispered.

"Don't be distressed," he said. "You'll come about."

Faith smiled despite herself. "It's you I'm worried about."

"It's been an age since anyone worried about me. I'm not sure I like it." He opened his fist against her ribs just below her breast, and the impropriety in their positions struck her. She released him.

Regret etched his features—a regret to match her own. She straightened her shoulders. "Justin, about Beth. She's—"

"No!" he shouted, then he sighed, seeming to realize he'd been harsh. "You can't know," he said. "Her *mother* kidnapped her."

How could a man reveal such hate for his wife as Justin had just done in speaking the word *mother*? And how could a mother be a kidnapper?

Justin touched his brow with a shaking hand. "I followed their trail. I ... I think," he said. "I'm not sure."

"Justin. Beth didn't die. She's alive. Beth is alive." But not by so much as a blink did he react. "Did you hear me?" Faith asked, as he closed his eyes, shutting her out. When he opened them, he gave her a patronizing look. "She's well," Faith added in frustration. "Did I tell you that? And thriving?"

His smile turned wistful, as if, lacking her wits, she should be tolerated, even applauded for her feeble efforts.

"I once slapped Squire Kennedy's son for just such a look. I'm not addled. I speak the truth."

"You go to great lengths to ease a dying man's final hours." He closed his eyes to clear their moisture. "But you go too far."

"You're not dying." *God, let me be right.* "Soon you'll hold Beth—if you can keep her still that long—and you'll know."

As a tear slipped down his ashen cheek, Justin closed his eyes. The sun's slant cast shadows on the hollow, angular planes of his face. "Is Catherine here?" Then with more dispatch than Faith thought him capable, he raised his hand. "No. Of anyone, I need Cat least." His words were mocking and self-directed. Bitter.

"Forgive me," he said, reading her shock. "I'm not up to Catherine. I may never be." His voice faded as his dark lashes drifted against pale cheeks. He slept once more.

Faith paced the room and back, stopping frequently to check the rise and fall of Justin's chest. Lord, he thought Beth died and Catherine lived. Had his mind been damaged in the accident?

She left her sleeping patient to check on Beth, who accepted her cookie with a sober nod and tolerated being cuddled for a moment.

Justin slept that whole day, and Faith alternated between pacing and watching, imagining every dire consequence possible as a result of her decision to withhold his medicine.

Memories stirred her—the way he touched her hair, the look in his eyes when he thought she was ill, his rusty voice.

Justin awoke, regret filling him. He dreamed that when the pretty nurse said Beth lived, he believed her. But as dusk bruised the horizon, he knew she'd lied to ease him peacefully into eternity. He was dying. He breathed, deeply, to lessen the pain the acknowledgement brought. If he didn't collect himself, he might cry like a babe then what would his nurse think of him? Enough, he was at her mercy without allowing her pity. Upon his death, he would see Beth again, a thought sufficient to rally him.

He surmised it to be evening of the day he'd awakened. His nurse, Faith, sat beside him, bent over her stitching, concentration rapt.

Certain he'd never seen her before, he wondered why he felt as if he knew her, as if they were connected in some basic way.

His stomach pitched violently. "I believe I am hungry."

"Oh. Ouch!" She dropped her mending and stuck her pricked finger into her mouth, regarding him, her green eyes huge.

If he were not so ill, he would be enchanted. He frowned. Better to be ill. Best not allow another woman to spin her web. For good reason, the deadliest of spiders was named widow. Enough that Catherine had ensnared him—such a paltry sin in view of everything—for she had murdered their daughter as surely as if she took a knife to Beth's tiny heart.

Yet it was Vincent he sought revenge upon, with reason, if only he could remember what reason precisely. Justin tried to keep from succumbing to his frustration, determined Catherine must be held accountable.

Women were capable of every deceitful, vile, even deadly deed. If he would but remember that, he could be safe from this beautiful nurse. Yet as he looked into her eyes, he feared she already possessed more power over him than Catherine or his mother ever had, except he did not understand how or why.

Forewarned is forearmed, he thought, and wondered if he had the strength to fight a blind, mewling kitten, much less a vibrant, determined young woman with raven curls and sparkling emerald eyes. A woman whose seeming concern rocked him to his depths.

"I didn't mean to startle you," he said, fighting nausea.

With her mask of concern in place, he almost believed her sincere. What had she to *gain* from caring for him? Something, he did not doubt. He simply must learn what.

"I've made you ill with my ridiculous notions," she said, placing her cool hand to his brow.

Justin struggled with the roiling in his gut and took another deep breath. "Been asleep for weeks. Told me so yourself. Must have done something right." He wished her touch did not feel so splendid. He closed his eyes hoping she would keep her hand where it was. Her violet scent brought a fleeting memory. An angel of mercy, beautiful and soft. He tried to hold the concept, but the monstrous ill feeling in the pit of his belly plagued him.

She removed her hand—more's the pity—and brushed it against his cheek, another touch he recognized. Craved.

When Justin slept again, Faith spoke to Jenny and Sally together in Beth's room. "My patient will need most of my attention for a while. His illness has taken a bad turn. Sally, I need you to take full charge of Beth, but I shall spend every minute with her I can. Jenny, I'll count on you to fetch the necessities for my patient while Harris is away."

Their willingness removed such a burden. "Thank you, both of you." Afraid to be away from Justin too long, she kissed Beth's jam-sticky cheek, and could almost imagine herself being squeezed in return. "Be a good girl," Faith said, tucking a curl behind Beth's ear. "I love you."

Beth gave her Justin's wistful I-wish-it-were-so smile. Like him, she wanted to believe Faith's words, except she thought she knew better. Both would need tender care in the days ahead. And if it was love they needed, Faith would see they got it.

Upon her return, Faith regarded her patient. Her grandfather had looked healthier laid out in the front parlor the morning of his funeral, than Justin did right now.

She wheeled him back to the bed to transfer him into it. Holding him the way Harris taught her, she moved him ... but he woke. "Relax, Justin. Don't fight me."

He did relax, and she hauled him onto the bed, his breathing labored, brow damp. "I can handle you better when you're asleep," she said by way of apology. "Please say something."

"Weak," he whispered. "Like an old woman. Bloody degrading. Cold too."

Faith got another blanket. "Are you still hungry? I could—"

"God no." He shuddered. "More blankets."

He trembled uncontrollably, his complexion a muddy gray. Placing more covers over him didn't help. Faith had never seen anyone shake so. His eyes held a plea.

"Blast," she swore. "I'm killing you with my theories. I'm giving you your medicine."

"No," he said, teeth chattering.

Oh, Lord. "Is there nothing I can do?"

Shaking his head, he closed his eyes, his brow and hands cold as ice. Faith removed her shoes, climbed under the covers, and took him into her arms to share her body's heat. "We'll get through this together," she said.

He held her so tight, Faith was certain she'd be bruised—a small price to pay for his recovery, if recovery it were to be.

His chills interspersed with pain, Justin trembled, teeth chattering and gnashing in turn. Judging by the way he stiffened, groaned, and went limp, he lost consciousness, until another bout roused him again. And when it did, he uttered a string of ragged curses, peppered with succinct words—inappropriate she was certain. "Blast it, Faith, don't listen to me, I'm a vulgar son-of-a-bitch."

And that, she thought, must *certainly* soothe her sensibilities. She might laugh, if she didn't want so badly to cry. "Say what you will; I shall wipe it from memory with due haste."

His chuckle ended in a hiss; a new agony taking him in its grip.

Most of the time he didn't know who or where he was, why or how he suffered, much less what he said. The consequences of her decision to withhold his medicine had, indeed, become his.

Justin could very well die in her arms.

Time passed at the pace of a garden snail making its plodding way up hill. Faith's clothes were drenched with sweat. Justin dozed fitfully. Minutes turned to hours. Toward morning, when his trembling subsided somewhat, Faith eased from his side to run to her room to wash and change.

When she returned, he was as ashen as the first time she saw him. Now, they teetered at the opposite pole from twenty-four hours ago. *Not* receiving the medicine was killing him.

Faith fetched the vial. "Forgive me," she whispered, "But you need this." And she poured the medicine down his throat.

He choked and spat out the pungent brown liquid. For a second Faith gazed at her splattered gown—then she looked into furious dark eyes. Demon's eyes—wasn't that what his childhood nurse called them? *Be happy you'll never be pierced with the likes of his stare,* Vincent had said, and a piercing stab, she felt.

Then Justin became violently ill, putting period to her morning wash and fresh dress. When his spasms subsided, he bestowed upon her another dark penetrating stare and a long, low snarl of fury.

She cleaned him up in silence, and after a good-night growl, he slipped into an exhausted sleep. She sat and fretted. He remained in a coma when he took the medicine. He became deathly ill without it.

Her nursing skills proved worthless in the face of the paradox.

At the window, Faith looked beyond the firmament toward He who allowed Justin's suffering. "He has had enough!" she shouted. "Do you hear? Enough. Have mercy."

When Justin finally woke, after two agonizing days, the stubble on his cheeks gave him the look of a pirate—an angry pirate, inclined toward flogging and carnage.

Faith hid dismay behind bravado. "I do not know how a man who has imbibed strong drink appears, but I expect that's how you look right now."

"And exactly how I feel. No thanks to you."

If he wasn't absolutely right, Faith might defend herself, but she had intensified his torment rather than lessen it. Swallowing the lump in her throat, she raised her chin. "Whatever you think, I have done only what I thought best for *you*."

"I can almost believe it."

Ire replaced her guilt. "Try a little harder then, if you please."

His raised brow spoke of challenge.

She took up the gauntlet. "I insist that you eat *something*."

He crossed his arms. "My stomach will pitch anything you give it."

"In just that event, I sent for quince jelly." He looked entirely doubtful, but when she presented the filled spoon, he opened his mouth. As the victor in this battle of wits, Faith smiled inwardly. His hand to his stomach stopped her celebration.

She, with a quick basin, Justin poised at the ready, they waited, but the quince jelly did not get pitched.

"Did it help, do you think?"

"I'm ... not sure."

Faith raised a spoonful of soft marrow pudding.

Dread in his look, Justin accepted the offering.

The clock counted the minutes, and time augured success.

Hard on its heels, she offered another.

"Damn it. Wait." He took a deep breath. Nodded.

After he swallowed, his eyes widened then he shook his head and lay back. "All I can stomach."

"You'll lose your strength."

"Not to worry. None to lose." He stared at a trembling hand. "So blasted weak."

"I worry that you are too ill to go without your medicine. Let me give it to you."

"Makes me sleep." He caught his breath. "Might have for eternity. I know ... I am alive, however sick I become, this way. *No more medicine.*"

"You wish to stay awake and suffer?"

Justin touched her cheek. "I'd rather look at you than sleep."

Faith didn't want him to see how his words or his touch affected her. "I'll do everything I can to help you."

"Why so downcast?"

"It hurts me to see you like this."

"Hurts me more." His chuckle became a groan. Beads of sweat formed on his upper lip, his eyes glazed and his body went rigid. He looked as if he could scream in agony, but he remained silent.

She bathed his brow.

"Go away," he said between clenched teeth.

"What?"

"Go ... away."

"I will not!"

"Get out! I don't need you! I don't need anyone!" He groaned, pulled her close, and buried his face in her skirts. One hand dug into her hip, the other ripped her sash. And he passed out.

Faith lowered him to the bed. "I'll never leave you."

Justin's temperature rose, and Faith forced Calamint tea down his throat as he slept. She watched his chest for every breath, selfishly thanking God he lived still.

When he doubled over, teeth gnashing, she rubbed his back. She tried to soothe him in every way she knew—with her touch, her words, her presence. "I would take your pain as my own, if I could," she whispered, while through the incredibly long night, Justin continued to refuse his medicine.

By morning his fever raged. He kicked off his blankets and tore at his nightshirt. Faith removed it, and his grateful look nearly undid her. He couldn't drink the water he craved faster than it passed through his skin in perspiration—perspiration which did not cool him. She needed to lower his temperature.

Barley water did not help. Neither the Cinchona bark, a newly-discovered fever remedy Jenny brought from the apothecary in the village. It seemed nothing helped. If it were winter, she'd cover him with snow.

A memory surfaced—her as a child at Aunt Lizzie's, where they enjoyed ice chunks in August. Where she lived, in Arundel, squares were cut from the river Arun's frozen surface and stored underground between layers of hay for use later in the year.

Faith asked, and Jenny confirmed that an icehouse stood near Killashandra.

"Have ice fetched immediately ... three, no *six* large chunks."

Two hours later, to Faith's shock, Hemsted, Vincent's man of affairs, brought buckets of chipped ice, introducing himself as he entered. Faith had no time to answer his inquiries, and after a glance toward her patient, he went on his way.

She covered Justin with a blanket and placed the ice atop. Tiny chips, she placed on his tongue to quench his never-ending thirst. And through chattering teeth, he begged for more. The ice melted against his fevered body so fast, Faith had it broken into larger pieces the next morning.

Again, Hemsted delivered it. Again, Faith dismissed him.

Justin's fever raged for three days. On the fourth, though still elevated, it no longer seemed life-threatening. When Faith poured that morning's ice over him, Justin just about jumped from the bed. With a sweep of his arm, he sent ice skittering and shattering in every direction. "Blast it, Faith, if you want to freeze me for posterity, wait till I'm dead!" And she laughed. His temperature may not yet be normal, but she discontinued packing him in ice, though he devoured all the chips he could get.

Her next step was to bathe him with cool, sudsy water. Then she exchanged the oil-cloth beneath him for clean sheets and covered him to his waist. Bare-chested and clean, he slept like a babe for the whole day, giving her a chance to bathe *her* smelly self, and spend time with Beth.

That he survived the raging fever, Faith believed was certain proof that Justin would recover. But that evening, icy tremors seized him once again, and he opened his arms to her. That he trusted she would warm him with her body was the first sign he could trust at all. She wondered if he would later remember it as progress or weakness. When she climbed beneath the blankets, he pulled her against him and held her as if in letting go he would be lost. She derived as much comfort from him as he from her. Only night turning to day, and day back to night, augured the passing of time.

Faith bathed, ate or changed, when Justin slept, which to her relief happened more often. The cycle repeated itself, yet as the days flew, each lessened in duration and strength. By the fourth week, each lasted hours, rather than days. The phases between became longer, more restful, followed by periods of near-wellness.

When lucid, Justin watched her. And the more intimately she tended him, the angrier he became. Her bathing him, in particular, called upon his disdain. As now.

Faith sponged him feeling the tension in every cord and sinew of his body, and she sought his distraction in words. "How old are you, your grace?"

He frowned as if he couldn't believe what he heard. "You call me Justin when you lie in my arms."

"And you call me many things, none of which I would like you to make a habit of using."

He nearly smiled. "I want you to call me Justin. Please."

She nodded. "Justin. How old are you?"

"Thirty-four. You?"

"Twenty."

"My God. A babe. I am forced to depend on a child."

"A child who has been caring for you, lifting you, feeding you—" Faith saw his horror. "I am simply saying that I am an adult, certainly no child."

"You're right, of course. *I* am the child. Cannot even piss without help."

For the most part, she ignored him when he was coarse. But not today. "No, not a child; an old man. Doddering. Feeble-minded."

She laughed at his consternation. "Don't begin a word game you're not willing to lose," she said. "You scored not one hit with those singular verbal darts you toss." She nodded in satisfaction. "And your bath is finished."

The next time he became ill, as had become ritual, she asked if he wanted his medicine.

"I'll not take the foul potion. I cannot."

"Just a bit."

"Blast it, Faith. I would rather be alive and in pain, than trapped in hell ... alive."

The picture his words painted so moved her, Faith's heart nearly broke, and she squeezed his hand. "I'll not ask again."

He lifted their clasped hands to his heart. "Finally. It took you long enough. You're so persistent, so resolute. No matter how often I said no, you—"

"Were I not tenacious and unyielding, I would still dose you twice daily, at eight precisely ... and you might not be bullying me now, you might be six feet under. Did you ever think of that?"

He crossed his arms. "No. I did not."

"If you think to intimidate me—flat on your back, me towering over you—think again. You had best recover your strength and stand looking down at *me*, If you intend that I should shudder in my slippers."

He touched his lips to her fingertips, and the look in his eyes as he watched her above them, made her soar inside , as she savored every nuance.

He lowered his arms to his sides, still holding her hand, and gave her one of his wistful smiles. "I'm glad you're persistent and resolute. And stubborn. And determined. And hard-headed—"

"That's quite enough." This was as close as Justin Devereux would ever get to a thank you or an apology. And if he said one more word, she would cry. She cleared her throat. "Let's celebrate."

"What?"

"You know. A celebration. Because you're off the medicine."

Justin suspected his nurse was touched, but he'd humor her. "Certainly." He bowed—as well as he could in a bed. "May I have the honor of partnering you in this dance?"

Her laugh brought an odd need, a longing for something fringed with danger ... and still he yearned.

She stopped laughing, and bristled at his silence, her brows furrowed with worry. Lord, he was tired of her disquiet. He wanted her to laugh more. "You're right. A celebration is in order. Open yon windows. All of them. As wide as you can."

She gave him a head-tilt, a humor-the-idiot look, and he laughed. They were trying to humor each other. So be it. But she was smiling again. Confused, yes, but delighted. She opened several windows. "There you go. Plan to catch yourself a bird?"

"Wider still, if you please."

She threw open the casements, inviting the warm summer breeze in, a hint of honeysuckle on its wings, and stood waiting.

Honeysuckle. He liked the scent. And something akin to contentment filled him—odd considering his circumstances. Circumstances that might be deadly were it not for Faith Wickham. How had he managed without her? How would he go on if she left?

Justin supposed that if he worried about the future, he must be less concerned that his death was imminent. Which must be a good thing.

He caught her concern again. "Why so quiet, my faithful nurse?" He chuckled at his pun. "This is a celebration, remember?"

He raised a vial of medicine and gave his nurse a calculating smile, his *famous* smile, the one that, over the years, felled many a white-clad virgin, scandalizing her doting mama in the process.

But Faith's return grin was just as deadly.

Justin realized that grin had the power to slay him and his humor changed. "To hell with foul medicine!" He threw the vial. But it bounced off the sill and landed with a thud at her feet.

"You missed," she said.

He tried to recover his light mood. "Ah well, I threw it symbolically, if not actually, out the window."

Faith's eyes widened and she blushed.

"Good God, did you think I was aiming at you?"

"I ... I didn't know." Her eyes began to sparkle. "But now I do." She retrieved the vial from the floor. "To hell with sleep," she said and tossed it out the window.

His reaction to her enjoyment turned physical, so Justin thought his heart might fail, and he decided not to fight her, but to enjoy her. For as long as he dared.

She went to the bedstand and took up several bottles, tossing them as one. "To hell with death."

Clink, clink, clink! The vials hit the elm by the window, and a cacophony grew, squawking, flapping, as a swarm of rooks took flight from its leafy depths. And amid the bustle, one misguided avis entered and circled the room ... then as quickly flew back out again.

Faith turned to him wide-eyed, and they burst into laughter.

She tossed several more vials, sending to hell every manner of evil, including a childhood foe whose ears should grow so big, he should trip over them and break his fool neck.

Justin was captivated.

She fell laughing beside him on the bed. They wrapped their arms around each other to catch their breaths. Lord, he liked having her here. This, friendship, this *esprit de corps* was heady stuff. He had never experienced anything like. Daunting, to be sure, yet uplifting. "You kept some of the vials. You won't try to pour them down my gullet while I sleep will you?"

She chuckled against his neck where she fit so nicely. "If Harris finds us an apothecary to determine the ingredients, we might need them as samples." She yawned.

He'd ask her about the samples another time. "Go to sleep."

Moments later, he could tell from her breathing that she obeyed him. He closed his eyes to savor. He liked her here. He liked *her.*

Dangerous, he knew, and perhaps when he put distance and time between him and her nurturing heart, her laughter nothing but a fond memory, he might remember she was a woman like all the rest. But for now, he would enjoy these rare moments.

He pulled her close, inhaled the scent of her—violets. Tested the feel of her—silk. He saw images ... of her leaning against a window berating God for letting him suffer. By all that was holy, he'd never heard of anyone giving hell to God.

He could almost feel her hand rubbing his back as he'd writhed in agony, her tears warm on his shoulder. He'd watched those salty drops trail down his arm, and he became so moved, his own tears fell.

In his mind's eye, he saw the memory of moonlight revealing Faith in his arms, sharing the warmth of her body with him, taking his icy hands and sliding them into her bodice. She'd gasped at his touch. He'd pulled his hands away, but she took them back, and blushed, he knew, because her face had warmed his neck, a temperature for which he had been supremely grateful.

He saw her fear as she removed his nightshirt when the heat emanated from him in suffocating waves. Then her look of profound relief as she'd packed him in ice, her hands so cold she'd wrapped them in towels to keep her fingers from freezing.

He was too tired, suddenly, to separate one image of Faith from the other. The forms mingled. And within them shimmered the angel who had come to him while he suffered in hell. The angel who had set him free.

CHAPTER FIVE

BITTERSWEET, RIPE WITH orange berries and opening yellow pods, lined the stable drive. Summer neared its end. Harris should be back by now. Possible reasons for his tardiness seemed too alarming for Faith to contemplate.

She helped Justin to the opposite side of the bed so she could cover the near side with an oilcloth for his morning bath. Then she poured hot water into the basin and gathered towels and razor.

"Your wages must be extravagant to inspire such dedication."

The better Justin got, it seemed, the nastier he became. But Faith was in no mood for his irascibility this morning. "Speak not one word of payment for your care, else I'll throw the chamber pot at your thick head." She had even less patience for his arrogant smile. "Yes I became your nurse for the wages, and as to whether they're generous, I cannot say. But were they tuppence or guineas per quarter, I would give the same care. Now get your lazy self back to this side. You need the exercise."

"You, Miss, are being paid to tend me. See that you do."

Like her first morning at Killashandra, she was being bullied by an arrogant duke. "You are exactly like your brother."

"That's a bloody spiteful thing to say!"

If she'd thought him provoked previously, it was nothing to this. She shouldn't have mentioned Vincent, considering Justin's vow of vengeance.

"What, pray tell, do you know of my brother?"

"The benighted man harped on the subject of my wages using the same acerbic tones ... as if I should grovel with thanks for his generosity."

Justin scoffed. "Vincent is never generous. If he pays you well, he has something to gain by it."

Faith helped Justin wishing he hadn't confirmed that suspicion. "Nevertheless ... should I, a stranger to you both, have said, 'No wages necessary. I shall be pleased to care for such a nasty, disagreeable man from the kindness of my heart?'"

"You couldn't have described me so. I was unconscious."

She poked her finger into his hard, unmoving chest. "Correct! And would still be, if not for me."

He frowned at her poking finger.

She removed it and attended to dipping the washcloth in hot water. "I didn't know yet what a chuckle-head you were."

To erase Justin's scowl, she washed his face with undue vigor, ignoring his oath. In like manner, she washed his neck, shoulders and arms. "It seems to me, did I nothing to earn my wage, you would be correct to complain. But there is no lack in the care I give you."

"You nearly killed me with your care!"

"You had accomplished the near-dead state before I arrived." She rolled him over. "I earn every brass farthing."

"I cannot agree, as I do not know how much you earn."

"And you never shall!" As she washed his chest, his interest became pointed and disquieting, and she became self-conscious.

"You missed a spot," he said.

She looked up, to see if he was serious. "I beg your pardon." His probing eyes sparkled and Faith wished he would turn his avid examination from her face. Would that she could bathe him and forget it ... but the lout must bring it to both their attentions.

"I said, my dear, you have missed a spot." Even his voice had gained strength in the last weeks.

She had no doubt that he took pleasure in fanning the embers of her discomfort. "Where?" she asked,

He pointed obscurely, somewhere below his belly. "There."

"Where!"

"Your vocabulary seems to have taken wing, your wits along with it. I indicate your lack because I am uncomfortable, and would like to be washed more thoroughly. More zealously."

Lord, his words shivered her in the most incredible places.

He raised a brow. "Surely the procedure is not abhorrent to you. Because, my dear, you look as if you have taken a disgust of your work. And with the lavish wages my brother is paying you."

Faith shut her mouth and lathered the cloth zealously. Perhaps if it was thick with suds and she washed his ... parts with speed, the procedure wouldn't seem so intimate. She gathered the courage to work her way toward that dreaded triangle of mystery.

"Surely mine is not the first man's body you've seen?"

"Certainly not." How could a voice she'd prayed so long to hear, infuriate her so? Of course she'd never seen another man's body. Papa had washed grandfather, and Justin looked different from little Andy's.

Hands shaking, determined to finish, Faith arrived at the dratted location he indicated, making certain a thick layer of suds covered him. She did a thorough washing, scrubbing around and under parts she yearned to examine at her leisure. She lowered her chin to hide her color. *Examine at her leisure? Really?* She scrubbed harder.

"Bloody hell!" Justin pushed her hand away and nearly doubled over cupping himself.

That area *was* softer than she expected. "Did I hurt them?"

"I wanted to be washed not castrated."

"Cat's what?" she asked.

"You mutilated my—"

"Never mind, dolt." She didn't want to know what she crushed. She retrieved the washcloth and threw it at his head. "That's what you get, you disagreeable, bad-tempered...."

He caught her arm as she turned away. "Faith. I was teasing."

"Knowing full well how uncomfortable I found handling your private parts?"

"I like you handling my private parts."

Faith pulled from his grip and emptied the wash basin over his no-longer private parts. "Go to the devil, Justin Devereux."

"Damn it, woman, that's hot." He spoiled his rage by chuckling at her ire.

In her room, Faith leaned against her closed door. Checkered with outrageous curses—for her entertainment, she was certain—his amusement sounded wonderful.

Later she returned to find him naked and sound asleep on the dry side of the bed. And for the first time, Faith was able to study him, his wide shoulders, no longer defined by bone, but muscle, the dark hair on his chest that arrowed toward ... everything. She should be embarrassed, but she was not, and she could not look away. Even in repose—and she had once seen that particular man part otherwise—Faith thought him splendid.

Her mother had spoken to her of desire as the need for the physical expression of love between two people. But Faith had not really understood ... until this moment, when she responded physically, her body reacting of its own volition, to the beauty of his.

Entranced, she stepped closer ... and looked into dark knowing eyes, the lines around them blossoming with his smile.

Justin wanted to say, 'Caught you,' but she'd catch fire, so red were her cheeks. "I'm cold," he said, instead, and was thanked with a grateful expression as she covered him.

Then he watched her change the bed linen—the reason for its slogged state and her clandestine examination, sitting heavily between them. He liked the blush that stole up her neck. Not for the first time, he wondered where it began and wanted to ask. But she was distressed enough without him embarrassing her further. Did she sense this attachment between them? A connection forged by care, admiration, and something ... more? "Damn it, no!"

Faith looked up. "Cross again? Have I tucked a blanket wrong? I vow, you'd find fault with a fat goose."

"Sit down, will you. Your fussing makes me dizzy."

"Fussing is it? You would rather sleep in a wet bed?"

"I expect I have before."

She regarded her hands with interest. "Not since I arrived."

"I thank you for that." He took her hand. "Forgive my fitful disposition. It's difficult to lie here and be waited upon. I am become a burden, and I had rather be the savior than the saved."

Mischief sparked in her emerald eyes as she slipped his nightshirt over his head. "As you would rather be the seducer than the seduced?"

He smiled inwardly and decided to allow her attempt to cheer him. "Seducer? What makes you say that?"

"I hear that you were a rake of the first order."

"Good God, way out in Arundel? How old were you? Five?"

Her laugh, like cool water sluiced over his fevered body. They'd taken a turn in their relationship. It spoke more of man and woman, less of patient and nurse. And Justin wasn't certain he liked it. "I left raking behind when I married." *Aye, and his manhood as well.* "Pray, where did you hear such tales?"

"Mrs. Tucker."

"You befriended that harridan? I am impressed. Your talents

are endless, it seems. Can you tame a wild beast?"

She looked directly into his eyes. "Not yet."

"Perhaps, but you have awakened him."

Her green eyes widened.

"Be prudent with your maidenly innocence, my dear, lest you be ravished for the sport of it."

"Are maidens more likely to be ravished than matrons?"

"Yes, for maidens are tender and easy to the bit."

"Like lambs? Tender and tasty to the palate, you mean."

"Do I?"

Faith turned to tidy the room.

He had learned to measure her by her barometer of blushing agitation. And at this moment, it threatened combustion.

"Harris told me about your way with women. How they flirted outrageously. You were deemed quite the catch, he said."

"Harris is an old fool."

Her laugh was easy and melodious, and Justin savored it. "I have called him such myself," she said. "But I love him."

"Foolish child. How can you love someone you hardly know? You throw the word about as if the absurdity exists."

She straightened, alert, wary. "Does it not, in your opinion?"

He damn near snorted. "It does not."

"Believe as you wish. But you are more likely to be captured by what catches you unaware, physical or emotional." She tilted her head. "And I begin to believe love can be both at once."

Justin chuckled self-derisively. "And I called you a child." That would teach him to consider this woman dangerous in more ways than the usual. If he allowed it, she might make him believe in fairies and love-potions. Now that he was better, he should send her away, but at the notion, pain struck at his center, deep and agonizing. "Damn it, Faith! Stop fussing and come rest."

"You have a decidedly low opinion of my actions. But to humor you, your grace, I shall rest." She sat in her chair, lay her head back and closed her eyes. "For a moment."

She was probably more exhausted than he. Sooty circles rimmed her eyes. Her hair hung limp. Damn. She should see to herself, at least as well as she saw to him. "Faith?" God's teeth, she slept quickly. "Faith, wake up." He grasped her skirt and tugged. "Blast it, your neck will be sore."

She jumped. "Are you ill?" She stood so fast, she looked as if she might faint.

He held her hips to steady her, sliding his hands to her waist, learning her shape with his palms. "I wonder how you can care for someone else, when you cannot care for yourself."

"I have the sense to cosh you. You frightened me senseless. Are you behaving like a bear because you're hungry as one?"

He curled his fingers into her, stroking her waist ever so slightly. "No, but I may have a thorn in my paw."

She pursed her lips. "I must conclude then that both paws are injured, for they seem to be seeking ease against my person."

He surprised himself with his bark of laughter, as much as he apparently surprised her. He gave her waist a squeeze. "I hereby order you to go and rest. I shall call if I need you."

She stepped from his hold. "Are you ordering me to neglect you so you may discharge me without conscience? Thank you, but no." Her look changed. "You're flushed. Do you have a fever?" She placed her hand on his forehead, slid it to his cheek.

He turned his face into her touch, nearly kissing her palm, and noted the danger.

"Stop that," she said. From her look, you'd think he'd broken her heart with such attention.

"Blast it, Faith. If you don't lie down beside me, I'll shout down the house and everyone will know I'm well."

"You wouldn't."

Of course he wouldn't. "Do as I say, or you will find out." Stubborn, stubborn woman. "Come; you'll be here if I need you."

The set of her jaw told him she didn't intend to budge.

"Damn it, you have slept beside me before. Hell, you've slept entangled with me. Stay above the covers, if you must. I promise on my honor as a—"

"Rake."

"A gentleman. Have you no trust in me?"

She raised a brow. "You know the meaning of trust then?"

He ignored the taunt. "I'm hardly in a position to compromise you."

She laughed again. "I'm so very compromised now, there is little left over which to worry."

"There is much over which to worry, make no mistake." He only wished there were more. Though he had the inclination, his body refused to cooperate. But there was more to life than the sexual, was there not? And there could be pleasure for Faith, at least. He could ... oh wicked, dangerous thought.

"I confess, I am tired," she said.

"Finally, you show a modicum of sense."

"As usual, you act the hind end of a—"

"Hush. Come to bed."

Shaking her head, Faith grudgingly climbed onto the opposite side and curled up, facing him "Did you never wonder," she asked, "Why God made more horses hind ends than he made horses?"

"You'll get no rest, if you're annoyed," he said.

She released a slow breath, and fought her smile. He applauded her attempt. Her thick lashes fluttered against porcelain cheeks.

As Justin closed his own eyes, he wondered if Faith coming to nurse him was a gift, or a curse.

Justin awoke to find Faith's breast against his hand. He felt her budding nipple, closed his eyes and wished ... Damnation. He eased himself away. Distance held safety for them both. He was a man flawed. And married. And Faith Wickham deserved better.

He'd never known a woman like her. *Known* one? He couldn't imagine one. No amount of money could induce Catherine to endure what Faith had. He'd seen his suffering reflected in Faith's eyes. And no matter his yearning, nothing could come of a connection between them. He had ended, he reminded himself, half a man, and that half was married.

Even if he divorced Catherine, which he would, an unmarried woman could not consort with a divorced man. He nearly laughed. An unmarried woman could not sleep beside a married man either, but Faith did exactly that. Strange circumstances, he told himself, made unusual bed-mates. Still, to avoid society's censure, when he recovered, he and Faith must part. And with that realization came pain, sharp and stabbing, and Justin groaned.

Faith sat up. "What's wrong, love?"

She was so foggy, she didn't realize what she said. Hell, she probably called every mewling kitten, love. As always, when he became ill, she took him into her arms.

Justin held her. He needed her strength until desolation passed. She thought him physically ill, and illness did plague him. Illness of spirit. For suddenly he felt overwhelming grief, as if his struggle had been for naught and he might as well have expired as recovered. There was nothing for him here. He'd lost Beth, and Faith, well, *she* was nothing more than an aberration, a last favor from above.

"It's all right. I'm here," she said, sensing his despair. "You've lost so much. It must be difficult to come to terms with all of it."

Beth's death? Never. "Terms be damned. I'll never accept what happened, and I'll have retribution, make no mistake."

"Revenge won't solve anything. And you've healing to do before you're ready to take on the world. Be patient and we'll do it together. All of it. In time."

She would stand by him? While he ran his brother through? "You don't know what you're saying. Go home to that big, happy family with a mother and father who love you. That's rare, Faith, a family like yours. You know nothing of fighting." He looked into her eyes. "You know nothing of losing."

Faith struggled from his arms and rose. "I know of struggle and loss. I fought for your life, and I fought hard. Perhaps this time I won. But with my grandfather, I did not. And he lost more than I; he lost his life. Her eyes filled with unshed tears. "You're right. I'm nothing but a useless child."

"Don't cry."

"I never cry."

Not for herself. But she cried for others. He'd seen her. He couldn't keep from reaching out, from pulling her down with him. The kiss began tenderly. The taste of her intoxicated him. He teased her lips open with his, then she whimpered as he closed his mouth over hers. She was young, untried. He should stop.

Instead, he settled her across his lap and kissed her again. "You taste like honey." Her heart beat against his. He pulled her closer and gloried in her compliance. She stroked his nape, sliding her hand beneath his nightshirt before snatching it back.

Heat raced through Faith. She didn't know if it was shock over her wandering hand, or just plain lust. Likely lust, the kind Jimmy Kennedy told her about when they were twelve.

And she'd thought he was making the whole thing up.

But this was real. She was in Justin's bed, sitting across his lap, simmering like a pudding in his arms. How could such a gentle touch evoke such heat? And did she alone melt within the inferno? She thought not. Justin breathed hard, as if he'd been running. Under her hand, his heart beat strong and fast.

His kiss gentled; he stroked the side of her breast, and white-hot flames shot through her. If she stood, her knees would buckle, the pulsating surge within her incredibly shocking and remarkably pleasant.

It was bad. It was good. A rapture she never imagined.

When Justin stroked her naked breast, Faith sighed, floated, and opened her eyes to watch, mesmerized, as he encircled the delicate tip with his lips. "Justin!"

He looked up. Confused. As if he burned with fever still.

Faith slid from his lap, to catch her breath.

"Faith I—"

"We have to stop. I never ... I mean it was ... fascinating. But I...." She craved answers. When had this attraction begun? Where would it end? And would she survive? "I'm sorry."

"*You're* sorry." Justin's laughter resonated with insult. His look changed to anger, disappointment.

Faith's foolish apology echoed in her head. She really was an ignorant child. Even his narrow-eyed expression mocked her. She looked to where his gaze centered ... and nearly expired at the sight of her exposed breast, the nipple hard and aching. She gasped and turned, her haste ridiculous in its tardiness.

Willing her gathering tears not to spill, she pulled her chemise up to cover herself. And with shaking hands, she retied the laces she couldn't remember coming undone.

Awkwardness plagued her. How she dreaded looking into his eyes. Surely he knew she liked what he did, without her being foolish enough to say so. Fascinating indeed. Did this skill he possessed have any bearing on Justin's popularity with the ladies?

Suddenly she hated every woman he ever touched. Hated being one of them. She wondered if even a one, including herself, meant any more to him than a moment of stolen pleasure.

Without turning, Faith rose from her side of the bed. Sun rays needled into the room illuminating her in her foolishness. She smoothed her skirts. If only she could leave without facing him, but she needed to go around the bed to get to her door. So she raised her chin and trained her gaze on her goal.

As she passed his side of the bed, Justin caught her about the waist and drew her back. Once she was there, his hands at her waist, his thumbs stroking beneath her breasts, she couldn't seem to gather the moral strength to move.

"I'm sorry," he whispered. "I should not have." His hands slid down her hips and away.

Silence.

She needn't have worried about facing him. He lay back, shielding his eyes. "It was no good from the start," he said.

His words, like a knife, cut her. Had he disliked their intimacy? For her it had been ... why she had practically.... Her heart quickened just thinking about it. She would have said yes to whatever he'd asked, would have let him do anything.

She should be grateful she displeased him. Her virtue remained intact. Which mattered little, for she wanted him to pull her close and kiss her again, to say how wonderful she made him feel. She was a naive child, and the worldly Justin Devereux had kissed *women* who knew what they were about, who knew how to please a man.

In her room, she shut the door between, leaned against it, and touched her breast. A tender ache, not pain, not pleasure. Foolish her. She longed for something of which she knew nothing.

Pacing her room, she craved a few moments away. She checked Justin and saw he slept. Ten minutes later, she approached the beach she'd seen from the window. The hair blowing in her eyes gave her a good, solid reason to be annoyed. She pulled her shawl tight against the chill in the September wind. Gulls circled an outcropping of rocks, their cries in sympathy with her plight.

When she reached the shingle, she scooped a handful of pebbles and stepped to the lapping froth. The sea swallowed a smooth bronze stone with barely a ripple. Creeping foam pushed her back. "Beware of forces more powerful than you," it warned. And she understood, for she could as easily drown in Justin's kisses.

She walked back up the beach and sat amid ballooning skirts on dry, sun-warmed sand, hugged her knees, and gazed at the horizon.

Her first morning at Killashandra, Justin opened his eyes. Then she'd wanted to see them again. When she did, she wanted his smile, to hear his voice, his laugh.

She'd wanted him to awaken. And he did.

Then she wanted him to get well. And by all appearances, that wish was being granted as well.

Now she wanted him to love her. She drew a heart in the sand, and erased it. Why could she never be satisfied? In those first weeks, had she known the progress Justin would make, she would have been the happiest of women. Which is exactly what she would be ... happy ... and his nurse.

But she would never, ever, forget what they'd shared today.

Justin would recover and she would go home. Jimmy Kennedy would come down from Oxford. He'd begged her for kisses two years ago. At Christmas, she would see if he still felt the same ... if Justin recovered enough for her to leave by then.

After a trek down the beach, Faith climbed the sloped path through shoulder-high oat grass toward the trim lawns and formal gardens of Killashandra.

"Miss Wickham? Wait, please." Hemsted, Vincent's man, strode toward her. Then the cat from the library charged, making her lose her footing.

With a shout, her pursuer caught her. She shrieked, and even after he regained his balance, Faith was so shaken, she kept her arms around his neck.

Hemsted grinned. "I confess I wanted to get your attention, but it was not my plan to knock you off your feet." He carried her up the path. "Though to be honest, I cannot have asked for a more fortuitous outcome." He set her down and bowed.

Faith couldn't help smiling. He had an engaging manner. But she must remember to whom his loyalty belonged. "Did you want me, Mr. Hemsted?"

He indicated the path back to the house. "Shall we?"

She nodded and they strolled side by side.

"I wondered how your patient is." He shook his head. "Rather, I should say that his brother, my employer, wishes to know."

The sun caught his hair just so and the wind played with a gold lock tossing it against his brow and away. Though he seemed kind and easy to look upon, she must remain wary. "My patient is the same."

"Has he recovered from the fever? His Grace is anxious to know, as this was a first downward turn since the accident."

Faith grimaced inwardly. "I can imagine his agitation at the news." *Elation more like.*

"Yes," Hemsted said soberly, hands behind his back, face to the wind.

Faith examined his expression to see if he knew of Vincent's malevolence, but his look appeared free of guile. Lord, she *liked* him.

He stepped on uneven ground and caught himself. "Blast." He examined the grass. "Ah. The culprit." He retrieved and offered said culprit for her inspection.

With a start, Faith saw the familiar amber vial. They stood beneath the elm, of course, and Justin's window two floors above. Oh God.

Hemsted measured its weight, tossed it up and caught it. "What could it be? I know. A fairy bottle with three wishes."

Faith forced a smile. "What shall we wish for, then?"

Hemsted flashed a grin. "I would be no gentleman if I answered. And call me Max." He unstopped the vial and sniffed. "Ugh." In a flash he held it away. "Whatever it was, it's gone brackish." He dropped the cruet but pocketed the stopper.

Faith's heart beat so loudly, it was a wonder he didn't hear. What had they been thinking to throw the things out the window? But her gallant said no more as he walked her to her door. "Might you be free to dine with me tonight?"

Tonight she would be searching in the dark for evidence of Justin's recovery, every bottle of it. "I'm sorry. My patient will need me. This was the first time I've wandered and I'm not likely to do so again. Thank you for your rescue and your company. Good day."

Faith washed and changed before returning to Justin. He slept like a babe and hadn't even known she'd gone.

She would recover the evidence and see him well.

Then she would leave him.

CHAPTER SIX

J USTIN SAT BY the window, a book in his lap, dusk covering the world in smoky gray, Faith driving him crazy. He wanted his happy, smiling nurse back. He wanted to hear her laugh until he silenced her with his kiss. He ached to court her and wake beside her every morning, to make her cry his name in ecstasy.

He wanted everything he could not have.

Damn it. He did not want her. He did not want any of it.

It mattered not, because, since he broke her heart, when couldn't respond to her, Justin knew he would never be intimate with a woman again. Never father another child. Faith deserved better. Besides, he had no right to contemplate a future with Faith. Not when Catherine remained his wife.

He regarded her portrait. How angry he'd been at her for having it painted. He had excluded her from the family portrait he commissioned. By her own admission, she wanted no family. Yet out of spite, she'd had her own portrait painted and hung beside him and Beth.

Knowing its history, Vincent must have enjoyed ordering its placement here. Or, perhaps Catherine did, and he *supposed* this was as good a time as any to ask.

He touched Faith's arm, caught her attention, and removed her sewing from her lap. "Tell me. Is Catherine here at Killashandra?"

Faith paled visibly. "No, Catherine's not here ... exactly. Are you sure you wouldn't rather wait till another day when—"

"What do you mean, not exactly?"

Faith rose and poured tea. "I suppose since you're well enough to ask the question, you must be well enough to hear the answer."

"If she's not here, the answer can't be that bad, believe me."

The woman who faced *his* demons beside him looked as if she'd like to flee.

"Justin." Faith took his hand. "You remember the carriage accident in which you were injured?"

Pain shot through him. "Just say it, Faith."

She took a deep breath. "I shall ... in a minute. Would you rather a cup of chocolate?"

"Faith."

She rose and went to the bed to gaze at Catherine's portrait above it. "She was beautiful."

"Not on the inside ... what do you mean *was*?"

"Catherine *was* ... not as fortunate as you in that accident."

Justin could do nothing but stare. Faith's words made no sense. She touched his arm. When had she approached? "When I said not here, exactly, I meant ... she rests in the family vault not a quarter mile distant." She examined his expression and shook her head. "Catherine is dead, Justin."

"What?"

"I know you're confused about the carriage accident, but Catherine was killed."

Justin took a shuddering breath. "That's the one answer for which I was unprepared." He should feel sorrow or regret—he'd fancied himself in love with Cat once.

Faith's worry showed. He'd been silent too long. He squeezed her hand and gave her a smile meant to reassure. "I'm all right. Just stunned. Are you sure? I mean, could you be mistaken?"

"Vincent said she died in that carriage accident. I assumed you'd been traveling together."

"I don't believe so. I wish to God I could remember. My head aches for trying. Though my memories of the accident are vague, I didn't think Catherine could have been killed."

Faith tugged her hand away, her fury as clear as her worry a minute before. "How can you hear your wife is dead and remain perfectly calm? Have you no heart?"

"None that I know of. It would serve you well to remember that, Faith. I didn't need Catherine, and I don't need you."

Justin ignored Faith's pain. He'd needed to remind himself of her kinship to Catherine and his mother. Women. Vipers all. "I'm nearly as well as I can be. Soon enough you'll go home and marry the squire's son, Sir something, and have a dozen brats."

"Sir James Kennedy. And we plan on having six." With that, she was gone.

Faith sneaked out the servants' entrance. She must go around the house by the back, or risk being seen.

If only she knew how many vials they threw. She'd counted the remainder today. Half a dozen. It was likely they'd thrown only three, or four. Or ten. She groaned in frustration.

The wind off the salt-sharp sea whipped her skirts, flapping them so loud, she fancied someone must hear. She knelt under the elm, its denuded branches looking ready to snatch her in their grip. Her dress, wet through in a blink, she wandered on all fours, searching through slimy leaves for any number of pear-shaped bottles. If Hemsted or Vincent saw her....

A high-pitched cry sat Faith up. A near shriek. Leaves rustled. Cries grew shrill. Fast. Furious. Something skittered over her knees. Faith screamed and clambered to her feet.

A flying weight hit her, felled her. Fighting it, she stood, but it hung from her skirts for a beat, howled and ran.

A cat, that bloody damn black cat that frightened her in the library and nearly knocked her down yesterday. Faith held her heart so it would not fall from her chest, silent sobs shaking her.

There had been several cats. Tom cats on the prowl. Fighting over a female, no doubt. Lord. Oh, Lord. Shaking, Faith returned to her task, clinging to the ground for support, and calmed enough to return to her search. She found a break in the turf, recognized the path. She touched something, cold, wet, snatched her hand back. Reached again. She had one! She held her trophy against her, but she wasn't finished ... not by any means.

Justin swore. The evening had been long. Lonely. Where the devil was Faith? He'd think her in danger, such fear dogged him.

He shook it off, but trepidation tormented him until she came in at midnight. He had never been so relieved. "Sit with me," he said, hating to show how much he missed her, unable to keep from it.

She lifted a spoon to his lips. "Take this laudanum. It will help you sleep." She was all business and apparently still angry.

He opened his mouth to protest and she dosed him. Bitter liquid gagged him. He was furious and sick. "Don't ever do that again!" he said, when he stopped heaving. "Do you hear me?"

"All of England hears you."

He touched his stomach. "I've been dosed enough to last till my dying day, which, at this moment, I wish would come soon."

Faith slammed the bedstand drawer, then a window.

He wished she'd say something, but when she didn't, he did. "I'm a beast. A cad. A brute. An ill-tempered, ungrateful wretch. A useless—"

She crossed her arms and raised a brow. "Yes. You are."

"I'm sick and it's your fault." He pouted and knew it, but he couldn't stop. "I'm going to be awake all night again. How many days has it been? Never mind. It'll be worse if I know."

"Will you try some Chamomile tea?"

"I'll try anything." He raised a hand. "Almost anything."

An hour later, Justin realized the tea had relaxed him. Yet he was still awake, and Faith had fallen asleep. He touched a lone curl near his pillow. She would be angry when she woke, for she tried never to desert him when he lay wakeful. But she needed to rest, even if he couldn't.

She was not like Catherine. No matter how tired, she tended him without complaint. Times he couldn't bear himself, she remained and took his abuse. Sometimes she gave as good as she got, sometimes better. At others, she was skittish as a new colt. How could he blame her? He wanted her, and it made him angry. He couldn't have her, and it made him angry.

Faith stood by the window staring at the blue-green sea, worried about the vials waiting to reveal their secret. Autumn shivered rusty-leafed trees and purple thistle, and for the first time in her life, Faith prayed for winter. *Snow* would hide the evidence, if they got lucky this winter.

The devil slept in his chair. A good man, as Harris said. She only wished her heart did not leap when he looked at her. Daily, he improved, yet she feared one morning he would be gone. And she could not bear it.

How cozy he looked, though with a crimp in his position. Fearing he might become stiff and sore, she decided to put him back to bed. Asleep, he would be easy to handle.

She wheeled him to the bed, hoisted his unresisting body as Harris had taught her ... and dropped him. He looked so surprised, Faith laughed down at him. "You should have relaxed."

"This might come as a surprise, but I'm not used to being carried by ladies. Waking from sleep to find it so, muddled me."

"That may be, but now how do I get you up here and into this bed?"

Sprawled on the floor, he leaned on an elbow, head in hand. "A few years ago, I would have given my fortune to hear you say those words."

With the toe of her slipper, Faith tapped his elbow out from under him, but he regained his balance. Pulling on her skirts, he tugged her to the floor and kissed her. "I could pull myself along the floor to the bed. Then if ... excuse me ... *when* you lift me, there won't be so far to go."

"Go ahead, but if you find it painful, stop."

Justin managed to get to the bed, as pleased as her by his success. He even pulled himself up by the bedpost. She helped him the rest of the way. "You must be tired after that," she said.

"We'll both be tired and we'll sleep better. Go to your own bed tonight. It's best."

Looking at her hands to hide her disappointment, Faith agreed.

"Stay first, talk to me for a while before you go." He reached for her, but changed his mind. "Why did you believe I would die if I didn't take that medicine? Really?"

"That's what his gr ... what I was told when I came here.

"*Who* told you that?"

"The man who hired me."

"Vincent."

"Justin, I—"

"I think you had better finish your sentence. His what?"

"His grace."

"And his grace is...."

"The Duke of Ainsley."

Justin furrowed his brows. "I thought *I* was the Duke of Ainsley. Yes. I'm sure of it. Explain, please."

"You were ill for so long—"

"Just get it out, damn it."

"Your brother, Vincent, is the sixth Duke of Ainsley."

"But I didn't bloody well die."

"Your condition was not expected to change. The House allowed him to inherit. He's your guardian. You were in that bed a month when I arrived. You had been described as neither alive nor dead. And, Justin, that was not an exaggerated description."

"My tenants will be left to flounder."

"They have been seeking your brother, or so Mrs. Tucker says."

"God help them. He isn't here, is he? No, of course not. With money at his disposal, I'd hardly expect him to rusticate."

"He's in France ... courting a lady."

Justin raised a brow. "A lady? Hardly likely."

"He led me to believe he planned to marry while in France."

"My poor tenants." Justin threw off the covers as if he would jump from the bed, and Faith shared his frustration when he could not. "Damn it to hell. No one, matters more to Vincent than money. Lord, I wish I knew how Catherine died. She was his mistress. They might even have cared for each other. A match made in hell, you might say." Justin laughed. Crudely, mockingly.

Faith sat. "Your brother and your wife? No wonder you didn't mourn her." If Vincent loved Catherine, it didn't show when he mentioned her death, Faith thought, and her fears trebled. "Justin, Vincent could come back any time. If he sees you're getting well—"

"Come here." He pulled her down till she rested against his pillow. "I didn't mean to distress you. No need to worry."

"There is every reason to worry, and well you know it."

"You told me that in time we'd face all of it ... together. Did you mean it?"

A few days ago, she'd vowed to leave him, but when he put it that way... "I meant it."

He took her lovingly into his arms, a possession she thrilled to, and he kissed her. Thoroughly. Dizzy thorough. She needed to hold him or lose her balance.

He pulled the least bit away, her lips still pulsing for his, and he grinned.

She touched her fingers to his, to hers. She had been boldly and bracingly kissed, so their lips were left warm, pulsing, hers aching for more. "That was not the kiss of a sick man!"

"Why, thank you, Faith. Now, off to your bed before I loose my manners. Scoot."

He watched her go and couldn't help smiling. Just now, her eyes wide from the wonder of a kiss, she reminded him of a startled doe. A false impression that. Faith was the strongest woman he'd ever encountered and he didn't mean strength of limb.

He meant strength of heart ... and soul.

Knowing Vincent as he did, there was no doubt in his mind his brother wanted him dead. The greedy bastard had probably thought he was so close when that carriage went over the cliff.

Vincent must have lured him there for just such a purpose. The setting, as Faith retold it, away from everything, sounded so perfect, the carriage so terribly close to the edge. But to be so vile as to kill a child? Justin was beginning to distinguish the difference between his nightmares and reality, yet the puzzle pieces in his brain did not yet fit.

Did Catherine know what Vincent planned? She may not have wanted a child, but even she ... no, he wouldn't believe it. This was on Vincent's plate. Justin would stake his life on it. He nearly groaned at how close he'd come. He already had staked his life but *Faith* had won out.

She was correct about one thing. If Vincent knew he was recovering, his brother would try again. But Justin needed to live, to care for his tenants. Though if he were able to walk out of here, he would no longer need Faith.

But he did not *need* Faith. He needed no one. Besides, Faith had plans for her life. Squire Kennedy awaited her in Arundel.

Justin scoffed at himself. Then why could he not let her go? Why did the very idea bring him pain? God's teeth, *six* children?

Perhaps his jealousy was not based on need, but simple lust. Likely so. And why would that please him; he couldn't satisfy his own lust, not in a hundred years. So he *should* let her go.

What rankled was the notion of someone else sharing Faith's bed, bringing her pleasure, giving her children. Why? She was a woman like any other, was she not?

"Bloody hell! Stupid bastard."

Faith heard, rose and re-pinned her hair. "What's wrong?" she asked returning to his room.

"Sorry. I didn't mean to disturb you."

She lit a candle. "Are you all right?"

"Feeling sorry for myself. Cheer me up, will you?"

She settled into the chair by his bed. "I will do my best. See now, how *shall* I cheer you? More tales of my childhood? Jimmy Kennedy and I used to—"

"Absolutely not!"

"Shall I sing? Or dance?" She rose and did a fair imitation of a highland fling. "Or would you like to tell me what's troubling you?" She folded her hands in her lap. "Speak to me."

"I'm not sure. I've never felt like this. I'm stuck in bed while my brother neglects his responsibilities—*my* responsibilities. I worry about my tenants, but I am in no condition to do anything about them. How Catherine died is driving me insane, and Beth. Dear, sweet, Beth." He shook his head in despair. "Just stay and talk to me."

Faith's heart beat wildly. "I think you're ready for the best surprise of your life." She touched his hand and looked into his eyes. "But you must allow that I had no choice in waiting until your health improved. Promise you won't be angry, because, Justin, it was not only your welfare at stake, and should you have denied—well, it could not have been borne."

"You distract me, I must say, but you give me the headache."

Faith clapped her hands. "I'll be back in a blink. Don't move."

Despite his dejection, Justin was charmed. Had he ever seen her so excited? Rather enchanting, he must admit.

She returned moments later, offering her surprise ... a child. "Dear, God." Pain sliced him. He fisted his hands to keep from snatching at it in useless hope. He sneered at Faith. "I believed you more compassionate than this."

"This is Beth, Justin." Faith's pity nearly undid him. "Take her. She's not made of porcelain." She placed the child in his arms.

With a murmur, the sprite sought his warmth. God. Justin had no choice but to hold the little one, yet he could not bear to look at her. "I cannot." His voice broke. "My daughter is dead. Whose child is this?"

Faith reclaimed Beth. "She is your child, Justin. But this was a dreadful mistake, which is why I waited. Thank God she's asleep; she could never *bear* your rejection."

Justin felt a failure. "Why are you tormenting me?"

"Had I set out to torment, I would have dosed you to death. I might have let your fever burn you alive, or let you freeze beneath layers of ice."

"Enough." Justin shook his head. "Tell me true. Who is this child?"

"Her name is Beth Devereux. She is your daughter."

CHAPTER SEVEN

THIS CAN'T BE Beth," Justin said, afraid to believe. "I saw the carriage—"

"Did you see Beth inside that carriage?"

Justin fought confusion over the events with the pull of promise in Faith's eyes. "You have no idea how much I...."

Faith, his tormentor—no, his savior, stepped near, and the child in her arms whimpered.

A palsy shook Justin, one that had nothing to do with ill-health, and everything to do with bone-deep fear. If he allowed the hope ... "God, how I want to believe. But I cannot. I dare not."

Faith rubbed the child's back. "Believe."

Justin took a breath. He'd lived through his daughter's death—a thousand, times a thousand—in the hell of his nightmares. But had he lived it in truth? He was no longer sure that he knew the difference.

Without volition, he raised his hand to the baby-fine curls, but stopped short of touching them. Fear had a taste. Acrid and throat-burning. He saw that Faith hurt for him, but she remained silent. He took a breath, reached again. Stopped again. Faith sat beside him, against his pillows, cradling the child so he could see her face. She brought the small hand to his, palm to palm. He ached to his soul for this to be as real as it seemed.

The sprite curled her fist around his finger. Justin closed his eyes and bowed his head so Faith would *not* see his tears.

Faith felt the anguish Justin tried to hide. With a groan, he stroked the tiny fist with his thumb, then he gazed finally into the perfect little face, his own a study in longing. "I want it to be her so badly."

Faith touched their entwined hands. "After the carriage went over the cliff, you didn't see her fall from it. By your claim, you don't remember her being at the site. Why do you believe she was there?"

He shrugged. "Vincent," Justin said, and looked sharply up at her.

Faith smiled. "Justin, you thought Catherine lived. You were wrong. You think Beth died. You *are* wrong."

He gazed at her, at every nuance of her expression, as if he might read the truth there. She smiled so he could. "When you woke, you said Beth died in that accident. I told you then that you were wrong. Do you remember?"

"Yes, but..." Myriad emotions crossed his face. Hope. Belief. Disbelief. Pain. Struggle. Hope again. He reached for his daughter, exhaling on a ragged sigh. "She's bigger than B—she's bigger."

"The morning I withheld your medicine for the first time, Beth called you Poppy."

Justin swallowed hard. His hand shook as he fingered a bronze curl. Tears in his eyes, he grinned. "She never could say Papa." He kissed the small forehead. "*My* Beth?"

The little one's sleepy eyes opened. She traced his lips. "Poppy," she said on a yawn, and slept again.

Justin sobbed and caught his breath. "Faith, I ... If not for you, I would never have known. Before you came, I had given up, in my head and heart, as I waited for the grave. But you roused me from hell even so. You were my angel, and so I thought you, and knew it for truth the moment I saw you." He caught her hand, kissed it. "I can't believe that this is Beth I hold in my arms. What do you know about the accident? Where was she that day?"

"With Catherine's old nurse outside London. I was hired to care for you both."

"Care for?" Justin frowned. "Was she ill?"

"Frightened. She's better now, but having you back is what she needs."

"Thank you for your care of my daughter. And her father. I can hardly credit my brother with such a wise choice of nurse."

"According to Harris, Vincent was being forced to find you a nurse, under threat from a local Magistrate and a group of powerful men—"

"Scoundrels," Justin said with a grin. "Powerful scoundrels."

"*All* right. Scoundrels forced him to find you a nurse. Then Vicar Kendrick of our parish recommended *me*."

"Gabriel," Justin said. "Gabriel Kendrick, Vicar, I mean; he's another scoundrel, or a knave of hearts, whatever you will."

"Don't let him hear you say that," Faith added, brow raised.

"I'd say it to Gabe's face."

Faith scoffed. "Better you than me. At any rate, I only met your brother on the day I arrived. I believe he was disappointed. He accepted me only so he could satisfy the Magistrate breathing down his neck and leave Killashandra behind."

"I'm surprised he *left* after seeing you. And be glad he did."

Beth stirred, catching his attention. "She's beautiful, isn't she?"

"I don't know. She reminds me of you, after all. Mrs. Tucker says she acts like you, too. She delights in chasing kittens and riding your old hobby horse. And you should hear her talk. I'll reintroduce you tomorrow when she can appreciate the reunion." Faith took Beth, kissed her nose, and rose to take her back to her bed.

"I hate to let her go. Wait." He touched Faith's arm. "Come

back." When Faith did, he kissed Beth's cheek. "Sleep well, Muffin. I'll see you in the morning." He crooked his finger, and when Faith responded by bending toward him, he kissed her cheek too. "Thank you for my daughter."

As she carried Beth to her room, Faith was seized with a longing so strong, it weakened her. She felt as if Justin had thanked her for giving him a child—their child.

What would it be like carrying his child, nurturing it with her body? Her womb clenched with need, and Faith recognized the yearning. She wanted a life with Justin. Lord, she loved him. The kind of love Mama spoke of, the forever kind, God help her.

Justin gave thanks. He had Beth. He had Faith. He would soon have his health. Nothing mattered more than that. He felt more alive than he had in years.

Faith cared for his daughter. Loved her, she said. Perhaps she didn't use the word *love* as indiscriminately as he'd at first believed.

He missed Beth already. But he would see her again tomorrow. And every day after, God grant it.

He had to get out of this damned bed. He had to get well.

"I see you're properly cheered," Faith said upon returning.

"I have the inclination, if not the ability, to waltz you about the room. Consider it a promise for the future." He pulled her down and kissed her, consumed her. At her dazed expression, he kissed her once more. "I'm starving, but I'll become a bear if you feed me pap again."

Faith stood—unsteadily, he thought with pride—and smoothed her dress. "We can't risk ordering you normal food. Someone will guess you're better."

"Because someone will not be happy if I recover. You stopped giving me the medicine because you thought it was poison." He remained calm so she would know he was ready for the answer.

"Perhaps."

"Vincent coveted my title and money. Likely he planned the carriage accident, or something near, by luring me out of London. Failing that, poison does not seem illogical."

She touched her throat. "Not ... the carriage accident."

"Why not? If he wanted me dead by poison, why not the other?"

"I don't know. It's ... he's your brother. Perhaps he didn't know the medicine was poison."

Justin shook his head. "I wonder you suspected danger at all."

Someone knocking on the hall door interrupted their painful discourse, just as well. For now.

"Pap," Faith said, returning with a tray. "For the bear."

Justin sighed in resignation. "I'll feed myself. And you have to eat, too, else it will be you needing a nurse."

Faith placed a small table between them. "Fiddle. I'm as strong as Squire Kennedy's favorite bull."

"I would prefer not to speak of your young swain." He stirred his mushy peas and poked his marrow pudding. On her plate sat Cornish pasties, roasted parsnips, Yorkshire pudding and cabbage. Clotted cream capped a strawberry tart. Justin's stomach rumbled in anticipation, but that was not *his* dinner. "Care to trade?"

"Would you like to share?"

"If you're sure." He immediately attempted to gather some beef-filled pastry with his spoon, lest she change her mind, she assumed, but he failed.

She stabbed a piece with her fork and popped it into his mouth.

He rolled his eyes in delight to entertain her. Before they finished, he'd eaten more than she.

"We emulate our ancestors," Faith said. "Communal trenchers."

He grabbed her finger and licked a spot of clotted cream. "I think our ancestors missed a treat."

"What, pray tell, is that?"

He tapped her nose. "The taste of sweet Faith."

Her skepticism charmed him.

"You mock me when I call you delicious. Must I prove my statement?" He placed the tray on the bed-stand and moved the table aside, curving his finger in a come-hither fashion.

Faith took several slow steps and stopped before him.

He grazed her lips with his. "Sweet." He kissed her lips. "Not too tart." A longer kiss. "Heavenly. I may never be sated." He hauled her across his lap and continued his assault.

"Justin," she whispered.

"Does my kissing you make you uncomfortable?"

"No," she answered, wide-eyed. "It makes me shiver."

When her tongue met his, he ravaged her mouth, shifted uncomfortably ... and realization dawned. He was a man whole again, hard and ready. Aching. He grinned inwardly, aching to tell Faith. To show her, by God. But she was so innocent.

"What? Why do you smile like the cat that got the cream?"

He pulled her close. "Partly," he said. "Because you make me smile." He opened his mouth over hers, brought the kiss to a simmer, and adjusted his position to accommodate his desire.

A pounding at the door stopped them.

"Who?" Faith wondered aloud, disoriented.

Pride at his ability to drug Faith with his kisses diverted Justin.

"Miss Wickham! Open this dratted door. At once. I insist upon being admitted to see my brother. Now!"

Faith jumped up before Justin could stop her. She fled to the windows, yanking each panel closed. Thank God. He feared she would throw open the door, but darkening the room was mercifully quick-witted. He should know better than to worry over her reaction in any situation.

"Break it down, damn it," they heard Vincent shout from the hall, his brother having someone else do the work, as usual.

Faith watched the hall door splinter with each thrust.

Justin grabbed his medicine and something else Faith had attempted to give him, and sprinkled dark pungent liquid and thick golden syrup over himself and his bedding. A sulfurous odor filled the room. Faith turned toward him, and understanding was born. His life depended on Vincent's fastidious nature keeping him from getting too close. He began a gruesome imitation of retching. Faith nodded her approval. The door heaved and gave.

With each gasp, the medicinal odor filling his nostrils was so sharp, Justin feared he would be truly ill.

Vincent burst in. "How dare you lock me out in my own house." Placing his hand over his nose and mouth, he came to a halt.

Faith raised her chin. "Your Grace." She was a child, again, in the midst of a thunderstorm. Except this was no childish fear, but real. Grown up. Deadly.

Justin retched in earnest and Vincent was furious. Gone even was his veneer of civility.

Faith could easily succumb to her panic, but Justin's life hung in the balance. Moments only passed as she and Vincent faced each other. Abashed, he composed himself.

She had gained the upper hand, and she wielded the power. "You caused me to abandon him in his need. He is ill, dying. His affliction could spread throughout the house, leaving all within...."

But she needn't finish. Vincent had removed himself with such speed as to make Faith wonder if his presence had been a nightmare.

Justin's dry retching, his gasps for breath, as if each might be his last, moved her. She sat him up and propped pillows behind him. Still his stomach convulsed. "Try holding your breath for a minute to interrupt the heaving."

He couldn't respond.

"Justin. Your body is responding to the same action over and over. Break the pattern. Swallow or take a deep breath."

Finally, he swallowed, which made a slight difference.

"Again, darling—"

"Are you so enamored of a near-dead man, Miss Wickham," Vincent said from the door, making her jump. "That you would speak to him with such pathetic pretense?" He stood close enough to hear, far enough to miss the changes in Justin. Faith hoped.

"Your grace," she said digging her fingers into Justin's shoulder, reminding him to remain still and keep his eyes closed.

"'Tis a sick game you play," Vincent said.

She shrugged. "Justin is my only company."

Vincent became a predator, she his prey. "You're fortunate I returned. I can ... we can entertain each other."

Justin tensed under her hand. She lessened the pressure on his shoulder and soothed as best she could with what she hoped looked like an unconscious movement.

Vincent saw her stroking fingers and focused upon them.

Uncomfortable under his scrutiny, Faith removed her hand.

He snapped back to the present, as if from a dream, and shifted his stance. "Tomorrow evening you will dine with me downstairs."

"I cannot. My patient. Your brother is—"

"Too ill to miss you for the night."

"He cannot be left alone for a moment. You saw how tenuous—"

"Harris will stay with him." Vincent's furious jaw-action boded ill.

"Harris is not here."

"Where the devil has he gone? I do not remember giving him permission to leave Killashandra."

"To ... get more medicine."

Vincent smiled. "I thought there was enough."

"We wanted to be certain—"

"Considering your patient's condition, I suspect what we have will do, but it's best to be sure ... that we have enough."

With which to kill, she thought. "With Harris gone, I must stay with him."

"I'll send a maid."

Faith gave up. "Some nights are better than others. If he needs someone, I'll tell you when I see you." If Justin waited alone, it would be a good excuse for her to return early.

"Good. Until tomorrow evening, my little nurse."

Faith bit her lip to keep from saying she was not *his* anything.

Vincent departed as silently as he'd returned.

When Faith looked at Justin, his eyes were closed. She put the room in order. After replacing his blankets, she inspected the damage to the door. The jagged wood fit neatly and quite securely back into its proper spot. The lock, however, was another problem. Faith pushed a small chest against the door. Then she fetched a tiny bell and fastened it to the knob. The slightest turn would ring it. She nodded. It would serve.

"I forbid you to go to him."

Justin's furious voice startled her. "I thought you slept."

"I said, I *forbid* you to go to Vincent."

She returned to his side. "I am only dining with him."

"It's time to grow up, Faith. He wants more than your company at dinner. He said he wants you to spend the night with him."

Faith laughed for Justin's benefit, but she was frightened. "He meant the evening. And, I'm not a child. I dined with him before and he left the next morning. He'll leave again tomorrow."

"He came back for a reason."

"He wants to know if the medicine is working. I'll assure him you're failing fast."

"He wants you, you little fool."

She agreed, but she had no choice. "I'll be fine."

"I said no."

"You have no right to tell me what to do, or what not to do."

"Just a while ago, you would have given me any right."

Faith wouldn't let him use her love this way. "Until you can prevent my departure, you have no choice but to watch me go." She'd matched him for low tactics, and she hated that. But if she apologized, he'd think her weak.

He made a sound between a laugh and a sneer. "You will always do what you damn well please, will you not ... Catherine!"

He may as well have slapped her. Faith went silently to her room, closed the door between, and for the first time since his recovery, left it closed all night. She paced until the middle of the longest, loneliest night of her life, but she refused to go to him.

In silence, she performed his morning ritual.

With a few words, Vincent had severed their tenuous bond. Sadly, the connection which had taken months to form, took only moments to destroy. A sign it was weak at best and not worth this deep sense of loss. But she was furious with Justin for not seeming to care at all. Under these strained conditions, and with Vincent in residence, Faith decided Beth's visit must wait.

Dressed for her evening with Vincent, Faith placed Justin's dinner before him.

"Do not expect me to eat this slop." He pushed the plate away. "You look like a harlot."

"Of course I do. It's what you expect, is it not? I would never disappoint you. I could also act the harlot, if Vincent wished." *If she knew how.* "After all, I must earn the money he pays me. And that slop is all you will get. I can hardly ask for food if I'm dining downstairs. You're supposed to be too ill to consume anything, if you will remember."

She adjusted her bodice to a precariously low position, taking satisfaction in the tensing of Justin's jaw. "Better, do you not think?" When she left, breasts nearly falling from her dress, she punctuated her departure by slamming the door.

In the hall, she straightened her bodice and covered herself.

As she and Vincent ate, he studied her. "You're quiet this evening, my dear. If I remember correctly, you had an avid interest in anything to do with my brother when first we dined together."

"I find the subject decidedly uninteresting of late, your Grace. Tell me of your travels in France?"

Vincent looked suspicious, which made her uncomfortable, but he gave an account of his search for a rich, French wife. As he rambled, Faith floated peas along the gravy rivers in her plate, wondering how to get Justin something nourishing to eat.

Vincent cleared his throat. "Miss Wickham, do you attend me?"

"What? I'm sorry."

"Since you're not hungry, I'll speak with you in the library. Now, if you don't mind." He chuckled. "Or, even if you do. This way please."

She followed him to his study, disliking his smile as much as ever, wondering what he wished to speak to her about. With a taciturn man like him, thoughts were difficult to imagine.

"Miss Wickham, I must say, you're disgustingly lacking in your attention to your employer this evening. Kindly look at me, and listen."

Faith snapped to attention. "I apologize, your Grace. I am tired this evening. I am awake many nights with your brother."

Then she saw them. Slender-necked and amber. Lined up, three in a row upon his desk. Full vials of Justin's medicine.

Faith vowed never to set another mousetrap.

CHAPTER EIGHT

FAITH HAD BEEN with Vincent for nearly an hour, while Justin paced—inasmuch as he could in a wheelchair. He stared out at the night sky, frustrated as hell that he could do nothing save sit and hide when his family needed him. His family. The image included Beth in his arms and Faith by their side. That gave him pause, because he found himself as repelled as drawn by the notion.

Had he, despite resolving never to be so foolish again, fallen for Miss Faith Wickham, that too-innocent-to-be-believed child? He shook his head. Of course he had not. Faith was a giving, nurturing, voluptuous creature. But he dare not fall. Women were dangerous. And Faith behaved true to form, cavorting with his brother, doing God knew what, while he waited here in agony, and fear, for her safety.

Justin swore and rolled his blasted chair into the hall, intent on rescue. He was sick of hiding like a coward. But at the top of the stairs, he looked down, and smacked the chair's arms, snapping one clean off. He couldn't defend a pup much less a woman, against a man who would stop at nothing to gain his ends.

Inspiration hit. Defense came in many forms. A man in a chair, with a weapon, could be as strong as one standing. Justin wheeled himself to the library balcony, pleased at the strength in his arms. But once there, he saw his father's dueling pistols mounted much higher than he remembered. And it would be no use trying to get them if he couldn't load them.

He checked the desk, where the case was kept. Lead balls and flints. The powder flask and oil bottle were full. Rod, patches, turnscrew, spring cramp—all there. He examined the fireplace ... and hoped he found the mantle as sturdy as his bedpost.

Faith stared at the vials and smoothed her skirt to wipe her palms and gather her wits. Footsteps in the hall reminded her she was not alone, except that she should probably not count on Vincent's servants.

The mantle clock chimed the quarter hour.

Vincent's impatient fingers drummed a tattoo on the desktop, and he stabbed her with his gaze. "Explain. Now!" he shouted, and she jumped.

Heart pounding, she stepped to the French doors to gaze out and steady herself. Forging courage, she imagined herself the cat, Vincent the mouse. The image emboldened her. She turned and smiled. "I'm not the naive child you think me, your grace."

Infused with alarm, Vincent staggered and knocked over a chair, the crash bringing him to his senses. But the pungent taste of fear brought him the strong desire to punish the strumpet. She hadn't even flinched when the chair fell. Even now, she ignored him and returned her gaze to the window.

Vincent whipped her about. "Tell me," he demanded, shaking her, her alarm exciting, making him wonder whether he should beat her or take her.

She moved away and into the room, searching furtively, as if rescue were to be found in a dark corner. When she raised her chin, he laughed. Her fallacious courage might be spirited, but he wondered if she knew what a formidable opponent he could be.

Her eyes, the greenest he'd ever seen, widened as she took a step back for each he took in her direction. When the desk stopped her retreat, he smiled. As she poised to bolt, he lunged, devouring her with his kiss, invading her with his tongue, slipping his hand in her dress.

"No!" His quarry rebelled with astonishing force.

He stumbled, caught hold and tore her bodice, raking her breast with his nails.

Straightening, he saw the cuts, and smiled. The top of her breast bore the image of a music staff etched in blood. "I seem to have branded you."

She raised her hand to slap him. He caught it, but her momentary strength amazed him, and he fell against a table. At his bellow of rage, the starch went out of her. He shoved her in a chair, imprisoning her with his arms. "Why were those vials outside?" He grasped her chin and raised it to examine her. High cheekbones. Full lips. The rapid pulse in her lovely neck revealed her fear. Her cat's eyes pierced him so thoroughly, it was a wonder he didn't bleed. "The truth," he said. "There is no game I cannot win."

She licked her lips, inviting him to do the same, and when he did, she bit his tongue. With an oath, he pulled away, highly aroused.

"Justin kept waking," she said, her voice trembling.

"Double the dose!"

Faith watched in horror as Vincent growled and threw a chair at a glass-fronted cabinet. Even as it shattered, he narrowed his eyes on her and reached for a marble urn.

As fast, faster, she threw a Chinese vase.

Sailing by his ear, it splintered on the hearth.

His expression blanked. With shaking hands, he placed the urn on the desk. "Why did you do that?"

To hurt him, God help her. "I thought ... you'd finish sooner if

I helped."

His smile, easy, disturbing, made him seem almost human. He straightened his coat and ran his hands through his hair.

A loud rapping startled them.

Vincent opened the door, and the library cat slipped into the room. Someone spoke. Vincent chuckled. "Thank you, no. Miss Wickham was just having a tantrum. But she's fine now."

He shut the door and turned to her. "You made too much noise." He looked at the disarray. "And a nasty mess. What am I to ... how the devil did that cat get in? Ah. Hemsted. Where he goes, so goes Satan." He opened the door and kicked the cat out ... literally. "Feeling better now?" he asked Faith.

Good Lord, did he actually think that she had done this? "I'm fine," she said, afraid to unbalance him further.

"Look," he said, all concern. "You tore your gown." He made to console her, his hand on her neck clammy, his wine-sour breath too close.

She made to move from his hold. "It's nothing."

"No, let me help." He tried to straighten her bodice. She wanted to slap his hand away; instead, she stepped back, holding the torn fabric against herself.

He stared at it. "You're bleeding." He reached for her. "Let me see."

"No!"

His fury at her rejection made Faith panic. "Justin was suffering!"

"What?"

"That's why I threw the vials."

He stopped, collected himself. "You said he woke."

"In a manner of speaking. He was out of control ... mad." If Vincent Devereux didn't understand madness, no one would. And if she lived through this, she could go on the stage.

"You can't stop giving him the medicine!" he snapped.

"No, no. Look." She picked up an unbroken vial, and holding her bodice, she tried to open it.

Vincent came too close again, and Faith tugged hard, unstopping it with a vengeance, and almost-accidentally tossed the contents at him.

His jaw tensed.

"I apologize." She pulled the soiled coat toward his face, nearly strangling him. "The color is wrong. See? And the odor." She shoved the soaked fabric under his nose, making him gag, tearing his waistcoat. "It's plainly turned."

She looked into his eyes. "The man responsible should hang."

His eyes widened. His nostrils flared.

"I could hang him myself for mixing the medicine carelessly and causing Justin to suffer." Faith shook so hard, it was a wonder she could speak. "If you will excuse me, your grace, I must see to my patient."

Vincent seemed to awaken, as if from a trance. "About my manners. I was ... overcome ... by your beauty."

Did he now remember his actions? Her shock must be apparent.

"If you would allow me to explain myself." He paced as one caged. "When I think of my brother, dying, and there is nothing I can do, it fills me with such ... rage."

Faith didn't want him to read her alarm, but his sporadic sanity frightened her more than his madness.

"Here now, Miss Wickham," Vincent said with gentle rebuke. "Surely you can forgive your employer."

A clear threat to her position, and she must heed the warning, for leaving Justin was unthinkable. She smiled as falsely as he. "There is nothing to forgive." The words tasted bitter. Desperation to be free overwhelmed her. She willed herself to remain, and not to turn tail and run, yet. "If you will excuse me. It has been a difficult day." She left sedately but without awaiting dismissal.

The moment the door shut, violent shudders seized her. Her skin was icy, yet moist with perspiration, her heartbeat erratic.

Hemsted stepped from the shadows, concern etching his features. He asked a silent question. Was she all right?

To discourage further inquiry, she gave him a relieved smile.

He relaxed, turned and stepped through a door, shutting it.

On shaking legs, Faith made her way toward her room. The hall seemed cavernous, the stairs too high, the corridors too dark.

Ill-prepared to face Justin, she sat in an alcove to let her tears fall.

Justin ignored his aching head. He'd smacked it on the hearth when he fell, but he'd gotten the pistols, by damn. He poured the powder, dropped the ball into the muzzle and tamped it with the loading rod.

The lower library door opened and Justin raised his head, alert. Vincent offered a glass of port. A man accepted. They discussed estates and profits—his—and left the library.

Where was Faith? Lord, she must be in his room and frantic at his absence. He placed the loaded pistols in their compartments, and returned the case to its drawer. If anyone noted their absence above the mantle, they would look here ... where they would be ready should Justin need them. Better here than in his room with Beth or Faith. One was too curious, the other too trusting. He patted the case of loaded pistols and shut the drawer.

In his room, he was sick with worry. Faith had not returned. Then she came in, hair tumbled, cheeks rosy. Catherine all over again. She didn't see him in the corner as she leaned against her door, hand to her heart, eyes closing. Dreaming of his brother?

Justin rolled his chair forward with the force of his anger.

Faith jumped and opened her eyes.

He took a breath, prepared to allow her to explain.

She raised her chin but said nothing.

His anger turned to disquiet. Her eyes spoke not of pleasure, but pain. He reached for her. "Faith?"

Her composure crumbled the minute Justin's look changed from anger to concern. When he took her on his lap, her strength disappeared and she wept.

"Dear God, dear God," he repeated, pulling her close.

As far as she was concerned, he couldn't hold her tight enough. She wanted to melt into him, never to be separated from him again. He rocked, stroked and soothed her. She felt so safe, she couldn't stop the first sob, nor the next, nor the one after that.

"Shh. You will make yourself ill. Please, Sweetheart."

Faith stilled as best she could, her sigh ragged.

Justin touched her cheek. "You're frightening the hell out of me. Please tell me what happened."

She shook her head. She couldn't, she couldn't.

"Damn it, tell me what that bastard did! Look at me," he demanded as he raised her chin so she was forced to stare into his furious eyes. "I'll shoot him if he hurt you. I swear I will."

"No, Justin. It's ... all right. He didn't ... actually."

"My God. What do you mean, not *actually*?"

She shook her head and hid her face in his neck once more.

Once more, he pulled her away to look at her.

She leaned against the missing chair-arm and he caught her, but her torn bodice slipped open. His hand shook as he raised it toward the four bloody scratches across her breast. He stopped short of touching her. "I'll kill him."

She pulled up the fabric to cover herself and looked away. "I'm so ashamed."

"Faith, whatever happened—and it can't be worse than my imagination—it was not your fault. I know Vincent."

Tears clouded her vision. "Before I left, you called me Catherine.

As if, as if...."

Justin shook his head. "Seeing Vincent after all this time, knowing he wanted you. I was reliving the past, afraid he would take you from me. I'm stuck in a bed or this blasted chair. I get so angry, I can't seem to help myself."

"That's what Vincent said."

"Sweet Jesus, Faith, you can't possibly think ... God, what have I done? Please, darling, I didn't mean it, though I know I don't deserve your forgiveness." He rocked her in his arms.

Faith pulled from his embrace. "Justin, are those tears?"

"No." He swallowed and pulled her back. "Ah, Faith. I'll never forgive myself for hurting you like that, or for being so useless to you."

She wiped his tears with her fingertips "You would never hurt me. I know that. And what happened *was* frightening, but I'm all right. I am. Just hold me for a while."

"Gladly," he said with a shaky voice. "But tell me the truth. Did Vincent hurt you?"

"Not in any way you can see."

"Dear God!" Justin wished he could absorb Faith into himself to protect her forever. He feared the question in his mind as much as the answer. "Faith, do you know what rape is?"

"No."

"It's a violation." He shuddered. "The worst kind. It's when a man forces himself on a woman ... inside her. Do you know what I'm asking?"

She couldn't look at him. "He didn't touch me."

"How then did he tear your dress? Scratch you?"

She sat back and took a deep breath. "He didn't force himself on me in the way you just said. He grabbed me and tried to kiss me. When I pushed him away ... my gown tore and I got scratched."

"The bloody bastard!"

"He was angry, frighteningly so. And he smashed things."

She explained how Vincent cornered her with the vials. "He wants you dead, Justin."

"And he just plain wants *you*. You know it too now, don't you, Faith?"

She went back into his embrace and nodded against his shirt.

He turned her in his arms and lowered the torn fabric to expose her injury. "I swear, Faith, by all that's holy, he'll never touch you again." He kissed her, carefully, gently, near and around the defilement, and cleansed her soul with his touch.

He swept her so thoroughly into a world of tenderness, she forgot, for a time, the world of fear.

When she calmed—when they both did—and put the night's horrors behind them, Justin spread salve on her cuts as tenderly as any nurse. Then he stripped her of her torn dress and dropped her nightrail over her head as efficiently as any abigail. When he tied the satin ribbons at her neck, their eyes met.

Justin cleared his throat, kissed her forehead and ordered her to bed then he covered her to her chin before he wheeled his way toward his own room.

"Are you sure *you'll* be all right?" she asked, stopping him with her question. "You were so ill yesterday."

"I'm fine. I brought what happened on myself with sprinkling that poison about. Then having Vincent here, knowing the threat he posed to you—"

"Me? I was worried about you."

Justin tilted his head. "We worry about each other. An interesting arrangement. Now go to sleep. I promise you'll not find me at death's door on the morrow." He came back to her bed, where she sat poised to get up, and motioned for her to lie down. She lay facing him while he tucked her in once more and kissed the tip of her nose. "You'll not lose me, Faith."

The castle shone gold in the sunlight, the path she walked lined with lady-slippers. Yellow buds and lush green leaves hid the thorns in the bracken.

The robed presence had flesh on his bones, his no-longer unseeing eyes were midnight blue and clear, his smile heart-quickening.

Faith opened her arms to him.

But from the depths of the black whirlpool rose anger and rage. Doom came charging forth and murder danced before them in shades of purple and black, both bearing the scents of suffering and death.

The coffin was bronze.

Faith woke crying. She ran into Justin's room, but she couldn't tell if he was breathing. "Justin, wake up." She shook him. "Please be all right."

He opened his eyes, alert. "Faith, what's wrong?"

"I ... I was afraid something happened, that you ... died." Tears streamed down her face, "I dreamed your coffin was sealed and I ... I couldn't open it, and I had not said good-bye. You were gone and I was ... alone ... without you."

Faith's wide eyes begged understanding, her dark, curls tumbled in thick waves over her shoulders and breasts. She looked breathtaking with her gentle curves outlined by the gown's flowing softness, as they strained against their confinement.

Justin's heart lurched and his mind raged at the fact of Vincent hurting her. He needed to remove the ugliness, for both of them, replace it with something beautiful. "You're cold." He raised the covers. "Come, let me warm you."

She got in beside him and settled against him.

He reveled in the scent and feel of her. Violets and silk. He quelled a strong, disturbing desire to investigate her every mysterious facet. "You smell as good as you taste," he said.

There followed a comfortable silence wherein Justin matched each portion of her anatomy to a corresponding portion of his, then he pressed his lips to her brow. "God, you feel good in my arms. This is where you belong," he whispered against her temple.

"I don't think Vicar Kendrick would approve, now that you're well."

"You warmed me. I'm warming you."

"You were ill, freezing."

"You were frantic, trembling." He slid his hand to her back, and fit her more intimately against him. "I'm taking care of you."

"When Beth is a young woman, should you come upon her and her young man in this situation, how will you react if he says he is caring for her?"

"Ah. Yes. Well. Since I wouldn't be certain his intentions were as noble as mine, I own I might have to break his neck."

Her chuckle brought his. "Go to sleep, green eyes. I'll not stop breathing." Her lashes tickled his neck as her eyes closed and contentment etched itself into his soul.

Faith slipped from Justin's bed and went to her room, dressing with particular care. Before returning, she smoothed her new dress at waist and hips and fluffed the full sleeves.

"You look particularly fetching this morning," Justin said as she returned. He *knew* that she'd primped for him, aggravating man.

"Did you sleep well?" she asked, but the minute the words were out, she knew they were wrong.

He winked. "Yes, I did. Now, what's on our schedule today?"

"First, breakfast. Then your bath."

"I'm glad I'm better. I'll enjoy my bath so much more."

He was not going to make this easy. "Since you're recovering so rapidly, I think you can manage to bathe yourself this morning while I prepare your daughter for a visit."

"My daughter," he said with renewed awe.

Faith accepted his breakfast tray when it was delivered and returned bearing welcome news. "Jenny said Vincent left, again, for France. But I hate that he could come back anytime."

Justin squeezed her hand. "I'll get well and we'll leave before he returns."

"Lord that sounds good." Did he plan for them to leave together? "I know some exercises that may help you recover the use of your legs more quickly."

"I'll try anything."

"Good. We'll begin later." Faith put everything he needed to bathe and dress beside him. "There. Prepare yourself for your daughter's visit. And I do hope you enjoy your bath."

She gave Sally the morning off, dressed Beth in a pinafore that showed her eyes to advantage and arranged her ringlets like a crown. Then she taught her to knock on her father's door.

"Enter, dear ladies."

Beth squealed and called, "Poppy," as she ran to him, and he took her on his lap.

After Justin hugged her, and kissed her, and got his emotions under control, they chatted, teased, laughed and tickled, while Faith tidied the room ... and worried.

Jenny said Hemsted was asking questions again. Suppose he decided to visit the sick room? Faith hated to keep Hemsted's presence a secret. But Justin had enough to worry about.

And poor Harris. If someone found his questions threatening ... Faith knew her imagination was running wild. Harris could handle himself. He'd cared for Justin alone until her arrival.

"Faith?" Justin called. "Beth fell asleep and, though my arms are strong, I don't think they'll hold her for an extended time. And she's too precious to drop."

Faith placed Beth on Justin's bed.

"I have to learn to walk," he said. "I can't stand not having control of my body."

"Your legs should have some strength. I exercised them before. If we start again today, you may be walking in no time." But the bed was occupied. "Lie on the floor and we can start."

Faith watched, arms akimbo, as Justin lowered himself to the rug.

"You look pleased with yourself," he said. "I think you like towering over me."

Faith knelt and slid his dressing gown and night-shirt well above his knees. "I can hardly wait for you to tower over me." She grasped his ankle with one hand and his thigh with the other, bending his knee back and forth. Straightening the leg, she pointed his foot toward the ceiling, then lay it flat again, and repeated the procedure several more times.

Lifting her skirts, she hobbled around him on her knees to his other leg. After several sets, she felt his thigh muscles. "You're too stiff," she said, straddling him, and he groaned.

She massaged his thigh thoroughly, enjoying the strength beneath her hands. Heady pleasure this, stroking the man she loved. But when she looked at him, his seemed pained. "You'll feel better in a minute," she said, kneading harder. "I think we need to do this more often."

Justin groaned again, agony distorting his features, perspiration glazing his upper lip.

Faith sat up. "Good Lord, I'm hurting you."

He shifted and raised one of his knees. "Ah ... no, you're not ... hurting me. But, perhaps we had better continue another day."

Still straddling him, Faith rested her back against his raised knee. "Absolutely not. If you ever want to leave this room, you have to move these muscles. She stroked his thigh. You just finished saying you wanted control over your body."

"Interesting you should remind me."

"Do you think you can bear it, if we continue?"

"I expect I can, if you can."

"Good." She pushed his dressing gown up further, and pulled back at the sight. "Oh, my."

"Don't stare, Faith. It'll only get bigger. And harder."

CHAPTER NINE

J USTIN WATCHED FAITH fight her fascination, but she couldn't look away from the physical evidence of his desire, blatantly outlined beneath his dressing gown. "It's ... dancing," she said.

He chuckled. "You did say I was stiff." Could she possibly realize how much he wanted her at this moment?

"Does it hurt?"

There was his answer. As naive as he thought. "Not ... exactly." The more she gaped, eyes wide as saucers, the more aroused he became.

"Its huge!"

He couldn't control his laughter. "Why, thank you, Sweetheart. That's the nicest thing you ever said to me." He urged her down beside him and brought her close. His face in her neck, his arousal nesting exactly where it belonged, his eyes closed, acute pleasure purling through him.

"You must be getting better more quickly than I ... is it warm in here?"

"Lord, yes." He was set to ignite.

"Should we continue the exercises?"

"I think we have to stop for now." He pulled away to read her expression. "Unless you want to lose your virtue right here on the floor?"

She pulled from his embrace and stood.

"I didn't think so," he said, with no little amount of regret. "Besides, I have a better place in mind for that."

She wheeled his chair to him. "I guess it would be best for Harris to exercise your legs from now on."

"You're right ... if exercise is *strictly* the intent. And I suppose, for the time being, it must be."

Faith's discomposure was obvious as she fussed while settling him in his chair. This must be her first experience with mutual sexual awareness. With sexual awareness of any kind.

Her breast came within inches of his face as she straightened the pillows behind him. What would she do if he nuzzled her just there and slid his hand up her leg while he did?

Reluctantly, he resisted the temptation to find out. For now. She was curious to learn; he was anxious to instruct. He wanted to touch, to savor, to penetrate. He groaned. Oh, how he wanted.

She pulled away. "Are you in pain?"

Marveling anew at her innocence, he pulled her to his lap.

She wrapped her arms around his neck as he planted quick kisses on her brow, her eyes, her face. "I lose control when you touch me," he whispered, sliding his hand to just below her breast.

She inhaled at his touch. "I like it when you touch me, too," she whispered, face pink.

Inflamed, he teased her lips with his, coaxed them apart, sipped and tasted. The world disappeared. She responded with the innocence of newfound passion, her kisses reaching his soul.

"Faith," he moaned as he briefly took his lips away then kissed her again, his hands moving finally to explore a gentle swell, tease a bud. She mewled and strained forward, responsive as all hell. He placed his hands on her hips to pull her closer.

"Poppy? Fay?"

It took great effort for Justin to pull his mind from passion. When Faith stood, or tried to, she wavered slightly and he grabbed her waist to steady her. She covered his hands with hers and looked into his eyes for a long moment. Rosy-cheeked, she turned to regard his daughter.

Beth stood on his bed, arms wide, calling, "Fay," and giggled when Faith sprinted in mock charge toward her.

Energy renewed, Beth spent another hour entertaining them.

After Faith gave Beth back to Sally's care, she returned to him and they ate a quiet lunch together. Justin could tell she was as preoccupied as he. "This afternoon, I want you to help me stand," he said, cutting the silence. "The best exercise might be attempting to walk and I would like to try."

"It might be a little soon." Faith worried her lip. "But, if it's what you want, I'll help as much as I can."

She moved furniture aside to clear him a wide path. He used his arms to raise himself then she helped him stand.

"Goodness, you look much bigger from here," Faith said.

He was dizzy but refused to mention it, or give in to it. "Feels good to look down at you."

"Now that you're standing you seem ... more wide-shouldered, perhaps, as well as taller."

"Am I putting too much weight on you?"

"No. No, it's all right. How do your legs feel?"

"Shaky, like they belong to someone else." He tried to take a step, but Faith was not prepared and they fell.

"We seem doomed to spending a good part of each day here," Justin joked. "Shall we give it another try?"

Faith helped him up. "Warn me next time you want to try anything fancy." When she let go and stood aside, he remained standing on his own for a good minute.

He stood again that night and four times the next day, Faith cheering him on. Each time he tried, he stood longer then the time before. After several days of practice, his legs stopped shaking. Before long, he could stand alone for nearly five minutes. A week later he executed his first step with considerable effort on both their parts.

"We did it!" he said hugging her. "I think the only thing wrong with my legs was lack of use. Thank you."

"It was your determination, Justin. You've been relentless."

"I couldn't have done it without you. I could stand up to Vincent now, if he barged in here again. How grand would that be?" He flexed his fingers. "I wonder if I can still throw a good punch." He lost his concentration and faltered.

"Enough for today." Faith turned him back to the bed. "More tomorrow when you're rested."

The following days for Justin were filled with slow plodding steps, the nights with deep sober contemplation.

He fought an inner struggle over Faith's seeming uniqueness among the women of his acquaintance. One side of him said, yes, she was genuine, loving, good. The other said no woman could be. He ached for wanting her, which was, in turn, driving him to the brink of insanity, raising him to dizzying heights, and frightening him to death.

The threat Vincent posed was real and it was serious. Not only was his life in jeopardy, but if Vincent discovered Faith's hand in his recovery, hers would be too. He shuddered to think of it.

And what about Beth? If something happened to him, she would be abandoned again. Though Faith loved her, she would have no right under the law to keep her. And there was no one on earth he would rather have care for his daughter than Faith.

The best way he could think to provide for Beth's future, would be to give her a mother who already loved her. He couldn't take the chance Beth might be left in Vincent's care again.

He must speak to Faith without delay.

That evening after dinner, he indicated the chair beside his, facing the hearth. "Sit down, Faith, please."

When she did, he took her hands and searched her eyes. "You've given me so much, my daughter, my very life. Though I can never repay you, I find I need something more." He paused. "Something extremely important to me."

Faith wondered why Justin was so formal. "You know I'll do anything to help you."

"You mentioned that my old friend, the Vicar, recommended you to Vincent. Could you send Gabe a message to come here?"

"Of course, but why?"

Justin ran his hand through his hair. "I've given much thought to my situation."

Faith had the impression that, were it possible, he would pace.

"If Vincent really wants me dead ..." He hesitated. "He might ... no, he *will* try again. And if he succeeds—"

"Justin no."

"Don't deny the facts, Faith. It's not my intent to frighten you, but we have to be realistic. I'm concerned for you and Beth." He looked at their clasped hands, squeezed. "I would ask the Vicar to marry us while he's here." He looked directly at her. "If you're agreeable to the arrangement."

Arrangement? Faith sat straighter. Feeling weighted down in the region of her heart, she removed her hands from his.

"If anything should happen to me," he said. "As my wife, you would be Beth's legal guardian. Since there are trusts in place for my wife and children—nothing Vincent can touch—both of you would be well cared for."

"Justin. Stop." Against a sudden chill, Faith rose to stir the already blazing fire, glad to have her back to him so she could recover from the pain of his cold proposal.

"If you find the thought of marriage to me distasteful," he said to her back. "I'll understand."

She turned in surprise.

"I ask that you consider Beth before you make your decision." He spoke with a hurried, nervous edge to his voice. "I'll not pressure you, for you must consider the potential danger in aligning yourself to me. Please take some time to think about this. Whatever you decide, I would like to speak with Gabriel. Could you send him a note tomorrow?"

Faith tried to speak, but no words would come. She blinked several times to stop her tears.

"Will you at least consider it?"

Who was this cold, hard man?

Then she remembered. He was the man who trusted no one.

She'd thought he was beginning to care for her. What a fool. He'd been right all along. Faith Wickham was a silly little girl.

"I'll ... consider it. Good night, Justin." She went to her room and shut the door between. Throwing herself on her bed, she looked at the gold brocade canopy above her. The man was a simpleton. He'd asked her to marry him, but did he say he cared for her? She slapped a tassel. He speaks not of tenderness, but common sense ... nonsense more like. He attempts to use persuasion to win a heart already, foolishly, filled with love. "Oh!" She rocked to a standing position. "More fool you, Justin Devereux!"

Faith bathed and donned her nightgown and sat on the settee before her hearth. She watched the flame shifting from orange to yellow and back, and wished she might say no, just to see what the oaf would do.

But she couldn't. The arrogant man was destined to be hers, every chiseled inch of him. She'd known it from the first.

She would marry him, of course—she had love enough for both

of them—but she would make him suffer the torments of hell before she would give him her answer.

The next morning, when she went to Justin, he sat by the window, examining the vase in his hand, pretending he was *not* waiting for her. He set it down when she entered, as if it was inconvenient to do so, and asked, offhandedly, if she had an answer for him.

She opened the curtains. "About what?" she asked, staring out, seeing nothing. A minute later, when he said nothing, she turned to him.

His jaw was set rigid. "Marriage," he said. "To me."

To occupy her hands and eyes, and keep them off him, she swept the hearth. "You mean the arrangement for me to become Beth's mother?" She didn't so much as look his way.

"I mean, about marrying me. You have to do that, you know, to become Beth's guardian."

She set aside the broom and strode right up to him. "Let's speak plainly. I will be Beth's mother or nothing."

He gave her a fierce scowl. "Damn it woman, you cannot be her mother, unless you marry me. Now, do you have a response or not?"

"Not." She sent for Vicar Kendrick first thing, as Justin requested, and spent the rest of the day with Beth.

The Vicar wrote to say he would be there in a week. Those days passed in quiet exercise, but each began the same way. "Faith, have you an answer for me today?"

"Not today," became her usual reply.

Conversations became businesslike, Faith became more miserable.

Justin stopped asking, and she did not offer a reply.

The following Monday, as Beth tied a rose silk ribbon around Justin's face, it was apparent to Faith that he was preparing to ask again. He looked just that forlorn when he set himself to it.

Between his dejected look and the ribbon—the end of which

he was attempting to spit from his mouth—Faith couldn't keep her weak self from smiling.

At her look, he pulled the ribbon off with purpose, but when he saw Beth's disappointment, he tickled her. And when Beth caught her breath, Justin looked at Faith with such hope, it was almost her undoing.

"It's been over a week, Faith. Can you answer my question?"

"What question was that?"

"Damnation."

"Damnation," Beth repeated.

"Hush, darling," Faith said smoothing Beth's curls, trying to hide her smile.

"To become my wife. Do you think so little of the offer?"

Faith looked at the man she loved, and though her heart went out to him, she wanted him to understand what it felt like to be on the receiving end of a cold offer. "For such an arrangement, an answer is unnecessary until the Vicar arrives."

"Perhaps I seemed unfeeling—"

"Perhaps?"

He reached for her hands; she placed them behind her back. His look hardened. "I didn't mean to sound harsh," he said with as little emotion as his proposal held. "I ... wanted you to realize the danger involved. I ... care ... perhaps more than I'd like." He made to grasp her by the waist, but she skirted his reach.

Someone knocked on his door.

Faith returned with breakfast. "Have mine," she said, placing it before him. "I'm not hungry. Beth and I are going outside."

"Bloody hell."

"Bloodyell," Beth said.

"Come along, darling, Poppy is tired." Beth kissed him on the cheek, his smile so filled with love for his daughter, Faith ached to have him look at her that way.

As she left his room, a spoon bounced off the door frame, beside her, but she did *not* look back.

"You're one damned stubborn woman, do you know that?" he shouted after her. "Perhaps I would be better off if you said no!"

Good. He deserved to be frustrated, the thick-skulled village idiot.

Faith woke to the same blood-curdling scream as on her first night at Killashandra, and she ran.

Justin struggled wildly, his cries satanic, his sobs heart-rending, calling Beth over and over.

Faith tried to calm him with soothing words, to stroke his brow, but she couldn't stop him from thrashing about. She held his arms by his side. "Wake up, Justin. You're having a nightmare. You're safe. Beth is safe. Darling, please open your eyes. Look at me."

He stopped struggling and looked at her ... with the same unseeing orbs of her nightmare, the empty eyes she'd seen that first morning, and she gasped in terror. "Justin! Wake up!" She shook him, called his name, but it was no use. He was gone.

Justin was gone.

Gone from her forever.

She'd treated him abominably and now she would never have a chance to show him how she really felt. The wail of anguish that was torn from her incited him to renewed combat.

Heart beating apace with her struggle, Faith tried to use her weight to hold him down, but he threw her aside with incredible strength, and she landed in a heap on the floor, while he continued to grapple with some unseen assailant.

Returning to his side, Faith sought divine help. Astounded by his strength, desperate to stop him, lest he do himself harm, Faith straddled him as she'd seen Harris do, but he fought her with the desperation of the damned, hurting her in his frenzy.

She protected her face with her hands as he reached for her, but he grabbed her shoulders, digging into her bruised flesh, and shoving her to the far side of the bed. "Justin, stop. Please." She dragged herself up and tried to grab his wrists. But he used her hold on him to his own advantage, and turned her, twisting one of her arms painfully behind her.

"Stop it!" she screamed as loud as she dared, afraid to alert anyone to the happenings in the sickroom.

He towered above her, crushing her twisted arm beneath her.

"Justin! You're hurting me!"

Eyes wide with horror, awareness registered on his face. Justin stopped moving, as if he were seeing her for the first time. He took in the crumpled bedding, their awkward positions, and let her go. "Faith?"

"You know me!" She began to sob. She couldn't stop, even as she pulled her sore arm free. "You're not gone." She touched his dear face. You're here and you're ..." Mine, she nearly said. "Oh, Justin. I thought...."

"My God!" He cradled her as if she were made of spun sugar. "What have I done?" He set her away, to examine her, remorse in his expression. "If I hurt you ... oh, Faith, I'm so sorry."

"You were fighting demons," she whispered, loving the feel of his lips on her neck, raising her chin to give him access.

He kissed her eyes, her tear trails. "One demon, yes."

"Who?"

He took a breath, held her face between his hands. "Vincent wouldn't let me stop the carriage from going over the cliff. He tried to keep me from rescuing Beth."

When Justin let her go, Faith felt adrift. He gazed at the ceiling, searching. "That's not how it happened. I think ... Faith, I remember. I think I remember the carriage accident."

"Tell me."

"Did I hurt you? Really?"

Faith saw the life in his eyes, felt his lips on her fingers, and thanked God he could see and speak to her. "I'm fine," she whispered. "And so are you."

He tucked her face beneath his chin, which she thought a fine place for it to be, and he squeezed her. He told her of his search to find Catherine and Vincent after they had taken Beth, of the cliff in Bognor, where he found the carriage. When he told her Vincent said Beth was in the carriage, he faltered.

"If it's too difficult...."

"I want to. Are you warm enough?"

Faith smiled. "Tell me."

He took a breath. "When the carriage went over, the cab whipped about and the door tore from its hinges. I knew Beth would fall out and be dashed against the jagged rocks below." His sigh was ragged. "Tonight, in my dream, I was fighting Vincent, though I never did. What I did was run to grab the carriage, to hold it back, but it dragged me over with it."

Faith held him tighter. "I can't imagine it." She shuddered. "And I'm glad I can't."

Justin lay his cheek against her hair, his heart slowing. "If Vincent discovers you helped me, you'll be in jeopardy too. It's driving me crazy, thinking he'll darken our lives this day or the next ... to finish the deed."

"You'll be ready, Justin, when the time comes to confront Vincent. We'll see to it."

"I could kill him for making me believe Beth was in that carriage. Cat didn't want Beth ... for other than a pawn. She wanted to trade Beth, to keep me from divorcing her, so she and Vincent could continue their relationship accepted by society."

Shock rocked Faith to her core.

"To get Beth back, I agreed, promising Beth and I would go away. I think Catherine was satisfied. But Vincent was not."

"Where was Catherine when you ... the last time you saw her?"

"Standing beside Vincent, a good fifty feet from the cliff."

"I can't understand, then, how she died."

"I'd wager Vincent has the answer."

Faith had lived in a world where no evil existed, and though Vincent had frightened her with his apparent madness ... "It's hard to believe anyone could be so evil."

"I'm not sure your parents did you a service, keeping the world at bay. There are evils all about us. You have to realize that."

"There is nothing wrong with raising happy children. My parents loved each other and all of us and we knew it. That's an extraordinary legacy to pass on to your children."

"Faith, you walked into the house of a murderer with your parents' blessings. You almost helped him carry out his plan. You were too innocent to know what was happening."

She pulled from his embrace. "My parents allowed ... urged me to come and help you. I knew something was wrong, so I stopped your medicine. I saved your life, ungrateful man. I'm not a child." She hadn't helped him without help from above, she knew, but it was important Justin see her as a woman, not a child.

"Hush." He pulled her back against him.

She should push him away. She really should. Instead, she punched him where she could hurt him, his kneecap.

"Do you feel better now?" he asked.

"No."

"I don't deserve you."

"You don't. But I'm glad you told me. I hope you feel better for sharing your pain. Your nightmare is over, you know."

"Is it?"

Faith knew, given Justin's experience, that she would have to show him how good life could be. Telling him would be useless.

"Lie with me and let me hold you," he whispered.

It was easy for Faith to comply. When he'd looked at her so blankly, she felt as if part of her had died, too. Right now, she most wanted to be in his arms.

Justin sighed in contentment. "You do know how to make a man forget his problems, Faith."

"I try," she said, knowing exactly what he meant.

Justin let Faith's peace flow through him as her body settled along the length of his. "Are you certain you're not hurt? I thought I was fighting a man, and I imagine I was rough."

"I'm strong. I held my own against that demon inside you."

"Aye, and I'll wager you have the bruises to show for it. At dawn's first light, Faith, I'm going to examine every blessed inch of you."

"I'd like that."

Oh, God. His body responded quick enough. Did she want him as much as he wanted her? "Then I'd as soon not wait for dawn."

After several, long, silent beats, Faith's gentle hands began to wander over his back, and her life-giving touch washed over him like sunshine after a raging storm.

Justin gave over to the sensations pulsing through him. "You are something," he whispered against her hair. Intoxicated, he kissed the pulse in her neck. Then he pushed aside the fabric of her nightdress, the better to tease her with his tongue.

With a breathless gasp, Faith's hands sifted through his hair, pulling him closer, urging him to continue.

He intended to fulfill her every unspoken request.

With his lips still at her breast, he slid his hand from her hip, ever so slowly, toward the inner silk of her thigh.

"What are you doing?" She stopped his hand's journey, trapping it between her knees. "You can't."

"My poor innocent chi—"

"Do not call me child!" She brought his hand back to her breast. "Is this the body of a child?"

He kissed that very beautiful exhibit. "Most assuredly, you are not a child. But I am a cad. You have no experience of men. And I—"

"Have much experience of women. How many?"

"Does that matter?"

"What matters, I suppose, is that our lives have come together now. You startled me when you touched me there. I didn't know ... I *don't* know ... what to do, or what to expect."

"Will you put yourself in my care?" he asked.

"There is no other to whom I could answer yes."

He was as shaken by her easy trust as he was humbled by it.

"We've come a long way together have we not, Justin?"

"I'd like for us to go the rest of the way." He brought her into a stream of moonlight so he could look into her eyes. "'Tis more than a business arrangement I want, Faith. Become my wife in deed as well as name. I want us to raise Beth together, for you to be her mother. I never thought to want another by my side, but I want *you*. To share my life and learn the passion that can exist between us. May we begin now, Faith?"

"Yes, please."

Justin gazed in awe at her curls crowning his pillow, her emerald eyes shimmering with passion.

Warmth purled through his ready body, and a sense of destiny engulfed him, as he recognized Faith as the missing half of him. He drank in the sight and scent of her. "I feel as if you've always belonged to me. Does that make sense?"

Faith nodded. "Don't try to explain it. It's ... mystical."

"Mystical," he whispered sliding her nightgown up her legs, stopping at her knees, waiting for permission to continue. "May I?"

"I want our bodies to be as close as our souls are."

Justin watched awareness, and full-blown desire, wash over her. He stroked her inner thigh again, until her whimper filled him with sudden, hard need. He wanted to bury himself in her warmth, to become one with her.

Leaving her gown at the apex of her thighs, he untied the last satin bow at her bodice. She helped him slip the gown over her head, and wonder filled him. Faith Wickham, a woman of innocence and passion, and all his.

Her gown got tossed and he gloried in her womanly form. "Exquisite," he whispered palming her waist, then drinking from her lips again.

When he made to lay her down, Faith put her hand to his chest, in restraint. He stopped, wary, but her eyes danced as she raised his nightshirt over his head. Then she ran her hand along his chest, speeding his heart. "I've had the strongest notion to do this of late," she said. "Do you mind?"

"Only that you stopped. Touch me as you will. Anytime."

"We're agreed then. We both wish to be touched." She budded his nipple. "And kissed and held." She slid her hands to his shoulders and brought him over her.

Skin to skin, for the very first time, their sighs mingled.

Justin rolled them to their sides. "I don't know how I survived until you entered my life," he whispered.

"Barely," was her pert reply.

This was the most splendid moment of Faith's life. The man she had loved, from almost the first, gazed at her with passion. She cherished each angle and line of the scoundrel's face.

He poised above her now, tense, anxious. "Would that I could take you without hurting you."

"Come inside me, Justin. Please." *For you are my life.*

He surged at her invitation, and though she suffered a moment of discomfort and amazement, Faith welcomed him with joy.

Justin moved slowly, until he filled her, the satisfaction of destiny and fate soothing her. And when her discomfort passed and she could feel him unmoving, for her sake, she raised her hips to take him deeper.

At the invitation, Justin buried himself in her. And when she sighed and relaxed, he slipped from her in one long, sleek stroke, her cry of loss bringing him back again. And again.

He touched chords never played and they made music fit to reach heaven. He showed her his rhythm, and as if she'd always known it, they swayed and dipped in harmony.

Justin led her to a sparkling crescendo, bringing her so high, she feared to go beyond, and when she thought she could not, he made her soar again.

Faith followed her love to the brink of everlasting, and left the world behind. They shared a perfect ascent and surged to an all-consuming zenith where they marveled and held. Then, at a contented, leisurely pace they returned to a world forever-altered. Faith luxuriated in the serene moments when their hearts beat apace, slowing, calming. And she slept.

"Faith," her lover whispered, stroking her deeply and intimately. "Now you *must* marry me," he whispered, not bothering to hide the satisfaction in his voice.

Faith's bubble burst. "*Must* I?" Silent moments passed.

"It's a good bargain, Faith, this marriage between us."

Loathe to put space between them, she remained by his side. "Yes," she whispered, sadly. "A bargain of an arrangement."

"Then you agree?"

She couldn't speak for the lump in her throat.

"Answer me, Faith. I'm a sick man, remember."

"Yes," she said swallowing. "Your infirmity was abundantly evident just now."

He pulled her against his warm, delicious front and caged her legs with his. "Go to sleep, my stubborn lady. You will marry me, else I'll tell Vicar Kendrick that you're a fallen woman. Though I think he's fallen a time or two himself."

Heartsick, Faith could not work up the energy to be amused when she should. "Have you ever seen a man have apoplexy? It cannot be pretty. Best say I have fallen cap-over-tail for you."

"Good," Justin said, nipping her earlobe.

"Fine," Faith returned. "I don't like it above half, but we'll lie."

CHAPTER TEN

HARRIS RETURNED EARLY in the morning and headed for Justin's room near eight o'clock. Though he carried a new vial of medicine, his intention was to keep Miss Faith from using it. There came a time in life, he decided, retainer or no, when one had to speak. And for him, today was that day.

The door to the bedroom was locked, but he had a key. As he used it, he saw the door had been broken and repaired. Odd that.

He went in, determined to speak his mind … and stopped at the sight of his bare-legged Mistress entangled with his near-dead master. The tray slipped from his hand.

At the resounding crash, his master sat bolt upright. "Have a care, man. You'll wake the dead."

Harris, hand on his pounding heart, fell into a chair. With shaking hands, he wiped his brow and stared at the vision staring back. "Wake the dead? I already have! You were damned near dead last time I saw you."

"That bad, was I?"

Harris nodded, unable to believe he was having a conversation with his master. And that very ghost glanced at his wide-eyed nurse, covered to her chin, and grinned back. "I am recovered."

Harris sensed the tension crackling between the two, and it was the kind shouldn't be witnessed. He grinned. "I'm thinkin' it must have taken somethin' wicked to rouse you from hell."

"Wicked, yes. Faith did it," his master said proudly.

"Has my mistress found some miraculous cure, then?" Harris asked, laughter beyond his control.

The wicked nurse slithered low under the blankets, but his master pulled her against him, for all the world as if he owned her. "She has *magnificent* ... curative powers."

"Justin Devereux!" she screeched. "I don't know which of you I'm angrier with. The smirking half-wit beside me ... yes you, Justin. Or you, Harris, with your daft grin. If you will stop your gawking and childish humor, and depart, you may return in an hour. We'll explain Justin's recovery then." She wagged her finger. "Mind, no one suspects Justin's improvement so you had better—" She raised a brow— "Close your mouth. Now, Harris."

Harris shut his jaw on a chuckle and retreated, laughing anyway when he tripped over their discarded nightclothes.

Justin caught Harris's bold wink before he shut the door.

Back ramrod-straight, arousing as all hell, Faith rose, dragging the blanket with her, leaving him exposed, and wrapped it about herself, fury in her emerald eyes. "I can't believe this!" She threw her hands in the air, almost losing the blanket.

He tried to help her catch it and she ripped it from his hand. "You enjoyed that, Justin Devereux. Sometimes you can be such a half-wit." She strode from the room, majestic in her anger, making him laugh the harder, and want her the more.

He finally stopped laughing and grabbed his dressing gown from the bed. Perhaps this arrangement might be as beneficial to them—if he survived Vincent's scheme—as it would be for Beth.

He had never felt this way, exactly, about another woman.

He desired Faith, yes, yet this was stronger, deeper, and both more and less sexual, than he'd ever known. It was not simple lust with Faith, though God knew, last night had been one of the best in his life. As if they had met on some remote spiritual plane at the same moment they melded on the physical.

Heady stuff, that, he thought, as he moved to his wheelchair and went to the windows. He watched the sea, but saw her face in moonlight, lips swollen from his kisses, parted and inviting.

Before long, her soft tread whispered of her coming. "Come to me, Faith," he said without turning.

She stopped behind him, but he reached around and brought her onto his lap, cheek to cheek and lips to lips. But even after the kiss, she remained wary. "Forgive me?" he asked.

She considered his request for a moment. "Perhaps. Someday. Maybe."

"It was only Harris, after all."

"Your lack of perception boggles. You are such a bird-wit."

He nuzzled her neck. "You're right."

"And well you know it." She rose at his body's response, but he stroked the blond lace along her bodice. "You look fetching." With quick action, he had her back on his lap and stole her lips.

Harris coughed.

Faith stood. "Harris," she said. "You startled me ... us."

"Sorry. Old habits. From now on, I won't come in till you open the door. Can you tell me about this cure, now?" He cleared his throat. "Tell me, true, how did it come about?"

They related the tale, Justin giving Faith credit, and Faith giving it back, Harris nodding all the while. "I can't tell you how it was to walk in here and see you returned to the living."

Justin tried to keep from smiling. "What did you find in London? Faith tells me you were searching for the doctor and the source of the poison you were feeding me."

Harris straightened. "I didn't know I was hurting you!"

Justin touched his arm. "No man has ever been more devoted. Thank you for what you did for me." Justin took Faith's hand and entwined their fingers. "Now then, tell us what you discovered."

"Stevens, the doctor tended you in London, told your brother that with care, you could be hale and whole again, but he was dismissed with the excuse you were being brought here to recover. He warned against the move and he did not prescribe the potion."

"Do you know anything about the doctor who did?"

"Old sot can't tend animals, let alone people. Far as I could see, he only *called* himself a doctor. You were right Missy, about Blackstone having money of a sudden. Likely hired out'a gaol, cause that's where he was cooling his heels before your accident, your grace. Ain't no one thought much of his doctoring. Known better for his drinking and gambling."

Harris turned to Faith. "You scared him, ringing a peel over him, cause after he left here, he took ship for America."

"I chased him away!" Faith cried. "He can't help us now."

Justin squeezed her hand. "We'll come about. The medicine?" he asked Harris. "Did the apothecary say who sells it?"

Harris shook his head. "An apothecary in Seven Dials said an urchin from the Rookery, never the same one twice, comes to his door with your medicine every few weeks. Likely enough vermin between buyer and seller to keep us looking for the culprit. I did find a bloke to give us a fair accounting of what's in it." Harris fished in his pocket. "Wrote it down." He handed Faith the paper.

She scanned it. "This Mr. Baldershaw says that from the red-brown color and bittersweet taste, he believes it's, in part, a decoction of the poppy. The opium made you sleep, Justin. It also contains licorice and cloves to make it taste better."

"Doesn't work," Justin said.

Faith grimaced. "He soaked bread with the medicine and fed it to gutter rats. Oh, Lord, they died!" Knowing she might have made a different decision, Faith shuddered, appalled.

Encouraged by Justin's nod, she continued. "The opium is mixed with sherry to strengthen the effects. He thinks it could have hemlock or deathcap powder, no more than a few grains of either. Oh, here he says, it's likely Hemlock, which keeps the victim's mind functioning while destroying his body."

"The nightmares," Justin said. "Me tied at the base of a black pit while I watched Beth tumble to her death, over and over again."

Harris frowned and turned to gaze out the window.

Faith squeezed Justin's shoulder and he placed his hand over hers. The clock struck the hour, marking Justin's life, rather than his death, and Faith gave thanks.

"Since the poison did not result in death, Mr. Baldershaw suspects it was made with the spring root of the hemlock. He says it's much less potent in spring than at any other time of year and only an amateur would make the mistake." She shook her head. "Thank God for an amateur. These ingredients together, he says, would produce sleep, strange dreams, delirium, and discomfort or pain, depending upon the amounts."

"It works," Justin said dryly.

"If taken in larger doses or over a long enough period, death would result," Faith said with a shudder. "If, after a prolonged period, one were to stop taking it, severe symptoms could result. We know about them. He goes on to suggest the victim might have formed an immunity to one or more of the toxins or a combination of them. He says milk expunges the effects of the poison. Knowing you were given milk often, no one will ever know for certain how or why you survived."

Harris sat, looking worn. "He didn't believe you'd been taking it twice a day for so long. When he saw how little was the dose, he thought the person who made it particularly clever, or particularly ignorant. Its having opium in it might help him find where it came from. He'll ask around but it'll take time since he must take care. I waited to receive the answer, but it never came. Could have sent a note, Miss Faith, but soon as Baldershaw give me this, I came back so you'd stop dosing him.

"I'm glad," Justin said. "Anyone could have read the note and we were worried about you."

"Sorry, your grace. I feared you might be dead, but not worried." He nodded at Faith. "Thought she was daft. Light, air, cleaning, bathing, changing the curtains, as if that would help, and wanting it done yesterday. Bossy she was, ordering—"

"That's enough, Harris," Faith said. "We have to stop Vincent before he tries again. You must return to London to find out who supplies and buys those ingredients."

"Be careful," Justin added. "Talk to Baggins at my London house about the accident. Ask what happened when I was brought back to Grosvenor Square afterward. And Catherine's old nurse—get her name and direction. Cat might have told her something."

"Harris," Faith said. "See who found Catherine and Justin after the accident. Vincent's servants might have answers."

"Good thought, sweetheart. I wonder if it was Marcus or Grant who found us, or even Gabriel or Carry. I sent a man to alert my friends when Beth went missing. Locate them, Harris, but don't approach them, yet."

Harris bowed. "If you please, your grace?"

Justin stood. "Yes, Harris?"

The surprised man paled then all out smiled. "Happy I am to have you back, and better than I thought." He shook his head. "I can't believe it."

"I have much to live for." Justin brought Faith close.

"Knew it the minute I clapped eyes on her," Harris said. "I said, 'the master'd like you b'God,' and she thought I meant Vincent, and her back went up like a cat." Harris smiled. "With your permission, your grace, I'll be on my way 's'afternoon."

"God speed, Harris."

It was mid-afternoon by the time Faith walked Harris to the stairs. "Have a care, Miss. There's a bloke downstairs, Hemsted, Vincent's man, asking questions."

"Has anyone told him anything?"

"Mostly, they ignore him, being Vincent's man and all. Them that's saying anything is so they'll keep their posts, and that they make up. Take care." He tipped an invisible hat and left.

Faith returned to the sickroom after telling everyone Justin was failing. He opened his arms, and after learning how close they'd come, there was nowhere she'd rather be.

Later, Vicar Kendrick knocked at her bedroom door, and as far as the household was concerned—after hearing the false news of Justin's decline—the prelate's arrival could not have been better timed. Faith welcomed him with enthusiasm.

"My dear Ms. Wickham, you have positively bloomed in your position as nurse to the Duke of Ainsley, but—" He stood back to consider her more closely, his brows furrowed. I must say, I did not expect you to exude radiance in a house about to lose its master."

Faith knew that she should not be surprised at his censure. She had not been truthful about the reason for his visit. She led him further into the room. "Reverend Kendrick, behold my patient."

Her patient had been seated, and hidden by the high back of her settee, facing the hearth, as it was, its back to her door.

Justin stood, revealing himself, and extended his hand. "Gabe, it's been too long."

"Ainsley!" In the way of old friends they embraced, more or less, stiff backed, hard slaps and all that. Faith smiled inwardly at the emotion-filled, yet unemotional, male ritual.

"I must say, Faith, you led me to believe … and not ten minutes ago, the housekeeper said...." Vicar Gabriel Kendrick looked from his friend to the parishioner for whom he had

"This house would surely *have* lost its master had you not sent Faith to me. I thank you."

Vicar Kendrick turned to her. "Another credit to your nursing skills. A miracle of sorts, I think. Congratulations, my dear."

Emotion welled in Faith. "Would that they could all be so successful."

Her spiritual leader patted her hand. "I know, my dear. But cease blaming yourself for your grandfather. It was never your fault, because it was never in your hands. You're doing the Lord's work in the way He asks. Do not accept responsibility that is His," he admonished.

"Well," Justin said. "It must have been His plan that I survive, for Faith has given me more than my life." He embraced her shoulder, and his friend's smile vanished. "See here, Ainsley—"

Faith stepped forward and touched the Vicar's arm. "Please, sit, and let me explain what's transpired since I arrived."

"I asked Faith to send for you," Justin said, "because we wish to marry, and we'd like you to perform the ceremony."

It was hard to tell if the vicar was shocked or relieved, Faith thought. "No one can know about our marriage, not even my parents. Justin's life is in danger and you must keep our secret."

"Your parents will never forgive me."

"They will, for Faith's life is also at risk," Justin said. "I do not speak idly. The threat is ruthless." Justin took a paper from Faith's bedstand. "Here is Lord Ponsonby's direction. Though he can be trusted, simply tell him that during a moment of awareness, I asked Faith to marry me to care for my young daughter, and please ask him to keep our secret. As Magistrate, he can secure a special license. I want this marriage to be above reproach. I'll take no chance with a havey-cavey affair."

The Vicar nodded. "A special license will eliminate the need for the banns to be read or to hold the ceremony in a church or chapel. Other details must be dealt with, however, but I will deal with them in short order and return on Friday."

After Faith rocked Beth, she found Justin by his bed. He'd turned back the covers. "I've been waiting for you."

The freezing rain clicking against the windows added to her unease. "I think we should sleep in our own rooms."

Justin's surprise turned to contrition. "Of course. I didn't mean to presume, but in my heart, we are wed."

"We are not," she said. "And it *is* only be a marriage of convenience." He'd even made that clear to the Vicar. They would marry for Beth's sake, and no other. Sadness held her in its grip.

He frowned. "Last night—"

"Was an indiscretion it would be wrong to repeat."

"It did not seem indiscreet," he said. "But beautiful."

She turned from the entreaty in his eyes to look out the window. They were on a course that could be as destructive as the carriage accident, their "marriage" the runaway vehicle. Without care, it would crash, and they would shatter.

But if they traveled with care, they might—perhaps—journey peacefully. "Please," she whispered, not daring to look at him.

He stepped behind her, because his struggle to come to her on his own had not been a silent one. When he slipped his arms around her, his hands at her waist, her resolve faltered. "Let me hold you while we sleep," he whispered, his lips caressing her ear.

She allowed herself the luxury of leaning into him and closed her eyes to savor. He was a warm hearth on a winter night, a shady tree in the summer sun. But a hearth needed tending, or it might smoke, a tree pruning, or it might die.

Reluctantly, she faced him. "It wouldn't end there."

"I hoped you wouldn't realize that." He trailed his fingers along her cheek and down.

With determination, Faith stepped away. "Good night." The memory of his grimace would be a cold companion in her lonely bed tonight.

During the days that followed, Faith resisted Justin's sensual assaults. She loved him, but couldn't speak the words for fear of silence. She wanted him to trust her, but he never would.

For Beth's sake, the marriage must take place, but the road they would travel in life must be constructed with care, or their journey would end in disaster. A physical union, while beautiful, could break a marriage without the proper foundation. She considered mutual trust to be the strongest groundwork. And it must come first.

On Friday morning, with Justin's directions, Faith went to his parents' apartments—with the excuse of seeking blankets—to fetch his father's clothing so he might dress for their wedding. Vincent had likely taken over his old apartment—for no one would want his father's ostentatious lair, not even Vincent.

But the Vicar didn't return Friday. His note said Ponsonby was in Scotland for a month. On what was to have been their wedding night, Faith was hard put to ignore the desire in Justin eyes. But she was resolved. Trust first, intimacy second.

That night, she dreamed that when the Vicar pronounced them married, Justin kissed her. And when she opened her eyes, he *was* kissing her in fact ... in her *bed!* She fought succumbing to the sensuality in his look and the promise in his touch. "What are you doing here?"

"You should be proud of me," he said. "I walked all the way from my room, alone. But my legs are tired and shaking. Let me lie down and rest, before I fall and hurt myself."

His hand and arm trembled; he did need to lie down. Faith scooted to the far side of the bed, but his condition was not so dire as to keep him from pulling her into his arms. "Justin Devereux!

Where is your nightshirt?"

"I thought you could keep me warm." He kissed her.

Faith's determination was sorely tested. Resolute, she pushed from his embrace and rose from the bed.

"The devil, Faith." Justin raised himself on an elbow. "Where in blazes are you going?

"To sleep in *your* bed."

She shook her head at his groan. This was going to be a long month.

CHAPTER ELEVEN

WITHIN THE HOUR he would wed. Again. With more trepidation than he would like—battle scars, he'd wager—after six long weeks of waiting, Faith would finally become his lawfully wedded wife.

He placed his father's lapis stickpin in his linen neck cloth. Nothing to fear from marriage. Not with Faith. He was glad the day had arrived. Happy. Jubilant. And he had Vincent to thank. He grimaced. Fancy having Vincent to thank for *anything*.

Upon that incredible thought came another. Fancy considering thanks rather than blame. Justin supposed that somewhere deep inside, he'd always known Faith was different. Had she not proved it in so many ways?

Yet, too near the surface for comfort pressed a niggling fear. Panic, it was called. Experience—the kind that left a bitter taste in a man's mouth, on every level.

Taking a deep breath, consigning uncertainty to the devil, Justin faced his old school chum, a scoundrel of a vicar, though he supposed Gabe might have changed. Or at the least, he understood the sinners in his flock better than most shepherds.

"What think you, Gabriel? Am I a fit bridegroom for so beautiful a bride?"

"Aye, and permit me to compliment you on your bride. Faith has a selfless spirit. She is as beautiful within as without."

"A diamond of the first water? A veritable paragon?" Justin asked, hiding his tease.

His friend's back stiffened. "Indeed, your grace."

"Cut the defensive stance. You are a *bit* prejudiced in her favor?"

Catching the humor, Gabe chuckled. "Well...."

When Faith came in, Justin knew he was not the only man struck by the sight. Lights danced in the emerald of her eyes. Her porcelain skin, which *he* could nearly feel beneath his fingertips, was tinged by her charming blush. Her raven hair shone in streaks of near blue in the candlelight. Her gown of ivory silk with pink rosettes and sash, accented a waist so tiny, and breasts so full, he ached to explore. He had to fist his hands to keep from reaching for her.

Faith nearly lost her breath at Justin's perusal. "Do you like the gown? It came with the rest of ... my new clothes."

"I like you in it." Justin kept his heated gaze so trained on her, Faith warmed to the point of catching fire.

The Vicar cleared his throat, stifling desire, cutting the tension. "You look beautiful." He kissed her hand.

Grateful, Faith turned from her brazenly-handsome bridegroom in fawn pantaloons and azure tail-coat, shaken by such a mad dash back to sanity from the sweet rush of carnal urgency.

"It's fortunate you and your father were of a size," she said to Justin, her voice so normal, she appreciated the deception.

He kissed the inside of her wrist. Currents raced from there to unimaginable places. Lord, she needed to get hold of herself.

"Thank you," he said, and she didn't remember why.

His clothes. Now she remembered. "Vincent could never wear your father's things." She prattled and knew it.

"He favors my mother." Justin's odd, suddenly detached voice caught her attention. Of Vincent, Justin spoke with passion. Of their mother, he could barely gather a modicum of interest.

"You rarely speak of her."

He tilted his head. "I hardly knew her." A simple fact.

Much as his answer shocked her, she saw it as another reason for his inability to trust. How she wanted to heel him.

The Vicar coughed. "Shall we proceed with the ceremony?"

By her hearth, the Vicar spoke the words that bound her to Justin for eternity, while the blustery breath of winter rattled the battlements in protest. December the 15th, 1827.

The vicar cleared his throat. "I can't remember when a wedding meant so much. Take care of her, my friend, or you may find yourself the object of my wrath."

"I can take you and we both know it." Justin's smile gave her a glimpse of the lad he might have been.

"Maybe when we were boys." The vicar, too, for that matter. "Be good to her. Be good to each other."

"We will," Faith said. "Imagine me, with a husband of noble character."

"You deserve nothing less," the vicar said. "Neither you." He slapped Justin on the back once more.

"Thank you, Gabe. I wanted only you to perform the ceremony."

"I only wish Faith's parents could share our joy. I pray they forgive me for keeping this from them."

"They will be happy you were here for me."

The vicar nodded solemnly, doubtfully, and opened his bag. "I pray so." He took out a familiar tome, the parish register, in which was inscribed her birth. She touched it. Home.

"Faith, you will inscribe your maiden name. Justin, sign below it. Notice that Lord and Lady Ponsonby signed as witnesses. When I explained the need for secrecy, they agreed to witness with me as proxy. They sponsored me at the school where we met, Justin, which is why they sought my help in getting your nurse, Justin." He gave Faith the quill. "The biggest problem was permission for Faith to wed. Age twenty one is the age of consent. Ponsonby reluctantly accepted my favor, but if your parents oppose the union later, they will be within their rights to petition for annulment."

Justin frowned. "But an annulment would mean—"

"He believes you at death's door, Justin." The Vicar donned his coat. "God be with you in your struggle against evil, and guide your path to justice, and forgiveness."

The men shook hands, their friendship and respect evident. "You have given me a great gift."

That, oddly enough, nicked at the granite of Faith's resolve to delay their physical intimacy. She stepped into the vicar's open arms. "God speed," he whispered, and then he was gone.

She felt adrift, the forces around her strong and unknown.

She turned back to the room and Justin's arms offered shelter. "My turn to kiss the bride," he whispered against her temple. In her dream, he told her now that he loved her. Silently, she begged for the words.

His dark eyes smoldered with arousal.

Say it. Please say it.

His lips touched hers, teased them apart, unrestrained, passionate. "I'll never get enough of you." The words were wrong, yet she returned the sentiment. Never enough.

When she was in dire peril of allowing her determination to drown in kisses, he stepped away, his grin decidedly wicked. "Do you know what I would like right now?"

Contrasting urges to laugh and scream warred, but Faith smiled. "I cannot imagine … neither am I certain that I wish to know."

"I would like to bathe in a tub." He crooked his finger but she stepped back. He bore the eyes of a sorcerer, compelling and dangerous. "As my wife, you can no longer refuse."

Was he speaking of baths? It was conceivable he would be so relaxed afterwards, that he would have no strength for his conjugal rights ... and pigs might fly. She sighed. At least the bath would postpone the inevitable.

Difficult to deny what one most craved. She faced a hard battle tonight—oh, horrid word choice. She shook her head. "Go to your room and shut the door. I'll ring for Jenny. You shall have your bath, and soon." He kissed her with great fervor, tried for another, but she evaded him. With a laugh, he finally allowed himself to be pushed into his room and shut in.

It took nearly an hour before Faith could open his door once again. "Your bath awaits, lord and master."

"You changed from your wedding dress," he said, disappointed.

"What would Jenny think to find me dressed like that?"

"She would, of course, have assumed you married the dying man in the next room."

Did his behavior, or her guilt, make her uncomfortable? "Justin. What's wrong with you?"

"From the moment I saw you in that dress, I imagined myself removing it."

"You were supposed to be listening to the vicar's words." She wasn't certain how to deal with Justin as a husband. "Get into the tub."

Eyes dancing, he stripped with shameless abandon.

Faith wanted to vanish at the evidence of his arousal. Guilt grew. And why should it? Theirs was a business arrangement. It wasn't as if he loved her. And a relationship built on lust was a house built on sand ... precarious. Easily toppled.

Rather than guilt, her determination gained strength. She raised her chin. She was right; they needed to begin with the proper foundation ... or relinquish themselves to a sad future.

Justin took her hand. It was evident her silence worried him.

"Help me, wife, into that wonderfully hot, steamy water."

She was disappointed he chose playful banter, for it was time to come to a pact about how to begin this "till-death-do-us-part" arrangement. But their discussion would come in due course, and she couldn't blame him for craving a real bath, so she humored him. He found it awkward, needing more agility than he'd regained, to step into the copper tub, and nearly lost his balance.

When, at last, he sat, he sighed, eyes closing in near-ecstasy. "Next time, I shall invite you to join me, Lady Faith."

Faith looked up, soap in hand. "What did you call me?"

"The title will be yours when we recover it. But, Faith, you are now an obstacle to Vincent's inheriting. Should something happen to me, he would get the title, but little else. All goes to my wife and children … which is why he wanted Catherine."

Faith faltered in her resolve. Justin's fear of marriage, his mistrust of love, sat upon a foundation so much stronger than sand, but solid as marble. It was called experience. With such festering scars, how could she fault his fear of new wounds? If only he would trust that *she* would never inflict them. She sighed. "I'm happy to thwart Vincent. The money is trifling, the title, less important. Wife is title enough." She was married to the man she loved. And if she told him, would he believe her?

"And the property?" he asked.

"We need somewhere to live, but my parents would take us in."

His bark of laughter grated. "God protect us from that."

"Justin Devereux. My parents are good people."

"I'm sure, but I won't live with them to prove it." He trailed his finger down her neck, across her collarbone, lower, slower. "Kiss me, wife." His expression held promise.

Aching to respond, unable to summon the strength to stop, or remember why she should, Faith got singed by the fire in his eyes. Her resolve turned to dust as she stepped into a miasma of desire. But her determination to make of this marriage more than an arrangement nagged at her. Justin's lips were a breath away. Another sip. Just one more.

She fought the pull.

Sanity returned on the wings of a satisfied chuckle. And she dropped the soap and slapped her hand against the water, the backlash raining sober reality.

"God's teeth!" Justin swore.

Shaken by thwarted desire, Faith sat back on her heels.

Water dripped from Justin's hair and the tip of his nose, his bony knees peeked through the surface of the water, his indignance comical. The picture tickled her so, Faith laughed herself senseless, his surprise making it funnier.

Losing the struggle between consternation and mirth, Justin laughed too. "Wash me, woman, I have plans for this evening."

Warmth purled through her. She supposed there were worse destinies than losing this battle ... and if she allowed it to happen, she would have the rest of her life to learn what the worst was.

Justin closed his eyes, content. A surprising peace filled him. Faith skimmed his body in a slow, sensual massage. Her lathered hands kneaded his shoulders and back, made soapy swirls in his chest hair and skimmed his nipples, arousing, branding. Then she slid her hands lower ... and stopped.

He opened his eyes when she started on his legs and chuckled at her blush. He couldn't wait to discover where it began.

He was hard as a pikestaff and near ready to spend when she began to work toward that part of his anatomy she had neglected, the part that anticipated her touch with almost painful need.

Unable to bear it another moment, he brought her hand to his flesh and closed her fingers around him. "Ah." She explored his length, surprising him, and looked as heated as him. Passion had come alive between them. Soon, he would make her sing with it.

Faith was afire, but she had to stop. How had she gotten into this? How could she tell the man sleek and throbbing beneath her fingers that she would be his wife in name only, when she wanted him in every way? She absently traced his nipple with the tip of a finger as she considered her dilemma.

It wasn't just respect and love their marriage needed. As his second wife, she needed to be a dear friend, a cherished partner, a trusted confidant, a beloved mother to his child, an exciting, passionate lover—everything his first wife was not.

Justin tried to bring her hand back to where it had been, but she resisted and placed both hands in her lap instead.

His look questioned; she turned away. More than anything, she wanted to heal the wounds Catherine had inflicted, the ones left to fester. She was more determined than ever to heal this man with love, if he would allow it. But how to show her love while refusing to take him to her bed? A dilemma.

Justin stroked her face. "Why, my darling, has anguish replaced the passion in her eyes?"

Faith sighed and stood. Time to be honest; he deserved nothing less. "Our marriage is an arrangement. Your words."

He opened his mouth to protest. She shook her head to stop him. "I know to you, that also means intimacy, but to me, a marriage is more. It's love, Justin. I realize you don't grasp, much less believe in the word, neither the feelings that go with it. But I vowed I wouldn't—we wouldn't lie together unless there was more than a bargain between us."

"Faith, I—"

"Wait, let me finish." She fetched the bucket by the door. I've been furious since you asked me to marry you in that cold way. I need to show you how it left me, how I felt the day you proposed the *arrangement*. This, I believe, will bring you the chill I felt that day." She emptied the bucket of ice over him.

"Damnation!" He rose with a speed she didn't think he could, his look hard, stinging like a slap, and she stepped back.

He struggled from the tub, but did not want her help. Her guilt palpable, her determination went the way of his arousal. His step was ungainly; he nearly fell. It made him angrier. He snapped his dressing gown off the chair, shrugged into it and tied it at the waist with a yank. "I see how cold my offer must have left you," he said through clenched teeth.

Faith stilled. Of anything he might have said, that was the least expected. *Did* he understand? Or did anger drive him?

"Love is a myth, Faith, invented by the likes of Mrs. Radcliff," he snapped, stepped away from her, and faltered. She reached to steady him, but his look froze her.

Fatigued, he sat on the settee, his weariness rooted deeper than the physical, which frightened her. He was bone-weary of playing fox to his brother's hound, which was understandable, and she just added to his burden by making him doubt the wisdom of their marriage. "Justin, I—"

He held a staying hand. "In light of these feelings you have just revealed, exactly where does this marriage of ours stand?"

She shrugged in sadness. "I don't know, but I need more than an arrangement, Justin. A marriage needs more than passion."

"Yet a lack of passion can be fatal to a marriage. I've had that kind. And it was not good. I want better for us." Shoulders set, he raised his chin and looked straight at her.

Lord, she had to make him see. So much depended on this. "A marriage needs—*I* need—respect, understanding, trust. And passion, but it must be built on the rest or we have *nothing*." She knelt and reached for his hands but he folded his arms.

She lay her cheek against his knees, to steady her trembling and seek wisdom from a higher source. After several clock-ticking minutes, wherein he did not touch her, no matter how she prayed he would, she looked into his eyes and stood. "We are speaking of the rest of our lives, Justin. Did you not listen to the Vicar? "In sickness and in health, until death us to part.""

"I believe we have mastered the sickness and health part." His levity rang hollow.

"Until *death*," she snapped. "A long, lonely business *arrangement*, and no bloody bargain!"

He sighed. "What do you ask of me, precisely?"

"That you try to understand how I feel."

"I am trying. How can I prove it?"

"Make no demands on me tonight. I need something solid between us, before we become … intimate again."

"The vicar said you should obey me."

"Do you order me to allow you the use of my body then?"

"Damnation, Faith, that's not what I meant. Fear not, I have no desire to take someone who does not want me."

She started to speak. He stopped her with a finger to her lips. At least he was touching her. She closed her eyes to cherish the sensation.

"I did not mean that the way it sounded. I am trying to understand. What I ask is this; sleep by my side, let me hold you in my arms. Only that, until you are ready for more. I too want to make this marriage work." He stood.

Shocked, grateful, certain when he was rested he would want more, Faith put an arm around his waist. "Let's go to bed."

A child's giggle penetrated Faith's consciousness. She woke to see Beth perched atop the blankets straddling her father's chest. Nose to nose, she stared into his eyes.

Justin's chuckle and Beth's laugh were like music.

Faith sat against her pillows. "I forgot to tell you; since I've been sleeping in here again, Beth occasionally joins me before Sally comes for her."

Justin placed a kiss on his daughter's nose. "Morning, Muffin."

He looked at Faith, "An unusual way for a man to wake the morning after his wedding. But then the wedding night was out of the ordinary, also."

"I ... I'm sorry about the ice."

He grimaced. "Probably the only thing that could accomplish what it did." He smoothed Beth's bronze curls. "Faith, you mean more to me than I can express." He took a shuddering breath. "Frankly I find even that admission frightening. You'll never be sorry you married me. My word. But you ask a lot."

"I begin to understand." It was all she could do not to beg him to make love to her. But his candor made a good beginning and she did not want to take a step back. "Thank you for that."

He smiled—more than his doubtful half-smile, but not one open and easy, either. "What time does Sally usually come for Beth?"

"Around seven."

"Good, we have two hours together." They tickled and played until Beth yawned. Justin tucked her against him, took Faith's hand and brought it to his lips. "Shall we three escape and leave Vincent to his wealth, for mine will be with me."

His words washed gently over her with a soothing touch. Faith placed her arm around him and their daughter. "Shh," she whispered. "Beth's asleep. Here, I'll take her back to her own bed."

When she returned, Justin had propped himself up in bed, and he watched her. "You're the mother Beth needs."

"Would you mind if I taught her to call me Mama?"

"People might wonder why she suddenly began."

"My God, I'm getting careless. It's too soon, you're right."

He squeezed her hand. "Harris should be back in a few weeks. Perhaps then we can make plans to deal with Vincent."

"I'm afraid of what Vincent will do next, and his man has been asking questions, checking the food brought up—"

"You didn't tell me that."

"I didn't want to worry you, but Hemsted, his man, is terribly interested in what's happening with you."

Justin sat up. "Sometimes I wish I could walk out of here, declare myself alive, and have my life back the way it was."

"The way it was?"

Justin smiled. "No, not exactly." He pulled her down beside him. "I would have you by my side with no fear for the future. But we have to find a way to ensnare Vincent."

"By proving his guilt."

"If ever we can. I wonder how Harris's search is going."

"I received a letter from him yesterday while the Vicar was with you, before I began to dress for the ceremony. He has found nothing. He will spend Christmas in Horsham with his sister and return to London after. One of his contacts is following leads and he hopes answers will be waiting when he returns. He bids us be patient." She sighed. "It could take months."

He stood. "Months with the two of us shut up alone together." He slid his hands around her waist. "I want you for Christmas."

She touched his face. "Christmas, at the earliest."

Beside Justin, Faith tossed in her sleep. Celibacy was difficult for them both. Thank God his exercises used up so much energy. He had slept by her side since their wedding, a grueling test of respect and understanding. Perhaps even trust, for he trusted when her enigmatic needs were satisfied she would be a passionate wife. But how to satisfy those needs?

A challenge. Trust, understanding, respect. He did respect her. But trust? He didn't think there was much he wouldn't entrust to her. And perhaps he was coming to understand her frustration with this arrangement of a marriage … somewhat.

He worried with a family like hers—affectionate, close—she might expect more than he could give. But more than ever, he believed it was time to try. Because the prize was greater than any ever offered, and if he lost … it didn't bear thinking about.

He could tell by her breathing that she slept. Good. He slipped from bed. With stealth, he went to his room and donned his father's clothes. To fetch Faith's gift for Christmas, in two days time, he must walk—God grant him the strength—to the opposite wing of the house and his parents' apartments.

As he approached the stair at the center of the house, he remembered when he and Vincent slid down opposite rails, their mother frowning at the bottom. She explained later that she couldn't catch them both, so she had chosen to catch Justin.

He could still hear Vincent's scream as he landed and broke his arm. He was three years old, the younger by four years. Truth to tell, Justin had been surprised that the reigning queen of society had elected to catch either of her sons. But she'd shipped them off to old Fishface soon after, for an education said she, though it was more of a hell-raising, and they did *occasionally* come home for holidays … at her whim.

Eventually, Justin entered the queen's jasmine-scented sanctum and was transported to the event that led to this midnight excursion.

"*Maman*, you sent for me?" 'Twas so odd to be summoned to this room, Justin expected to be expelled, but he saw her smile in her mirror, her dressing-table a forest of glass bottles and enamel jars. Then to his shock, the lady with the rouge-pot lips stood and kissed him, clasping him to her breast.

She stood him away and examined him. "Ah, my son, you are soon a man and do not appreciate a selfish, clinging mother."

He was not a man yet. And she had never been a clinging mother. Selfish, yes; even then he knew that. For years, he'd hidden his yearning for this mother he hardly knew. Now he allowed himself to be held for a moment, pretending it was one of those dark nights he'd called for her, when she never came, because she wasn't there.

But he was not a halfling anymore, so he pulled away.

Tears silvered her cobalt eyes. "There is something I must say." She placed the palms of her hands against his face. "Never let it change you, my son. You will feel the same for me, and your brother, and your father. Do you promise this?"

He answered as she wished. "I promise."

"You, Justin, are your Papa's only son."

He was glad she no longer touched him as he tried to absorb her words, but they made no sense. He looked at her, really looked, her smile as false as her beauty. A mask. "Vincent—"

"Is my child by another man. Your father was not faithful, so neither was I. You remember your cousin who lived with us?"

"Justin Reddington. He was sent to America."

"He was your father's bastard. Your father named him Justin to spite me and brought him here to throw him in my face."

Justin reeled. "Why was he sent away?"

"Because, if he was not, I told your father I would present him with more bastards. A wife pays for her sins as well as her husband's. Someday, you will understand. *Eh bien.* Now you know. And you still love your *maman?*"

"Yes," he'd said, because she wanted him to, but something in him broke. A child had paid for his parents' mistakes. Children. For he and Vincent were not immune to the damage.

Sweating, hand trembling, Justin pulled himself from that horrible time in his life and concentrated on his purpose here. Sixteen was young to become world-wise, but it happened to him that night. Sometimes he hated his mother for that, even now.

He'd hated his parents for betraying each other and their sons, all *three* of them. Mostly, he hated them for casting Justin Reddington, an innocent child, adrift in a harsh world.

Justin Devereux's ability to trust had died in this room. He'd known it even then, and he couldn't change any of it.

Lady Madeleine Beaumont Devereux's pedestal had toppled.

Justin remembered her taking his hand—as if she had not just rocked the ground beneath his feet—and she led him to her fireplace. "Here, my love, is a secret and a gift." She felt beneath the mantle and pushed at the eye of a bronze gargoyle.

The fireplace swung away from the wall. Behind the structure hid a landing and a stairwell. She led him inside, located a knob, turned it, and took a pouch from a drawer. "Here is my gift. My *mama's* and her *mama's* emerald ring." She replaced the pouch and patted the drawer when it was shut. "It waits for your bride, Justin. Choose her wisely."

At this moment, the sea-wind battering the windows, Justin's heart was cold and heavy. He looked around the moon-lit room, dead now like the beautiful Madeleine. She'd kissed him for the last time here, beside her fireplace. She had never kissed him, that he could remember, but she had twice that day.

She died in her sleep two days later. A canker of the stomach. She'd known she was dying and the ring was her parting gift. As were her words. She loved him.

He'd forgotten the ring, until he began to drive himself insane looking for a Christmas gift for Faith. His children—assuming they would ever create any—would never know the need for affection he'd experienced. He saw daily how much she loved and showered that love on Beth.

How surprised Faith would be when he gave her the ring. "Thank you *Maman*," Justin whispered, understanding her better, perhaps, if not precisely *forgiving* her. He understood human imperfection so much better now.

It took a while to locate the correct gargoyle. "Ah," he whispered, pressing the creature's eye. Icy air galloped into the room as the fireplace opened on a groan. Inside, he located the knob he must turn to open the casket, but it did not budge.

He fetched the poker from the fireplace and rapped, recoiling at the echo in the stairwell. A dog barked somewhere in the house. The knob turned. And in the drawer, he found his mother's emerald ring. He slipped it into his pocket.

The dog's bark growing louder gave testimony to its approach. Justin pulled the hearth panel, closing himself inside. In the pitch-black passage behind his mother's fireplace, he waited.

An echoing flutter grew fast and clamorous. A bat—no two— dipped by his ear. "Terrific." That damned barking cur stood beside the fireplace, now. Too close.

Voices called to the beast. A man and a woman.

Justin glanced at the stairs. It would be the devil to reenter the house if he took them. It was freezing out and he didn't know if he could manage the stairs. His legs shook from walking.

The noisy hound must have his scent. He opened the panel and let the beast in, closing them both in. The dog set up a low growl. Justin hoped he was snarling at the bats.

Justin saw gleaming white teeth, while that snarl became louder, more threatening.

With little choice, Justin moved toward the stairs.

The dog lunged.

CHAPTER TWELVE

KNOCKED TO THE floor, Justin rolled to protect his face. And that's when the cur licked his ear. A tail slapped his leg, a slobbering whimper accompanied the dog's joy. "Toby?" The damned dog whined in ecstasy. "Shh, shh." Justin scrubbed behind the canine's ears. "Good boy," he whispered, getting his face washed. "Shh, boy."

The bickering voices dimmed and a door closed.

Faith woke when she heard a dog bark somewhere in the house. Justin no longer slept beside her.

She checked his room, Beth's, and her dressing room, her heart pounding madly. Had Vincent discovered Justin's recovery? Was Hemsted, his man of affairs too curious? Had she been careless? Had Vincent sent someone to abduct Justin … to finish the deed?

Her imagination was getting the best of her.

Likely a stable dog. Perhaps Justin got up to investigate the barking … and then he was accosted. If she wasn't so frightened, she'd laugh at herself.

One thing was certain, she couldn't sit around waiting. She had to do something, so she checked Beth, made sure she slept soundly, donned her wrapper, and left the room.

Justin sat behind the fireplace scratching Toby's ears and belly 'till quiet reigned and they emerged. In the hall, Justin scratched one last time. "Back to your kitchen rug, Friend." But the mongrel he'd rescued in a storm, six years before, would not step from his side. He slapped Toby's rump. "Off with you, now." But to no avail. Justin shook his head. "Come along, then. You're twice Beth's size, but she'll love you."

Approaching the center of the house, Justin stopped to rest in an alcove, on a gilded chair he'd once pretended was a throne, when Faith came running from the opposite wing, stopped at the top of the stairs, looked down, and gasped.

Justin stood, but it could be a costly error to show himself.

A man appeared at the top of the stairs, nodded and smiled at Faith. "It's me. Hard to see in the dark, I know."

Faith relaxed visibly. "Mr. Hemsted Good evening."

"Are you all right, Miss Wickham?"

Mr. and Miss. Good, they didn't know each other that well. Justin leaned into the shadows.

"I'm fine, I … wanted something to drink. I can't sleep."

Justin frowned. Foolish thing to tell a man. When the blighter touched Faith's arm, anger stiffened Justin's spine. Somehow sensing it, Toby charged the pair like a rabid beast.

Hemsted saw the dog, grabbed Faith, and to Justin's horror, Faith crumpled to the floor.

Justin made to run, but his legs didn't remember how, and they buckled. He caught himself and fell back into the chair. Toby sat at the top of the stairs wagging his tail.

Bloody dumb dog.

Hemsted lifted Faith in his arms and carried her toward her room. Their room, damn it. Justin swallowed his roar of rage. Faith would kill him, herself, if he gave them away. So he remained hidden until the bounder came back and went downstairs.

Justin reached their room in record time.

Faith lay on her bed, unconscious, her gown and wrapper loosened—nearly to her waist! He'd kill the bastard! He locked the door and went to her. "Faith?" he whispered, unable to accept that his bastion of strength had crumbled. True, she hardly knew Hemsted—though Hemsted seemed to think she should—and Toby could be frightening, but to faint. Faith?

Toby settled on the hearth while Justin bathed Faith's face and neck with cool water. Finally, she whimpered and turned her head. Justin raised her and put a cup of water to her lips. "Drink sweetheart, that's right. Just a little. There." He placed the cup on the bed-table.

Faith opened her eyes and turned ashen. In a blink, she was up and running. In her dressing room, she was abominably ill. He held her head while she retched, bathed her face, and gave her water to rinse her mouth. "You're safe, sweetheart. Everything will be all right. I'm here." He walked her back to bed and tucked her in. "I could strangle that man for touching you."

"He didn't touch me."

Justin trailed a finger down the exposed valley between her breasts and tugged a hanging bodice ribbon. "Who did this?"

"You should worry about him learning the truth about you, not about ... are you jealous?"

Justin ran his hand through his hair. "Of course not. He could be dangerous, that's all. And he unfastened your gown."

Someone knocked on the door. "Miss Wickham. Are you all right? I have brandy. May I come in?" Hemsted tried the knob, making Justin glad he'd locked the door.

Faith sat up, pushing him off the bed. "Go to your room," she whispered. "I'll open the door and tell him I'm fine."

He shook his head. "No."

Her hands on his chest, she backed him into his room. "I have to answer him," she whispered. "Or he'll force his way in."

Justin huffed in resignation, but he retied the ribbons on her gown and shut her wrapper to her neck. "There."

Faith's smile, as she shut the door, calmed him.

Certain Justin was listening, Faith cracked her door open. Hemsted was, indeed, holding a glass of brandy. He smiled with relief. "Good. You're looking better."

"Thank you. I am. I'm sorry, I—"

"You have nothing to be sorry for. I frightened you, though it was not my intent. I have a ridiculous fear of dogs and thought to protect you." He looked at the hearth. "That him?"

Faith was surprised to see the creature, nose on paws watching them, brows raising at opposite intervals, and she giggled. "Guess he isn't as dangerous as we thought."

Hemsted had a nice smile. "I guess not. Do you need anything before I go?"

A moan came from her patient and Faith's face warmed. "I have everything I need. Thank you. My patient needs me."

Hemsted stood there 'till she shut and locked the door.

In Justin's room, she glowered. "That was stupid."

"I'd like to wring his bloody neck."

"Shh. He's a nice man, and he was worried about me."

Oh what a look Justin gave her.

"Jealousy is beneath you," she said.

"Jealous? I'm mad as bloody hell." His look softened. "And worried, about you." He examined her face. "When you fainted, I thought my heart would stop. Faith, you frightened me."

"I frightened *you*? Someone is trying to kill you and you go missing." She crossed her arms and stepped from his entreaty, fisting her hands so she wouldn't reach for him. "Where the devil were you? I thought you'd been kidnapped. That Vincent took you ... to murder you. Don't smile, you half-wit. And no excuses, if you please. I awake from a sound sleep to hear a dog barking ... and you are gone! Gone,

Justin."

He looked like a child with a purloined kitten. "Faith, I realize that exploring at night was probably stupid—though I could hardly do so during the day. I couldn't sleep, and it's not like I had anything to occupy me, after all."

When Faith cuffed him, he chuckled, opened his arms, and she stepped in, hating herself for liking it.

"I thought if I knew where Vincent put us, I'd have an escape route, if we needed one. It didn't occur to me you'd wake and find me gone. I'm sorry I frightened you."

"You were a thoughtless idiot."

"I was … am." He chuckled.

"How dare you laugh at such a time."

"You're beautiful angry, all fire and spirit. I may inspire you to fury in future just to watch your eyes spark like that." He teased her top lip with his bottom one, ran his hands down her back.

Those sparks he'd mentioned were traveling now, touching down in the oddest places. She shivered.

"I wouldn't blame you if you never forgave me," he said, kissing her. "I beg your pardon, truly," he whispered, warming her, and Faith supposed there was nothing to do but forgive.

After that kiss, Justin declared a victory of sorts with his grin. "Am I forgiven then, for being so foolhardy and thoughtless?"

"My heart near stopped when I couldn't find you."

He frowned. "Am I asking too much to continue this farce? Perhaps we should just deal with Vincent in the open."

"No! He'll find another way. I'm fine. Really. I was frightened, that's all. You have to stay hidden until Vincent's fate is sealed. It's the safest way."

Christmas Eve arrived, almost by surprise. Faith dressed Beth in a red velvet frock for their secret family Christmas, while Jenny and Sally primped for the servants' party.

"Sally, did you have someone purchase the d-o-l-l?"

"I walked to the village yesterday while Beth was with you."

With Beth in her arms, Faith saw Jenny and Sally on their way. "Now we can have our Christmas party. You, me, and Poppy." When someone rapped on her door, Faith set Beth down and opened it. "Mr. Hemsted. Good evening." Justin was *not* going to like this.

"Happy Christmas, Miss Wickham. May I come in?"

Satan, Hemsted's shadow-cat stepped inside. Good thing Toby was with Justin. "Well, I ... we were just about to have Christmas—"

He stepped into the room. "I'll stay but a moment."

Beth put her finger in her mouth, regarding him warily.

"Does that cat really go everywhere you do?" Faith asked.

He chuckled. "It does."

Had he heard her ask the cat about poison, or seen her search outside at midnight? Had *he* given the vials to Vincent? "Does it ever go anywhere alone?"

"Tom-catting at midnight." Hemsted shook his head. "It doesn't tempt me."

Faith stifled a giggle as he knelt before Beth. "Hello there. I've seen you romping outside." Beth put her arm around Faith's leg, and leaned into her. Hemsted smiled. "Merry Christmas, Beth. I have a gift for you."

"You needn't have," Faith said.

"I wanted to." He pulled a bright wooden cone from his pocket and held it in the palm of his hand. "Take it. It's a top."

Wide-eyed, Beth stared from him to the toy.

"Do you know what a top does?"

Beth shook her head.

"Watch." Hemsted put it on the floor and gave it a twist. It turned with color-hazing speed. When it staggered and fell, Beth got right down and started it whirling again.

Hemsted smiled and stood. "You look festive in Christmas

green. By God, your dress matches your eyes. All you need is holly in your hair. Every man's Christmas wish come true."

Faith didn't know how to respond, or how to make him leave. She smoothed her dress. "Thank you."

"You don't look like you'd throw furniture in a fit of pique."

Faith was stunned until she remembered the night in Vincent's study when Vincent told him *she* was having the tantrum.

He laughed. "Your response says it all. I suspected as much."

She laughed too, reminding herself that beneath his charm, he was Vincent's man still. And Justin must be simmering with every word. She hoped he could keep his temper in check.

How could she get the curious man of affairs to leave?

Hemsted placed his hand on Justin's doorknob.

Faith shook her head, warning him off.

Countering her, Hemsted nodded and turned the knob.

Faith placed her hand on Justin's door so fast, Hemsted raised his brows. "I'd like to see your patient."

"No! He's been ill all day and has just now gone to sleep."

"But Vincent is concerned."

Like a snake whose venom has gone to water. "If we disturb him, there'll be no Christmas for Beth." Her voice's reflexive tremble, though caused by fear, made her seem near tears.

Hemsted's look softened. "Or for you?"

She nodded, and to keep him from seeing her relief, she regarded his hand on the knob.

He removed it. "Another day then. I did tell Vincent I would check his brother's progress."

"You may tell him there is none." Faith looked at her hands. "I fear Justin will not...." It was impossible to say the words.

Hemsted touched her hand. "Vincent will be sad to hear it."

She examined his expression to see if he believed what he said. Was he a party to Vincent's scheme? But true and deep regret etched his features, leaving Faith no wiser, but the flash of perception she caught disturbed her. She cleared her throat. "If you will excuse us, it's nearly time to put Beth to bed."

"No!" Beth knocked on Justin's door. "Poppy play."

Faith lifted Beth in her arms. "She wants her papa."

With sincere regret, Hemsted nodded and said good night.

Faith locked the door behind him and released a slow breath.

When she opened Justin's door, his fury was startling. "I forbid you to encourage him."

"Justin, I ..." What could she say?

Beth threw herself at Justin's legs and he lifted her up.

Faith touched his arm. "He meant no harm."

"He's Vincent's man!"

"Yes." Faith stared at Beth's top on the floor, feeling as abandoned, but Justin hugged *her* too and desolation vanished.

"I would as lief throw that T O P in the fire."

"She likes it."

"I was afraid she would."

Faith was charmed by his chagrin. "She'll love what we have for her too. Come. I have a special evening planned."

"So do I." Justin's look warmed her.

After Beth opened her gifts, Justin set her carousel-horse down and tugged its cord; the head bobbed and the legs trotted. Beth was so happy, she ignored her doll, until Faith showed her she could carry it while she pulled her horse. A short while later, both in tow, Beth climbed into her father's lap.

"Our first Christmas as a family," Faith said. "I hope Beth will always remember tonight."

"She'll have better memories in future," Justin promised.

"I remember eight barefoot children in nightclothes, singing outside our parents' door at dawn on Christmas morning."

"It must have been great to be part of a big family."

"Your family now, too."

He kissed her brow and shifted Beth. "Vincent and I rarely participated in Christmas celebrations. But one year, when our cousin, Justin Reddington, lived with us, during an adult play, a scene called for bird sounds. So we freed a sack of morning doves over the stage. But they were nervous after being bagged—and Cousin Kate's screams didn't help—and, well, they made a mess. It took days to get them all outside. Mrs. Tucker lit into us every time she found a memento of their visit."

Faith laughed. "You had cousin who was also named, Justin. That must have been confusing."

"Yes."

Faith sensed Justin's reticence. "Tell me more."

"Uncle Hal always trod on Aunt Sophie's train during rehearsal, so Vincent clipped the stitches in the waist right before the actual play. Aunt Sophie had eliminated her petticoats on so warm a night, and when the skirt fell, she fainted. Uncle Hal laughed himself sick, and *we* went without supper for days."

"It's hard to believe you and Vincent were friends."

"The three of us were friends, before Justin was sent to America. After that, Vincent and I got along somewhat, until he turned sixteen and woke one day hating everyone, especially me."

Faith smoothed his furrowed brow with a finger. "I'm sorry, Justin."

"Bedtime for my girl," he said, disliking her sympathy, revealing how deeply he'd been hurt by Vincent's rancor. When Beth woke and wanted her top, Justin's dismay was comical.

Once Beth was settled, they tucked into their adult feast.

Justin placed a small laden table before the settee and rubbed his hands together. "I hope Mrs. Tucker was generous."

"I told her I loved holiday fare. There's more than enough."

Justin devoured everything down to the plum pudding. "That

was delicious. The only thing missing was Boar's head."

Faith wrinkled her nose. "Ugh."

"I like singing as the Boar's head is brought in.

Faith put her arms around him. "Sing the song every year if you wish, but never make me serve it."

"Every year," Justin said, wistfully. He raised their single glass of wine. "To future Yuletides."

"Justin, I have something for you, sort of."

Justin's surprise was apparent. "When did you have an opportunity to find something? We were never apart."

"It was easier to acquire than I would have imagined."

Justin shook his head. "Contrary as ever."

"I'm not contrary, I'm tenacious. Papa said so."

"Obstinate, and I say so."

"And so I can be. Now guess."

"Just let me see it."

She shook her head. "No, first guess what it is."

"This could take all night."

"We have nothing better to do," she said.

One aristocratic brow rose. "Oh, don't we?"

Warmed by the promise in his look, Faith shivered. "Guess."

He pulled her to his lap—Every man's Christmas dream, Hemsted was right. Justin coaxed her with kisses. "Tell me," he said. She placed her hands on his chest, and warmth flowed through him, his heart beating faster. "Tell me." God how he wanted her.

Her eyes closed slowly. "I ... forget the question."

Lord, he didn't want to get ahead of himself here. "In that case ..." He placed a tiny box in her hand. "Happy Christmas, sweetheart."

After a surprised moment, she lifted the lid. In the box nestled his mother's ring, an emerald surrounded by diamonds. Rare and beautiful, like his wife.

Faith sat, speechless, as he slipped it on her finger. "The stone matches your eyes, though it has fewer facets." He lifted the beringed hand to his lips. "I have a confession. I fetched it the night you thought I was abducted. It was my mother's."

Predictably, she bristled. "I should beat you."

He sought her lips. Drank. Savored. "Yes, beat me, please."

Faith sat back, breathless. She held her hand near the candle to examine the ring, turning it to catch the light. "From mother to son. A good tradition."

"I don't expect to have a son." Justin brought her against him and tightened his arms about her. "I've yet to receive my surprise, though I like the one in my arms."

She sat back. "All right. Here's a hint. It's something you think never to have."

"My freedom from this apartment?"

Faith stood, smoothing bodice and skirt, making him ache to do the same. She shook her head, her hair settling about her shoulders in wild disarray.

"To hell with my surprise." He reached for her.

She stepped back. "Your surprise, Justin."

"Tenacious as ever," he said, exasperated. "Are you hiding it on your person then? And I'm to search for it? God's teeth, that will be more fun than receiving it."

Impatient, Faith placed Justin's hands on her abdomen. "Behold the package wherein lies your surprise." She watched his expression change, sober. "A son?" he whispered.

Tell me you love me. Now. It's time now.

Justin remained quiet, astonished. Faith's sense of anticipation fled, became unease, apprehension. He couldn't say he loved her, because he didn't. Perhaps he didn't want another child. She lost her joy. "What say you? About the baby, I mean?"

"What say I? You mean, what should we do?" Doubt, anger, clouded his expression.

Faith turned away so he wouldn't see her tears. He didn't want another baby. He hadn't even wanted her ... not for herself.

"Would you have the baby?" he asked.

He wasn't making sense. "I don't see that I have a choice."

He started as if struck. "I can't believe this is happening again."

Aching to heal the unnamed breach between them, determined to make him share her joy over their child, Faith touched his arm. But he stood as if he couldn't bear her touch.

She wanted this baby, desperately, and she needed to make him see how wonderful it would be. "Justin, I realize this will seem more curse than blessing when I begin to swell and people wonder how a near-dead man could—"

"Is that why you don't want our child?"

CHAPTER THIRTEEN

VINCENT SWIRLED THE brandy in his glass while he watched his wife, Aline Lamontagne Devereux, bat her kohl-lined eyes and flash her painted smile at every creature with a rod.

At least she amused him. This party was a bore. France was a bore. And Bergerac was a mole on the backside of a toad.

It was time to go home. To Killashandra.

Justin stood by the window watching Beth frolic in the snow with her nursemaid.

"What are they doing?" Faith asked from her bed, her color rivaling the white linens, except for the circles under her eyes.

"They're making snow angels."

"Stay back," Faith said. "If Beth sees you, she'll call or wave, and Sally will see you too."

He sighed and stepped away. "I missed so much of her life, I hate to miss anymore."

Smoothing the tiniest mound that was their child, Faith looked away. She'd been so sick with her pregnancy, Justin feared she must want the babe even less.

"Justin, you could love another child that much, couldn't you?"

Did she want to give him this child as Catherine wanted to give him Beth? So she could be free? "Could I?" He wasn't ready to let her know he'd take it, because she was breaking him, and he wanted to do some damage, himself.

A tear landed on her pillow. Another followed.

Justin couldn't understand her pain, but it seared him.

"It doesn't matter," she whispered. "You won't have to put yourself out."

He sat on her bed, but stopped himself from taking her in his arms. "What are you talking about?"

"I've been bleeding since this morning. I'm going to lose the baby." She curled into a tight ball and began to sob.

A knife pierced Justin's heart. Their baby was going to die. The child that was part of her. "Oh, Faith." He held her the way he'd wanted to since Christmas. All these weeks she'd refused to tell him why she didn't want their child. When he'd ask, she'd say the same, "If only you could trust."

It frustrated the hell out of him. He hadn't been talking about trust; he'd been talking about their baby, damn it.

Why didn't she want their baby?

And why was she crying because she might lose it?

Then the revelation came ... and it hit him hard. She'd been so angry he doubted her, she'd refused to answer. She wanted him to trust her to love their child. "Shh, sweetheart, shh. You'll hurt yourself and you'll increase the danger of losing the baby."

She looked at him with teary eyes. Eyes filled with hope.

He wiped her tears with his fingers. "You always wanted the baby, didn't you, Faith? And I couldn't see it."

"So much," she said. "I want it so much." Anguish brought new tears. "But you don't, and—"

"What the devil are you talking about?"

"Justin, you were so angry when I told you."

"Because you said you didn't have a choice but to have it."

Her eyes widened. "I didn't mean I *wanted* a choice. It was such a ridiculous question, I didn't know what else to say. I was so filled with joy, and you were so, so—"

"Afraid you were like Catherine." He shook his head. "It seems I'm always asking your forgiveness, doesn't it?"

"I'm afraid, Justin. I don't want to lose our baby."

Justin lay her back against the pillows and went to the hall door. "Stay. Don't move." He opened it.

"Justin! Where are you going?"

"To get you a doctor."

Spring slipped upon the world unaware. Daffodils were in bloom, but here, inside their personal Newgate, they were no closer to finding a solution to their problems than at Christmas. Time had become their enemy, and Justin anguished over a way to keep his family safe. Sometimes he wished he'd gone for that doctor, but with her nursing experience, Faith knew the only thing to be done was to stay in bed.

She told the staff she had a bad grippe, contagious, and needed rest, but in their little world, her role and his, as patient and nurse, had reversed.

Now she was getting better and their child was growing.

But they were in more serious trouble than ever. They needed to get away.

He couldn't sneak out at midnight with a pregnant wife and four-year old in tow. But with a little planning, if Faith could pose as his nurse again, before she blossomed beyond hiding, they might make it.

Where?

So much had changed, yet so much remained the same.

Hemsted—the irksome splinter in his nether region—gave Faith the news just after Christmas that Vincent was married.

His brother must want him dead more than ever. But for the first time in years, Justin wanted to live. Because of Faith.

With her pregnancy, it had been easy for them to abstain from intimate relations, as she requested. And her reasons were beginning to make sense to him. Even he wanted more than the physical intimacy they'd shared the night she conceived. Their role-reversal had made him understand something about caring ... which was frightening, if he allowed himself to ponder it.

During his illness, with him vulnerable and wretched, he'd expected Faith to be repulsed. Now, nursing her, he was more attuned to her, as if their spirits marched side by side on a plane too high to imagine. Sometimes he'd swear he experienced the same physical distress as she.

He wanted her well, the feisty, determined Faith again. He wanted to be free to share her life. He wanted her by his side to the end of their days, her hand in his, her smile like sunshine, her laughter a melody too sweet to imagine.

Yes, he wanted her body too, but he wanted her soul more.

They needed a fresh start. Away from here. But they would have no life at all, if anything happened to either of them.

Her condition was becoming evident ... at least to him. Soon it would be evident to all, putting her in as much danger as him. Vincent would not wait and see if their child was a girl, or the heir that could depose him.

The clock was ticking. In his head. In his life. In truth.

He wished to hell he knew how to beat it.

In his room that evening, Justin brought up their dilemma.

"It's worse than you think. When Jenny dressed me after my bath today," Faith said. "I popped a button clear across the room. She said I shouldn't be gaining weight after being so sick. She didn't finish her sentence, but her eyes got round as saucers. I think we need to tell her, Justin. Or I'll become gossip below stairs, and that'll be a short jump to Hemsted's ears, then to Vincent's."

Justin paled. "Sharing our secret with anyone is alarming."

Faith couldn't agree more, but she refused to let him see her concern. "Jenny is loyal, Justin. I'm certain of it."

"You're too trusting by half, Faith. You must realize that?"

"You're speaking about Hemsted. I'm speaking about Jenny."

He ran his hand through his hair. "You're right. And this is no time for us to argue."

"I agree."

When she heard a knock on her bedroom door, Faith crossed from his room to hers, Justin following as far as his doorway. "Who is it?" she called.

"Max Hemsted, Miss Wickham. May I speak to you for a moment? I have news."

Faith turned to Justin.

He raised his arms as if to say, "You see! There he is, after you again." Then he banked his expression lowered his arms in defeat, and stepped back to close his door with a gentle click.

She stared at it, fearing that more than a slab of wood stood between them. But there was nothing she could do now. When she opened her door, Hemsted beamed, and despite everything, she smiled. "It must be good news." *Please.*

He folded his hands behind his back. "Even if it were bad, I like looking at you."

She shook her head, amused, even gratified, but she bristled anticipating Justin's reaction. In a wifely act of rebellion, she went into the hall and shut her door. It was time Justin learned trust. This might not be his hardest lesson, but it would drive him crazy not to hear the conversation.

Twenty minutes later, Faith bid Hemsted a good-evening. She closed her door, leaned against it, and let her false smile go. Lord, she hadn't been this frightened since she planned to withhold Justin's medicine. First Jenny, and now this.

Danger rushed them from all directions.

Faith soothed her unborn child. "We'll keep you safe," she said. And no putting off the inevitable; Justin needed to know.

As she made the decision, Beth's door opened and Beth came tearing in, Sally and Jenny right behind. The sprite went straight to her father's door, grabbed the knob, and faster than Faith could move, Beth opened it and ran in. "Horsy, Poppy!"

Sally and Jenny heard Justin laugh and stepped forward to see into the forbidden room.

With a sigh of resignation, Faith joined them and saw, as did they, the man she loved shaking his head, a little chagrined, a lot handsome, which Sally's and Jenny's sighs confirmed.

They probably thought they saw a miracle—a distinguished man, gray at his temples, dashing in a mulberry dressing gown, his daughter in his arms.

They were clearly bemused and smitten with her husband.

Justin set Beth down, took her hand and approached. He bowed, tilted his head in greeting, and bestowed his knee-weakening smile. In response to their besotted grins, he slipped his arm around Faith's waist. "Well, Faith," he said. "I believe introductions are in order. Circumstances seem to be moving us forward with the speed of a snowball rolling downhill."

"You have no idea." Faith regarded her husband soberly. "Vincent is coming home."

Justin recovered after a sober bit of thought. "Our course is set then."

The abigail and nursemaid, even Beth, seemed to sense the gravity in the situation. Faith smoothed Beth's curls. "That snowball seems to be gaining weight and speed."

"Sit down, everyone. Please," Justin said. "We need to talk."

"The medicine I was giving Justin was poison," Faith began.

"As soon as I suspected, I stopped giving it to him, and in a long, slow process, he began to get well. We've kept his recovery a secret because...." She hesitated.

"*Someone* wants me dead."

Their loyal retainers' eyes widened.

"Now," Justin said. "Faith is my wife, she is increasing, and Vincent is returning, so we have no choice but to leave. If the situation is as I suspect, Faith's life, and that of our unborn child, are also in danger."

"We discussed this eventuality, and we'd very much like for you both to go with us," Faith said.

The girls' heightened senses of adventure became apparent.

"I would like to remind you that this could be dangerous," Faith cautioned.

"Yes, miss, my lady—your grace." Jenny giggled.

"Her grace will say her mother is ill and she must go home, that she's taking me and Beth, and both of you to help her." He turned to Faith. "Is that all right? It seems the best reason. You did say your parents would take us in."

"I could be with my mother when the baby comes."

Justin nodded. "Good." He rubbed his hands together. "With allies—he nodded at Sally and Jenny—it's time to move our army through enemy flanks."

"Justin Devereux. Are you enjoying this?"

"The army likely to win the war always enjoys a good battle."

"You've lost your wits from being locked up. I perceive no clear road to glory here. Tell me how *you* expect to leave?"

Justin shook his head. "You returned a dead man to life, Faith. Surely transporting a corpse can't be such a puzzle. On his back, my dear. On his back."

"Tell anyone who asks," he told Jenny and Sally, "That you're accompanying Faith, her patient and Beth, to her parents' home.

We're depending a great deal on both of you."

Sally and Jenny nodded as one, the weight of responsibility now heavy in their looks.

"Thank you," Justin said, leading them to the door.

The enormity of the move they planned astonished Faith, and by the time Justin returned, she badly needed his comfort.

"I guess this is it," he said.

Faith nodded. "It's frightening."

"Life and death frightening."

Faith wasn't ready to explore that right now. She'd barely made peace with their momentous resolve, much less the possible consequences. Instead, she considered details. "We'll leave word with Mrs. Tucker for Harris to come to us in Arundel."

"Don't you think it would be suspect for you to want my servant after managing without him for so long? Havey-cavey Hemsted will balk as it is over letting you go. If he realizes you want a male servant, he'll offer to go, himself."

Her husband's frown amused her.

"Send word to Harris, at my London house, for him to go to your parents. That way, no one here will know."

"This is a good solution. Why didn't we think of it sooner?"

"Events have forced us to act, and it's not a solution, but the beginning of one. We're lucky we're both able to travel, now that it's imperative we leave. First, I was too ill, and then you were."

"That's true. But how do you see this move as the beginning of a solution, Justin? I fear we only postpone the inevitable."

Justin hugged her. "Where's the mettle that allowed you to withdraw my medicine? Where's my feisty, fearless nurse?"

"Frightened ... and pregnant."

"The most imperative reason *to* go. Even if Vincent didn't notice that I'm well, he'd certainly notice you with child.

"From Arundel, I'll get in touch with the scoundrels, Grant and

Marcus in London. Gabe, I mean the vicar, would have written to keep them up to date on the entire affair. My friend Carry will come in handy, too. And if none of them are available, there's always the magistrate. From your parents' home, Harris will be able to come and go more easily. I'll be able to go outside, ride a horse. You, Beth and the baby will be safe."

Faith shivered. "Unless Vincent decides to come to Arundel."

Two days later, Faith stood at the top of the stairs looking down at Mrs. Tucker, Hemsted, all the servants lined up for her astonishing departure. If she made a mistake, just one....

Trepidation made her hesitate. She should return to their apartment. It wasn't too late. Except that it was.

Vincent was on his way.

She had not stepped foot below stairs for some time, due to her condition, which allowed the household to assume her patient could not do without her. Now, she adjusted her velvet pistachio cloak to make certain her girth was concealed, took a breath, and stepped onto the topmost stair.

Two footmen carried her patient's litter, and despite his closed eyes, smudged with kohl, his face dusted with rice powder, and the swaddling to conceal his vigor, Faith knew his heart skittered apace with hers. She'd felt his quickened beat when she kissed him before she opened the door to the footmen. That kiss had come from a nervous man, but surely not from a sick one.

Of everyone, Faith supposed she'd miss Hemsted most. He'd provided conversation when there was none to be had in the sickroom, and offered his hand in friendship. Justin's man or not, there was something about him that she liked.

He stood as if waiting for some last minute reprieve.

Faith stopped, but under the circumstances, kindness would be heartless. Best say good-bye and be done.

He surprised her by taking her hand. She'd appear rude if she snatched it away, though she was uneasy, given the fervor of his grip. "I think you know how sorry I am to see you leave, Miss Wickham. I shall miss ... your smiling face. I hope you find your mother fast recovered and that you come back to us soon."

Faith retrieved her hand with decorum. "Thank you, Mr. Hemsted. I appreciate your offer to apprise His Grace of my actions, and my reasons for them, though I cannot think it matters where I care for his relatives." The near-censure in her words caught her unaware. "As long as they are cared for, that is."

Hemsted gave her a wan smile before he looked to Justin, and Faith stepped between them and offered her hand for the last time.

He took it almost gratefully. "I'll make his Grace see that you had no choice. I know that Beth and her father are better off with you."

He was playing into their hands and she was a witch for enticing him. "You're too kind."

"Perhaps I'll come to visit you in Arundel, and see how they fare, if that's all right with you?"

Faith hesitated. To say no would be suspect. "If you wish."

He kissed her hand. "Until I see you next, then."

She was glad Justin had not seen the kiss. "I ... look forward to your visit." Faith turned to Mrs. Tucker and leaned forward for a hug, lest her child make itself known.

Mrs. Tucker wiped her eyes with the corner of her apron. "Good bye, Miss." She looked at Justin. "Take care of him. I don't expect it will matter where he ... sleeps." The woman sobbed as she turned away, and Faith felt terrible for the deception.

This was taking so long, Justin must be ready to jump up and walk out on his own. And Beth must be champing at the bit for that ride they'd promised her this morning.

Sally and Jenny would bring her down to their own carriage, after they saw from an upstairs window that Faith and Justin were inside the first.

Toby had been shut inside Beth's room, so he would stop licking the rice powder off Justin's face. At the very last minute, Jenny would convey Faith's order to let him out.

The coaches left in tandem. Faith couldn't believe she was going home with her husband and daughter.

She only wished her parents had some notion they were coming.

Inside their private carriage, Justin's litter sat corner to corner, cutting the cab space in half. When she looked over at him, he lay there watching her. "Close the curtains, will you, so I can quit this trap."

Faith examined the interior, split as it was by his stretcher. "Well, there isn't much room. Unless you sit on the opposite side of your pallet."

To her surprise, Justin did sit in the far corner, arms crossed, expression arrogant.

Faith guessed her farewell to Hemsted had rankled as much as she expected.

"I shall miss your smiling face," Justin mimicked.

"Justin, I—"

"I'm looking forward to your visit! Are you daft? What if he comes to your parents' house? What will he think when he finds you large with child and me walking around?"

"I didn't know the polite way to—"

"You should have said good-bye!" Justin snapped, but as soon as he saw her face, he climbed over the stretcher to take her on his lap. "I'm sorry, that was unkind. I wanted to plant him a facer. It wasn't your fault. You had no recourse but to accept his offer of a visit, else he might have been suspicious. You have become such a watering-pot."

Faith accepted his handkerchief and blew her nose. "It's not so much that I'm sensitive, Justin." She sniffed. "It's more that you're *insensitive.*" She placed the crumpled handkerchief in his hand.

He looked ruefully at it, placed it in his pocket, then settled her against him. "Forgive me and be done with it. You know you're fond of me, faults and all."

"Yes, well, that's what ... marriage is, being aware of your partner's faults and caring as much because of those faults, as despite them." She had nearly said, "that what's love is." *Would the pudding-head never learn?*

"I'm certainly fond of you with all of your faults," he said.

"I shall be eternally grateful," she responded dryly.

"Good. Now, I believe I've figured out how to investigate Vincent and the carriage accident myself."

"*You*, investigate? How?"

"I should die. Ouch. What did you pinch me for?"

"For speaking of dying when you've come so far."

He kissed her then and she wished it didn't feel so blasted good. "I mean, it should *appear* I have died. Vincent would feel as if he had accomplished his task and, perhaps, get careless about covering his trail."

"I'm listening," she said.

"Moving away from Killashandra gives us the perfect opportunity to put my plan in motion. Introduce me to neighbors and such as your husband, under a fictitious name, of course, for it has occurred to me that you must arrive with a husband." He patted the evidence of their passion.

Faith chuckled. "How will Vincent think you dead, when everyone at Killashandra knows full well that you left with me."

"That's why it'll work. Away from home, we can stage a fictitious funeral. About a week after we arrive, I'd say. You can notify the staff at Killashandra and send a note to Vincent through Hemsted. Tell him you'll care for Beth for as long as need be. Gabe, my friend, your vicar, can help with funeral arrangements."

Faith shook her head. "But surely Beth calling you, Poppy, will seem odd."

"She's my child from my first marriage. No one need know she was in your charge at Killashandra. I, for one, will be happy to see the last of this sham, but it must continue for a short time. Meanwhile, I'll be free to come and go as I please." He placed his hand over this new child of theirs.

Faith's eyes closed. She murmured, "Nice," and fell asleep.

Sometimes he wished he could say he loved her, because sometimes he could almost feel her yearning for the declaration. If only love were within him to give.

But he must be as true to himself as to her. She would want nothing less. After all, self-respect must be part and parcel of mutual respect, as well as trust and understanding, which he wanted as much as she. Hell, what he wanted was to love her. He simply didn't know how. Weary to the bone, he closed his eyes.

Before he knew it, Faith was kissing his ear. "Wake up. We're nearly there."

"You're feeling better, aren't you?" he asked, enjoying the playfulness that had been missing since her pregnancy.

"I am." She played with the hair at his nape and kissed him with lingering passion.

"Of all the times for seduction," he groaned as he returned her kiss. "We're about to descend on your family, and I fear we'll never be alone again."

Faith giggled. "As wonderful as this is, I'm afraid it's time you became an invalid once more."

"It's deuced difficult to look the invalid in this condition, Faith. You're a heartless wench. Do you know that?"

She laughed as she covered him with the blanket. "The outriders will carry you to the third-floor bedroom, and I'll come to you as soon as I settle Jenny and Sally with Beth, and explain everything to my parents. My brothers and sisters won't be up this late, so we can deal with them in the morning."

Soon enough, the coach door opened. Faith gave the outriders instructions and let herself into the house. "Carry him up to the third floor, first door on the right. Leave him on the bed then see to the luggage. The large trunk goes upstairs with the patient. Leave the rest here."

Faith motioned Jenny and Sally, with a sleeping Beth, to the small parlor. "Wait here. I'll bring you up in a minute."

Her parents emerged from the library in response to the noise.

"My Lord, it's Faith," her mother said.

"Yes, Mama," Faith said, and kissed her mother on the cheek, also by leaning toward her.

"Is something wrong?" her father asked.

"No. Yes. Mama, Papa, I've brought my patient and little Beth. We need to stay here for a while. Jenny will help with the work, and Sally will care for Beth. I thought they could stay in the spare room, and since Matt and John are at school, I could take their room with my patient.

Her parents could hardly send her away, and though they blustered and asked questions for which she gave no answers, they ultimately agreed.

After tucking Beth in, Faith went back downstairs, exhausted after three flights of stairs. When she got to the library, she found the two most lovable people in the world waiting for her. "It's wonderful to be home. I've missed you."

"You're looking a bit peaked, Love," her mother said and as she bemoaned Faith's appearance and need for rest. Her father helped her remove her cape.

"Thank you Papa," Faith said, only to be met with the most ludicrous expression she had ever seen on his face. "Papa?"

"Good God, Missy, you're increasing!"

Faith had always prided herself on her ability to handle any situation, but nothing could have prepared her for this moment. She'd taken such care when she first arrived but being home had simply disarmed her.

Her mother fell into the nearest chair and began to fan herself. "Faith, what have you done?"

Faith began to laugh.

Her father bristled. "This is no laughing matter!"

"I know it's not, Papa. It's just that ... well, you see, the patient that was neither alive nor dead ... he's definitely alive." She laughed at that too. "Oh, don't be angry. It's just that I'm so tired and you look so funny."

Faith understood her parent's surprise, but not their anger, not without allowing her to explain. Why hadn't she prepared for this?

"Young lady, how did this happen?" her father demanded.

"Good Lord, don't you know?" She was so tired, she amused the daylights out of herself.

Her father reddened. "What have you to say for yourself? You should be ashamed coming here like this to flaunt your ... your ... In front of your brothers and sisters. After all we taught you ... but I see we failed." He lowered his head, shaking it sadly.

Faith's eyes filled with tears, though she willed herself not to become a watering-pot. "Papa, you're condemning me without inquiry. I've never known you to be so unjust."

Her mother lifted a hand. "Do be quiet, both of you. Else we'll have the entire household to answer to."

Just when Faith thought her mother was about to bring order to their confusion, she fixedly regarded the doorway in shock.

Justin, now dressed in his most lordly attire, and silently commanding the respect due any indecently handsome peer of the realm, walked unceremoniously into the silent library, stopped to arrange the cuffs of his starched white shirt and gave her a wink.

Lord, he looked fetching. With a look, she told him how happy she was to see him, and her parents didn't miss the exchange.

He touched her cheek. "It's all right, Sweetheart." He faced his in-laws and bowed. "Justin Anthony Devereux, Fifth Duke of Ainsley, at your service." All ceremony gone, he took her into his arms, and she began to weep. "Everything's fine now, Sweetheart. Don't cry." He kissed her brow. "I came as quickly as I could. I heard some of what was said and I'm sorry you had to endure it alone."

He spoke as if there was no one else in the room, and made Faith wish there was not. Now their time alone seemed precious.

"Take your hands off my daughter! If you think, because you have a title, that you may make free with Faith before our eyes, that we will allow her to stay here and bear your bastard—"

"Papa!" Faith blanched, turned white as snow, and nearly as cold.

"Lord, Faith, don't faint on me," Justin said, leading her to the settee, torn between anger at her parents' treatment and concern for her. He knelt to chafe her hands. "Drink this," he said, offering the glass of brandy her father shoved into his hand.

With a second sip, her color returned, and though Justin was determined not to brawl with her parents at first meeting, he was angry at the way they treated her. He stood. "Sir, I mean no disrespect, but though you may order me to unhand your daughter, I have a right to tend my wife."

Satisfied he'd made an impression, Justin nodded. "Pray, be seated so I may sit beside Faith."

He wiped her tears with his handkerchief, glad for a chance to calm. "Give me a minute, Sweetheart, and I'll have you tucked into bed in no time."

John Wickham bristled and Justin was sorry for it, but they must be made to understand, in no uncertain terms, that Faith belonged to him now. He kissed her brow, resisting an urge to claim her lips.

Finally he turned to them. "I understand your shock to find Faith increasing, but we were married last December by your own Vicar Kendrick, who happens to be an old school chum of mine. He kept his own counsel at our urging and is concerned you will not understand his silence. I pray you forgive us all. Secrecy was imperative, several lives being at risk, including your daughter's."

Faith's father jumped to his feet. "No!"

Her mother paled. "What are you talking about?"

"There's no threat to your younger children, else we would not have come. My life is in danger, and now my wife and heir could be in danger too. Faith needs rest, so I'll hold explanations for morning, but please say nothing till we've had a chance to talk."

Justin was sorry for his anger. It was obvious Faith's parents loved her. "I want you to know that Faith means everything to me. I don't know how I existed without her, and I'll do everything in my power to make her happy. I understand, to some degree, how you must feel, but if you'll excuse us, it's been a trying day."

They left two bewildered people at the bottom of the stairs, and Faith turned into his arms before their door closed. "They were so upset," she said. "With everything else to worry about, I never considered their reaction. Thank you for coming. They looked so funny when they saw me. I'm certain I looked quite guilty."

He sat her on the bed and removed her shoes and stockings. Then he undid her buttons and eased her dress off. He noted the new fullness of her breasts as her body prepared itself to nurture their child.

Faith slept before he could fetch her nightrail. He tucked her in and kissed her cheek. "You're a tease even when you don't know it," he whispered.

From the window-seat, he gazed at the stars and vowed, for the safety of his family, to do two things—bury Justin Devereux and thwart Vincent Devereux.

His in-laws were at breakfast when Justin went down the next morning. "Your grace," John said standing. "I hope you will forgive an over-protective father."

"Call me Justin, and I will call you John and Cecile, if I may, as Faith suggested. No apologies are necessary on your part. I wondered how I would react if that were Beth, and I realized you must have held yourself in check."

Justin explained how Faith saved his life and the danger they faced. "I'd like to be introduced as Faith's husband, Justin Reddington. He's an American cousin, and I can carry off the charade, if need be. I do thank you for having us. We will try not to be too much of a burden."

"You're welcome for as long you need," Cecile said. "Had you sought sanctuary elsewhere, we would have been crushed."

Faith came in and kissed her parents. "Thank you, Mama."

Justin held her chair. "I thought to let you sleep, but you look well-rested this morning."

"I feel wonderful. You're safe. I'm home, and I'm ravenous."

Smiling, Justin piled her plate with sausage and eggs.

"I'm not expecting a pony, Justin."

He stopped. "Are you not? I had hoped...."

Faith cuffed him and her parents laughed, but Justin was chagrined to be on display after months of privacy. Now several children stopped as one in the doorway. Very much on display.

"Annie," Faith shrieked, as she stood and threw her arms around another beautiful young Wickham.

"Faith, you're home! I have so much to tell you." She stepped back and regarded her older sister. "But I expect it's not *near* as interesting as what you have to tell me."

Faith introduced the young ones as Andy and Lissa, then the twins as Jeremy and Amanda. When she stood behind his chair,

Justin was proud to be claimed by Faith. "This is my husband, Justin."

"Faith," Lissa said. "Are you going to have a baby?"

"Yes," Faith responded, obviously wary.

"Freddy Waring said the father places his seed in the mother, and that's how babies get inside their mothers." Oblivious to her mother's gasp, Lissa sat. "I asked him to show me and he said he would. Did you place your seed inside Faith, Justin?"

Justin strangled behind his napkin.

"Where the devil ... er pardon," John Wickham said. "Where does this Freddy Waring live?" he demanded.

"He's moved to America," the wide eyed child replied.

"Praise be," her father said.

Faith rose. "I'll get Beth. She'll love Andy and Lissa."

"Eat," Justin ordered. "I'll get her. Mother, make sure she eats."

As soon as he was gone, Faith's family spoke as one and she laughed. "Wait, I'll tell. Yes, he's the man I went to care for. We were married in December." She looked at her mother. "I want very much to be here when my baby is born."

Her mother clasped her hand. "I wouldn't hear of it coming into the world anywhere else."

Justin returned, Beth shyly cuddled up to him, until she saw Faith, and she opened her arms. "Mama."

Faith's heart fluttered. "Justin, did you tell her to say call me that?"

"I told her you were her mama now. She made the choice."

Later that day, Justin formally addressed Faith's parents in a closed parlor. "It's unfortunate you weren't present for our wedding, but perhaps you'd like to attend my funeral."

He chuckled at their horror. "Can you think of a better way to make a man intent on murder stop trying?"

So the Fifth Duke of Ainsley's funeral took place on a drizzly June morning. And though Justin hated the necessity, Faith wrote to Hemsted. "I did all I could for him, but alas, it was not enough. Justin Devereux is dead."

CHAPTER FOURTEEN

WHILE A PORTLY Marquis boasted of his grapes and vines, Vincent wondered how he'd tolerated this place so long. He'd wanted to leave weeks ago, but his father-in-law wouldn't hear of it and he couldn't afford to cross the rich bastard.

"If you please, your grace."

A footman beside him held a silver salver with a letter on it.

His companions stood in silence as Vincent opened it.

It was from Hemsted. 'I regret to inform you of the death of your brother—'

Vincent began to shake. '... cemetery ... Arundel ... advise ... arrangements ... child's return .... sympathies.'

Victory!

Vincent wanted to shout ... but he must be seen to grieve.

He lowered himself to a chair. *Don't smile.* But he couldn't help himself, so he bowed his head, and covered his eyes and his triumph.

Everyone watched. He had become the center of attention. His favorite place to be.

So he milked their curiosity, garnered their sympathy ... and rejoiced inwardly. That ripe little tart had assured his success by taking Justin on an extended journey. He'd hoped when he heard, that the carriage ride would finish him.

At first opportunity, he'd thank her in a most pleasurable manner.

His smile hovered, but happiness would not do. He visualized that which could utterly destroy him, if Justin were well and his wife were penniless. And he succeeded in his goal. Too well. It brought such anguish, his panic rose to the point that he shot to his feet to free himself from the horror.

The gasp of those assembled added to his anxiety. "My brother," he said, his voice breaking. "My brother is ... dead." He took a breath, realizing it was true. "I must go home."

His pain receded. It was only an act. He had what he wanted.

A short while later, in his personal carriage, Vincent finally shook off his agitation. "We must make haste," he told his wife. "I must see to my niece."

"You are also guardian of the money?" she asked.

"Yes." He smiled into the darkness.

"Ah, but you must be heartbroken. I am so sorry, *mon amour.*" Aline's kiss became an outlet for his rapture. For the first time in months, their passion stemmed from happiness rather than hate, and they did not wait to reach fulfillment.

Once they arrived at his wife's home, his home now, Vincent took her again. Perhaps he had not made a bad marriage after all. This had been the best sexual experience since his brother's wife, the fair Catherine, who, it turned out, loved her husband.

Damn it, Justin had always had it all, wealth, title, power, women ... a father who wanted him. He'd never found himself alone, abandoned, desolate ... at least until recently. Even then he'd been senseless, so he couldn't have known. Could he?

Had he suffered? All those months? His brother. His first playmate. Suddenly Vincent recalled a scene—twittering birds,

Justin rolling on the floor laughing. Vincent's chest tightened. And fast upon the tide of memory came sorrow. Guilt.

Catherine and Justin, both dead.

A horrific trepidation rushed Vincent.

It mocked him through a sleepless night, dogged his journey to Calais the next morning, and it wailed in the wind as he crossed the Channel toward England.

During a walk through the village, Justin met Squire Kennedy's son, him proud as a peacock, because Faith was his, and big with their child. He was still swaggering ten minutes later as they approached a copse. "Look," Faith said, eyes sparkling. "This is where I came to dream. Just move these branches. Careful or you'll get scratched."

He lifted some bracken and Faith beamed. "Isn't it wonderful?"

In the center of the tiny paradise, a brook ran beside a grassy slope, Pimpernel and Sundew at its edge. On the periphery stood a proud but gnarled beech tree, its upper limbs reaching for the sun, its lower branches for the brook. Justin let go of the foliage and, like a door to a secret garden, it closed them in.

"I forgot how beautiful it is here," Faith said. She led him to the tree where he removed his jacket and spread it on the grass. If he felt tired, how must Faith feel? He helped her down and sat against the tree. "Here, rest against me."

A robin chirped. A hawk screeched. The silence seemed blessed.

Faith glowed with sensuality as she raised her face to the sun. Justin stroked her hair, traced her ear. Such strange emotions she awakened in him—if only he could understand them—but wisdom danced just out of reach. And with the bewildering sentiment marched need, a physical exigency, banked, suppressed, ignored, but never, for a moment, absent.

They were alone in this sheltered Eden, secluded from the world, no abigails, nursemaids, children or parents. Faith was finally, joyfully well ... and *huge* with child.

She placed his hands below her breasts. For his sanity, he did not stroke or tease. But he sensed a need in her, and grazed the side of her neck, while *he* ached at the touch. "Tell me about the dreams you dreamed here."

"I remember no other dream than now, here, with you."

He settled her against him, his hand on her abdomen, and smiled as his child stirred in her womb. A simple moment. Perfect. "Sometimes, I think my life began when I woke to find you."

She turned in his arms, her wonder infusing him with peace. "How came I to be so blessed?" he asked. "I don't deserve you, I know, but heaven help anyone who tries to take you away."

"Kiss me," she whispered. "The way you did the night we made this baby."

She'd barely finished than he was ravaging her mouth, drinking greedy drafts, too long denied. They stopped to fill their lungs. Faith touched his cheek. "Do you remember our wedding night?"

It took Justin a moment to assimilate the shift. "The ice?" He remembered it well, for she had just poured it over him again.

"Our conversation," she said, voice husky, eyes luminous.

Ah, not a total shift after all. He did remember. "Every word." His bottom lip coaxed her top one, feather-light, erotic. "You know," he whispered. "I think we have achieved a fair measure of mutual ..." He traced her lips with his tongue.

"Kiss me again." Hearts pulsed. Words and time stopped.

Justin pulled away inhaling her scent, violets. He kissed her forehead. "I started to say ..." He took another breath. "We've achieved a measure of respect and understand—"

"Justin, please, it's been so long."

"God yes." He lay his wife in the grass and unfastened her gown. Since their marriage, he'd been holding his desire in check, waiting for her welcome, and this was it, unspoken, but unmistakable. And yet ... "Faith, the babe—"

"Mama said it's all right."

He pulled back. "You asked your mother!"

"Not exactly, but she said it's safe for several more weeks."

"But she thinks you conceived after we married."

Faith shook her head. "No. She doesn't. Come. Love me."

Justin hesitated, but he could no longer deny her, or himself, such perfect pleasure. Then, in a moment of insight, he realized that their single sexual encounter had not been merely pleasure, but an inevitable and cataclysmic communion of souls. And the knowledge rocked him. But when Faith opened her arms to him, he accepted the truth of it, the love, as his destiny.

He stroked and suckled her, bringing her to the edge of completion, over and over, until she begged him to fill her. And when he did, they rose swiftly together, until they reached heaven, then they floated above the earth like feathers in a summer breeze, their breaths mingling, their hearts beating apace.

And as languid as they, so became time and space.

The wind calmed. The sun moved lower in the sky. Peace. Until their child's antics startled them to awareness.

Justin looked into Faith's amazed face, wondering if her bemusement was from the baby's frolic or their passion. Whatever caused it, he experienced an infinitely sweet moment of oneness with her, and he was awed. He placed a reverent kiss on the swell of their child. "I think he's jealous."

Faith's laugh became a gilded treasure.

"I hereby decree that we shall return to this Eden every summer," he said.

"Mmm." Her eyes opened wide. "Ouch."

Justin rose and hovered. "Are you hurt? Lord, we shouldn't have. Are you laughing at me?" Relieved, absolved, he returned to her.

"Our son is practicing pugilism and I am his punching bag."

He watched her stomach reshape itself with his child's

movement. "Is he too big? I mean, I'm worried." He brought her hands to his lips. "When I think of his birth, I feel panic, akin to when I saw that carriage go over the cliff." He buried his face in her hair. "I'd give my life to spare you harm." He couldn't voice his fear that he would lose her.

She smoothed his brow. "There's nothing to worry about."

"You're not afraid, then?"

"I was ... because of what I didn't know. But I spoke with Mama yesterday."

"Which is when she told you we could—?"

"Yes. And what to expect. I feel better for knowing."

"Why didn't you tell me you were afraid? A fine husband I am, if you must face your fear alone."

"I didn't want to worry you, and you've been through this before."

"No I haven't. Beth's birth did not resemble this in the least. This time, my child's mother has such a grasp on me, I'm frightened senseless." He kissed her. "Do something, will you, Darling, to keep me from worrying? Tell me what your mother told you. Everything. So I can be reassured also."

"I will, tonight, but right now, I think we need to return."

Justin finger-combed her hair, then he dipped his handkerchief in the brook to sponge Faith's face and neck. When he buttoned her bodice, he lingered over the task.

"We look like street waifs," he said. "Do you think anyone will guess what we've been doing?"

Faith gasped. "Surely not. Mama and Papa would never...."

Justin's raised brow called forth her blush. "Yes, well, it's difficult to imagine one's parents." She stifled a giggle. "Yet I suppose with eight of us ... What about your parents?"

"I think they did it once."

"Twice. You forgot Vincent."

"I didn't, but I wish I could. Ready to go?"

"What if someone asks what happened? What will we say?"

"That Squire Kennedy chased us into the thickets?"

"Or that I climbed a tree and you came after me. Mama and Papa often scolded me for tree-climbing."

"In your condition? Forget that story."

"Justin, it's the truth they'd never believe. I'm sure of it."

He shook his head. "By the looks of you, the truth seems no more possible than tree climbing."

Faith looked at herself and grinned. "I know. What a scoundrel you are, Justin Devereux, taking your pregnant wife in the grass like a rutting stallion."

"Why, you brat, you begged me ... A stallion did you say?"

Harris awoke beside a woman of dubious character, recalling the notice in the Gazette that felled him. Justin Devereux was dead. Even after weeks of cheap gin and cheaper women, a fresh wave of grief washed over him.

He looked about the hovel they occupied, and guided by slits of light through its ill-fitting slatted walls, he found his clothes and gathered his possessions. Outside, he shook his head to clear it and stumbled in the direction of the mews behind the Grosvenor Square house, his eyes wet for thinking of his master.

He stopped. His master? What about his mistress? She must be beside herself. Why had he not thought of her before?

"Should've gone straight back, fool. How could you let her down at a time like this, and her with a babe on the way?" At the stable, he cleaned himself up and saddled his horse. Shortly thereafter, he set off at a neck or nothing pace, praying his mistress would forgive him for deserting her.

Late the next day, he arrived at Killashandra.

"About time you're back, old man," Mrs. Tucker snapped. "Not that there's need for you now."

"Don't be counting on keeping your position either. Who knows what will happen to Miss Faith and little Beth now?"

"They been gone for months and we've not been given the door."

"What? Miss Faith left my master here to die alone? I'll not believe it, not from what I saw the last time I was here."

Tucker straightened. "What *did* you see?"

He'd already said too much. "Who nursed master Justin after Miss Faith went away?"

"Old fool. She took Beth and the master with her."

"And you call me fool," he grumbled. "Why'd you just sit there like a goose without telling me?"

"I'd've told you sooner, had you not taken your own good time returning," she yelled to his retreating back.

By the end of July, Faith was so big, their walks were restricted to the garden and Justin was just as glad, for he was worried sick about the birth and wanted her near the house.

"I feel like a lumbering beast," she said, leaning on his arm. Despite her discomfort, she'd regained her cheerful disposition, and their mutual affection had flourished. And though Justin was chafing to get this damnable business with Vincent settled, he wouldn't leave her side.

"You don't have to stay with me every minute, Justin," she said. I'd think you had enough of being cooped up. You said you couldn't wait till you were free to ride out, yet you turn down every invitation."

He took her into his arms. "You can't get rid of me that easily." Faith raised her face for his kiss and *he* was more than happy to oblige.

"I don't know where you learned to behave in that brazen way." His mother-in-law's words sluiced over Justin like the ice on his wedding night. He stepped back but he didn't let Faith go.

"I vow, Faith, married nearly a year, expecting a child, and here you are carrying on outdoors in the middle of the day."

"I'm hardly in a condition to frolic, Mama."

With a grin, Justin hooked one arm around his mother-in-law's shoulder, the other around Faith's, and walked to the house.

During lunch, his father-in-law seemed preoccupied. "There's a horse-fair in York early tomorrow," he said, breaking the silence. "I could use your help, Justin, choosing a good mare. But I'd like to leave this afternoon, right after lunch."

Now Justin understood. They all knew he wanted to stay with Faith. "Much as I'd like to help, John, I can't leave Faith."

"Go, Justin," she said.

"But, the baby's due any day. And we'd be away overnight."

"Then I won't have the baby until Thursday."

His father-in-law hid his laugh behind a cough. "You could save me a lot of money, Son."

He should go, if only to repay their kindness. "Are you sure you'll be all right?" he asked, sensing Faith didn't want him to go. Sometimes he wished they were in his old room. Alone.

Faith touched his hand, soothing him. "Go. I'm not going to have this baby anytime soon."

A short time later, with great apprehension, Justin kissed his wife good-bye. "Take care of her, Mother," he said.

Faith watched Justin turn and wave twice, each time bringing a fresher, sharper pang of loneliness, until he faded from sight. "I love you," she whispered, desolation enveloping her. Her need to run after him and beg him to stay made her want to cry. But she bit her lip. If she started, there'd be no stopping her.

Her mother's arm came about her. "Come along, Sweet, and let Jenny help you with a sponge bath, then you can rest."

Faith sighed. "I guess." Why did she feel as if her heart had left with him? What was wrong with her, that a day apart should overcome her?

Faith woke later to someone calling her name and she nearly

cried when it wasn't Justin.

"Dear," her mother said, "There's a Mr. Harris here to see you. He's in the parlor. Do you want to get up and talk to him?"

"Harris, finally," Faith said, rising. "Yes, I'll see him."

"Are you hungry?" her mother asked. "Dinner was two hours ago." Her mother brushed her hair and helped her into her wrapper. It was comfortable and Harris wouldn't mind. He'd seen her in her nightrail, after all.

In the library, Harris paced, not sure what to say, not wanting to bring up painful memories. How could a supposedly healthy man just up and die after such a miraculous recovery?

When his Mistress came in, her hair about her shoulders, she looked forlorn and needing protection. Harris swallowed the lump in his throat, took her hands and sat silently beside her.

They began talking at the same time, and Mrs. Wickham, with tea and scones, eased the moment. "Don't stay up too long, dear," she said. "Good night, Mr. Harris, I hope your room is comfortable."

Faith ate little and was so quiet, Harris felt purely lost. "So," he said. "The child will be here before long."

She nodded absently. She was taking the master's death hard. To think his heir would be born after his death. Curse the gods. Aye, and a pox on Vincent Devereux too. He'd make the blighter pay, Harris decided, proof or no. "I'd give anything to see my master here beside you right now," he said, patting her hand.

"So would I Harris, so would I." Her mother must have told him how much she missed Justin. She yawned. Lord, she was tired.

"Here, now your grace, you'd best be doin' what your mama said and return to your bed. We'll talk when you're more the thing. I'll be staying for as long as you need me."

"Thank you Harris. I knew we could count on you." As she made her way back to her room, Faith was too exhausted to sort her thoughts. She'd slept so long already, she didn't see how she could be so tired, but sleep claimed her nevertheless.

Near dawn, she woke stiff and uncomfortable, and drenched in sweat. When she started to rise, pain came, ragged and breath-stealing. She gasped and stroked her distended abdomen. "Oh, Sweetheart, not while Papa's away."

CHAPTER FIFTEEN

WHEN THE WALLS stopped moving and the ceiling remained above her head, she rose and changed her nightgown, grateful her parents had given up their ground floor bedroom the month before. She needed to make her way to the kitchen to see if anyone was up.

Half way there, a second spasm stopped her. "Mama," she called, clinging to a stair rail to ride out the contraction.

Her mother rushed down, belting her wrapper. "Let's get you back into bed."

"Send Jem for Justin, Mama."

"Right now, Sweet. And Amanda will go for the midwife."

Her mother bathed her face. "Relax while you can. This is going to be a long day. You took nearly fifteen hours, you wicked child, but with Lissa I barely had time to warn your father."

"With Lissa, Papa needed warning."

Two hours later, the local midwife, swept into the room. "I can hardly believe I'm here to deliver my baby's baby."

The ticking of the clock became a hated sound.

After three hours, Faith was beginning to feel as if she was sinking into a whirlpool from which there was no escape.

After six hours, Mama began to worry.

From a distance, she heard the word, "Pray." Then she was running through a garden, grotesque thorns piercing her. She saw the cliff and knew if she wasn't careful, she'd fall off the edge into the turbulent whirlpool below.

But it was so dark, she couldn't see the edge. And if she fell, her baby would die with her. "Justin," she screamed. He'd saved her in her dream. Only he could save her now. "I can't go over the cliff, Justin, please."

"Too much blood," she heard.

The clock was set to mark the beginning of their child's life, but she'd been laboring so long; when would that life begin?

"More towels."

Someone was crying? "Mama?"

"You have to help us, Faith." Disjointed words came through a tunnel and echoed in her head. "Blood. Too much blood."

The pain made Faith scream fit to reach the next county.

Then she was floating above herself in the bed.

Faith's scream jolted Harris as he crossed the yard to the house. The babe was coming. Not for the first time, he cursed Vincent Devereux and pondered revenge.

The rider careening up the drive distracted him. He'd help the family by turning the visitor away.

As the lathered horse and its brawny rider neared, Faith screamed Justin's name in a bone-chilling outcry.

The rider leapt from his horse and Harris's heart leapt as the ghost of his master grabbed him by the shoulders. "My God, Man, what have I done?"

Harris swooned.

"No time for a man in his cups," Justin said as he ran inside.

At the door to their room, he stopped. So much blood.

"Get out. We have enough problems here," a matron said. Faith was white ... as death, and darkness threatened him.

"Go, Justin," Faith's mother said in despair. "We haven't time to worry about you too." She touched his arm. "Please. Go."

Justin threw off her hand. "Like hell I will." Kneeling, he wiped the matted hair from Faith's face and kissed her brow. "Faith, I'm here." But she didn't respond.

He watched horrified as her stomach mounded. Her scream, as if she was being torn asunder, tore him as well. "Oh, Faith."

Justin didn't know which was worse, her screams or her silence. "Sweetheart, can you hear me? I'm here." He saw his terror mirrored in all eyes. "She can't hear me. She doesn't know I'm here."

Someone touched his shoulder. "Tell her you'll keep her from going over the cliff."

"What?"

"She's been screaming about falling off a cliff for hours."

Oh God. Oh God. "I'll save you, Faith, and I'll hold you so tight you'll be safe forever."

"We're going to lose her," the midwife said.

"No!" Justin turned to his mother-in-law. "God won't take her." But they both knew he was fooling himself.

Unable to stop his tears, Justin kissed Faith's bloodless lips. "I'm sorry. I'm ..." He swallowed. "I'm getting tears all over you." He caressed her cheek. "Don't be mad, all right. It's not like ..." He sobbed. "Like ice or anything."

With the next contraction, her scream was weaker.

Faith was going to die.

Justin shouted her name loud enough to make God hear. "Faith, I need you. I'm the one who'll be falling off the edge if you don't come back. I love you, Faith. I love you so damned much."

"Justin?"

Had he conjured the thready whisper? "Faith?" Desperate, demented, he wanted to shake her to bring her back. "Faith," he sobbed with a shuddering breath. "If you love me, you'd better not leave me. Cause I'd die without you. I would." He wiped his eyes. "Beth and I need you so much."

Faith opened her eyes, their emerald depths rife with agony. She tried to raise her hand, failed. "Love ... you," she whispered on a long slow breath, and closed her eyes.

In stark terror, Justin turned to Cecile, his mother-in-law.

She squeezed his shoulder, but her consolation was useless; ice infused him.

"She's still with us," Cecile whispered.

Justin's heart began to beat again. "Thank God," he whispered. "Thank God." He raised her hand. "I'm here, Faith. I'll always be here." He kissed her palm.

She'd brought him back, and now he needed to do the same for her. "Come home to me, my love."

When pain gripped her again, he leaned close to murmur intimate words, love words, private and sacred.

"She must hear you, Justin," Cecile said. "She didn't scream that time."

But he feared it was because she no longer felt the pain. Still certain his touch, his voice, were the only ways to reach her, he coaxed her through the next pain. And the next.

Closer and closer, her contractions came. He stroked her cheek. "Would that your pain could be mine," he whispered.

She opened weary eyes. "Enough ... of your own." She licked her lips. "Not so bad ... now you're here."

With the words—her voice sweet as a hundred carolers—hope surged. He dipped his finger in water and wet her lips.

She kissed it and he was humbled. "Damn my hide, I should have stayed with you."

She smiled. "Love you ... too."

Her labor took a turn. Quick. Intense. Justin declared his love for her over and over again, not caring any longer who heard.

The midwife whispered instructions. He relayed them, urging Faith on.

"Hurts."

"I know, love. Not much longer now. Soon we'll have a beautiful babe." He looked at his mother-in-law beseeching her to affirm his words. Cecile nodded, and he was so bloody grateful, he had to take deep breaths to keep from blacking out.

"Tired," Faith whispered.

"Remember the love we shared when we created this child?"

Her smile was weak, her nod weaker.

"Bring him home now, so we can love him together."

Her eyes, focused now on him, held a spark of life that had been missing. "I knew you'd keep me from falling off the edge. You were the only one that could, you know."

"I know now," he said, her hand at his lips.

"Praise be," Cecile whispered. "She's back with us."

Justin coaxed Faith through another half-hour of labor. "That's my darling, my beautiful love. Give me a babe just like you, even if she's troublesome as Lissa."

Cecile chuckled. So, nearly, did Faith.

At dawn, nearly twenty-four hours after Faith's labor began, their son was brought into the world, his lusty screams filling the household with joy.

"A boy, hale and hearty," Cecile pronounced through her tears as she placed him in his mother's arms.

Justin couldn't speak, but let his tears mingle with Faith's as he kissed her.

Cecile tried to send him from the room, but he refused to go. Together they bathed Faith then he carefully, gratefully, lifted her and sat holding her while Cecile changed the bed. With the last hours haunting him, he held her as if he'd never let her go.

Faith's eyes closed as he smoothed the hair from her face and she sighed.

"You scared me witless," he whispered.

"You can put Faith back on the bed now, Justin."

With her eyes, Faith implored him not to let her go. "Go and rest, Mother. I'll put her down soon."

Cecile hesitated.

"Please Mama," Faith begged.

Cecile sighed. "Plain speaking, then. Faith lost too much blood. She needs to lie down, so we can raise her legs, so that baby of yours will have a Mama to take care of him."

That got his attention. When he rose, Faith whimpered, in protest or pain, and it pierced him. He placed her gently on the bed and knelt on the floor, his arms still around her. "I'd like to name our son Brian, for your grandfather," Justin said. "If that's all right with you?"

Faith nodded, and though her eyes were closed, she smiled.

Cecile smiled too. "My father would be pleased." She picked up the baby and kissed him. "We'll leave you two alone for now, but this little fellow will be hungry soon."

As soon as the door closed, Justin lay beside her, still holding her.

She opened her eyes. "You told me you love me."

"So I did. And with good reason. Because I do, with every breath in me."

"You never said it before."

"I didn't know what love was before."

Justin had fallen asleep with Faith in his arms. Cecile stood by the bed holding their son. The mite sucked his fist with noisy fervor. Justin let go of Faith and rose, embarrassed to be caught sleeping with his wife.

Thinking nothing of it, Cecile handed him the blanketed being, and the little wrinkled face contorted comically before giving forth a piercing wail.

Justin grinned. "How can something so tiny make so much noise?"

Faith woke. "You look like that picture of you holding Beth."

Cecile helped her with the new experience of feeding their son, and when Brian latched onto her nipple, she flinched.

"It won't hurt after a couple of days," Cecile said. "And it's easier with each child."

Justin paled. "Each child!"

"Don't look at me as if I have two heads, Justin," Cecile said. "It's never as bad after the first. I had a hard time with Faith, just like today, and here I am the mother of eight."

"I vow, Mama, it was harder on Justin than it was on me."

Cecile howled. "Men like you to think that, but don't you believe it."

Dressed for the day, Justin kissed Faith. I'm going to speak to Harris," he said. "He was damned fidgety when I saw him last."

Faith could barely keep her eyes open. "He was like that when I saw him the other night, too. I swear he was as sad over your absence as I was. See if he's all right."

"I'll not be long. Rest."

Faith drifted back to sleep as he watched.

He found Harris mending a fence beside Jeremy.

"Congratulations, your grace, on the birth of your son," Harris said. "Or should I say, for being alive."

Justin glanced at Jeremy. "Walk with me," he said, not leaving Harris any choice but to follow. "The boy doesn't know our scheme. Only Faith's parents and the vicar who married us know the truth. As far as anyone else is concerned, I'm Justin Reddington. The whole county went to Justin Devereux's funeral."

Harris told Justin about reading his death notice in the Gazette and of his shock at seeing him.

"I'm sorry, old friend, that Faith's note didn't reach you. I thought you were jug-bit when you swooned."

Harris winced. "Had enough of that to last forever." He rubbed his hands together. "Now, what's our next step in this grand scheme of cross-purposes and crooked answers?"

Justin grimaced. "To bring this deadly business to a close. When Faith is well, I'd like to return with you to London. It's time to get Grant and Marcus to help smoke Vincent out, and maybe even Gabe, too, if your vicar and my friend's up for it."

As Justin walked Faith into the garden one beautiful late summer day, she realized that his fear of losing her must finally have begun to ebb after all these weeks.

"I'll be back for you in an hour," he said. "Don't move from this spot."

"We'll be fine, won't we, angel," she asked their son.

After Justin left, Faith played with Brian until he fussed, then she put him to her breast. If not for Vincent, this time in their lives might be perfect. That he wanted Justin dead was more frightening than ever, because they were a family now.

Brian fussed as he nursed and Faith realized he must sense her anxiety. So she closed her eyes to concentrate on the beautiful day, the sun, the breeze, and her son's tiny hand on her breast.

"Faith. Sweet Girl!"

The unfamiliar exclamation shattered Faith's peace. "Mr. Hemsted!"

But he looked more stunned than she. "Miss Wickham. I had no idea ... that is to say, you have a child. How can that be?" The foolish question echoed in the silence, and his face reddened.

Faith covered herself with Brian's blanket. "Do sit, down."

He took the bench opposite. "Max, please." Despite his best efforts, his eyes kept straying toward Brian, suckling noisily. "Your child is young."

"Seven weeks today."

"You're well?"

"Quite robust, actually. What brings you to Arundel?"

"You." He colored again. "I've been worried about you since you left Killashandra. Now I can see my alarm was not unfounded. I guess when you care for someone, your instincts sharpen."

He cared for her? "Why do you feel your worry is justifiable?"

To Faith's chagrin, he knelt on one knee before her and took her hand. "My dear, Faith." He kissed her fingers. "You must be most unhappy."

"Why must I?"

"Poor darling. I have respect for your stoicism in these circumstances, but fate has taken a hand, and I couldn't be happier." He looked at the cloudless sky, as if seeking wisdom, then he gazed adoringly at her. "What I wish to ask, I do not ask lightly, nor is it something that has just occurred to me. As I said, I have been thinking of you for months."

When Faith tried to speak, he held up his hand. "Let me take care of you and your child. Marry me, dearest Faith, and make me the happiest of men."

"Oh, but—"

"Please say yes. If not because you care for me, yet, then do it for your son. An illegitimate child is ... I would call him mine. No one need know the circumstances of his birth."

Faith touched his hand. "You do me great honor, but—"

"Your son needs a father. I would be good to you." He lowered the blanket and gazed at Brian, touched his cheek. A tender gesture. "I'd be good to both of you."

She shook her head. She didn't want to hurt him.

He stood to pace. "Did the swine who deserted you leave you in disgust of men? Tell me you were not ... hurt," he begged.

She stood and went to him. "My child was conceived in love, Max. We'll be fine. Offer marriage to someone who can love you in return. It is my wish for you, my friend."

"Friend is not the word I would choose." He put his arm around her, Brian between them. "Let me give your child my name. Let me give his mother my love. You would come to love me, for I could show you such gentleness, bring you such pleasure."

He made to kiss her, but she turned her head. "I cannot marry you, Max. I'm sorry. Please try to understand."

"But your son is a bastard."

"My son bears his father's name, my husband's name."

"And that name is...."

"Devereux—"

"Vincent!"

"Reddington! Justin Reddington is my son's father."

Hemsted reacted strangely, as if taken by surprise. He shook his head. "Reddington, you say?"

"Yes. Seeing you made me think of Killashandra and my patient, Justin Devereux, and I misspoke. I met Justin Reddington there."

Hemsted's smile was enigmatic. "Indeed. And how did you manage to marry while at Killashandra?"

"Justin is ... a Devereux cousin. From America. He came ... to Killashandra when Vincent was in France and, and—"

"When did you marry?"

She should have let him think her child a bastard. She should not be trying to set his mind at rest. "What matters is that we are married, though the fact is not known to many." She touched his arm. "I ask you to keep our secret, Max. Can you? For me?"

"I'd do anything for you, Faith." He kissed her before she could react ... and Justin entered the garden.

When he saw them, he stopped—walking and smiling.

Faith went to him and took his arm. "Justin this is Mr. Hemsted.

He's in the employ of Vincent Devereux, as was I."

"As you still are," Hemsted said, wary, guarded, a man of affairs once more. "You have his niece. Or do you wish me to take her with me now? You have your own child after all."

"No!" Justin and Faith said in unison, with too much adamance, Faith was afraid.

"We love her like our own," Justin said.

"Yes," Faith agreed. "It would be terrible to uproot her again. She loves the baby. We'll keep her until his grace returns. Then, perhaps, we can discuss it. What do you think, darling?" The taut muscles beneath her hand told her Justin was furious.

He nodded. "I promise you, Mr. Hemsted, Beth couldn't be in better hands. Now, if you will excuse us, my wife needs to rest."

"Certainly. Good day to you sir. Faith." He walked away, but turned back. "If you pardon my saying so, Reddington, you don't have an American accent." His departing smile looked cryptic.

Justin removed Faith's hand from his arm. When the sound of carriage wheels heralded Hemsted's departure, he took her arm to steer her forward, but not in his usual, loving way. He didn't speak until he closed their bedroom door. "He was kissing you!"

"He was saying good-bye."

"Are you on such intimate terms then, that he should need to kiss you good bye."

"Just listen for a moment—"

"Tell me."

"Justin, I—"

"I said, tell me. Everything. Damn it!"

Faith's eyes filled with tears. Now he would never trust her. "He came into the garden while I was nursing the baby."

"What happened?"

"He thought that Brian was a bastard."

"And?"

"And I told him I was married, and he wanted to know the name my son bore—"

Justin's stance went on alert. "And you told him Reddington."

"I said Devereux at first, but—"

"Faith!" Justin's anger had never been so focused, so resolute.

"When I said Devereux, he thought Vincent was Brian's father. I said that I made the mistake because seeing him reminded me of Killashandra and my patient."

"Is that all?"

How could she say Max asked her to marry him? Justin was already jealous. After Catherine, who could blame him? "That's all."

"Are you sure?"

"Justin—"

"For once, I thought ... Never mind, I should know better by now. He'll go to Vincent with this."

"He won't."

"How can you be sure?"

"I asked him not to. He promised he'd keep our secret."

Justin's laugh was cruel. "As I said, you're a child. You know nothing of the world. Secrets, my dear, beg suspicion." He shook his head. "You trust too easily, Faith."

"And you trust not at all."

"And which of us do you consider more the fool?"

Faith raised her chin, for she could not speak past the lump in her throat.

"Try to rest," he said as he left the room.

Faith lay on their bed and let her tears fall.

Justin was leaving today, and Faith experienced a dreadful foreboding, one she couldn't shake.

"Don't worry," he said as he bent to kiss Brian, asleep in her arms, then Beth snuggled against her.

Faith imagined her dread must be visible for him to address her in other than anger for the first time in twenty four hours.

"I'll not be away long, and no one will recognize me. I'll be posing as a servant at my London house. If there's an emergency, send a note to this inn outside London, care of Grant St. Benedict."

Justin placed a quick, chaste kiss on her cheek, making her want to cry for what they'd lost. "I'll not stop worrying till you're back, safe." She didn't know what hurt more, their coming separation or this painful breach between them.

"I'd worry less were Hemsted ignorant of our marriage," came his oft-repeated phrase.

"I told you, I corrected my error. Hemsted thinks you're Reddington. And he promised to keep our secret."

"Vincent's man promised to keep our secret." Justin's chuckle was not a pleasant sound.

"He won't tell Vincent. I'm certain."

"You must have reason to believe him. Was it his flowery compliments?"

"Don't be ridiculous."

"His charming smile convinced you? Or was it that kiss I saw?"

"Stop it, Justin!"

He lowered his face to hers. "Or was there something that happened the night I went to my parents' apartments?"

"He cares for me," she shouted. "He loves me!"

Justin's head snapped back as if she'd slapped him.

Beth and Brian began to cry.

Justin stared at her as if he'd never seen her before. "Good-day, madam," he said, and went out the door, bag in hand.

Faith wept.

A minute later, her mother came bustling in, took the baby, handed Beth a cookie, and Faith a handkerchief. "If you ask me, he looked like he could sit down and bawl with the rest of you."

Faith almost smiled.

"This was your first fight. Don't worry. That man loves you and he'll be sending a note of apology in no time."

"No, mama. He may love me, but he doesn't trust me. And it would be too dangerous for us to be sending notes."

But that afternoon, a messenger arrived and her mother's look was smug.

Faith's hands shook as she wiped them on her apron and opened the note. Feeling the blood drain from her face, she sat in the nearest chair. "Vincent says if I want to keep Beth, I have to meet him at the London house in three days time. He's on his way there now." She bit her trembling lip.

"And so is Justin."

CHAPTER SIXTEEN

JUSTIN AND HARRIS approached the house after dark. Justin was exhilarated, yet he bore a heavy-heart. But if he let himself dwell on the way he'd left Faith, he'd fail them all.

First, he was going to stop Vincent, then he was going to fetch her and their children. No matter what she had done—and her betrayal still stung—but he loved and forgave her.

The Boltons, the new caretakers, welcomed Harris; he'd stayed there before, and Justin presented his letter of introduction, his own crest sealing it. Afterward, in the cubicle that would be his room, Justin sat on the small rope bed, Harris on a lone straight chair. A cracked ewer crowned a chest that bore testament to the indifference of the master—him. "This place is a dump."

"'T'aint right you staying here," Harris mumbled.

"It's not right for anyone to stay here. When things are back to normal, you can bet there'll be some changes." He put his hand on his man's shoulder. "I apologize for me and my kind."

Harris was appalled and discomforted by this breach of class distinction, so Justin changed the subject. "Ready to transform me into a gentleman, so I can break into Carry Muggeridge's house?"

"He one of the scoundrels?"

"Not one of the originals. More like a hanger-on, but handy in a *crooked* pinch."

Harris rolled his eyes. "Thought you wished not to be recognized."

"If I should be caught, a gentleman can name the prank a wager. A retainer would be clapped in irons."

Harris slapped his hands on his knees and stood. "We'd best get ye cleaned up, then."

At Carry's house Harris kept watch and Justin climbed inside.

The wait was long. When sounds of merriment approached, Justin cursed himself and jumped behind a curtain to be certain his friend was alone. God, he'd missed the drunken fool.

"Ye're a cool one, Carry, you are, ashking your … hic butler to take Lady Shilverley's wrap." The *lady* dragged out each fractured word. "Oooo," she cooed. "Good show, ol' boy!"

Justin peeked out to see the woman slip her hand into Carry's trousers as Carry nuzzled her.

Justin let go the curtain as if it caught fire.

Finally, Tess needed the *convenience*, and the second she left, Justin came out. "Hello, old friend. Is my face red?"

Carry didn't react. He didn't move or blink.

Justin looked him in the eye. "Carry? I meant to surprise you, not give you—"

"Aayyeeeeee! Aayyeeeeee!" Carry buttoned his pants and shook his head. "You came back to punish me, but I couldn't prove a thing. Knew it was a plot, but Vincent plugged the chinks." He stepped back. "I tried to set the runners on it. Laughed at me." The wall stopped his retreat. He wailed again and made a cross with his fingers.

Justin wanted badly to laugh. "Carry, I'm—"

Tess bounded into the room, and stopped, greed in her eyes. "Shee here," she intoned. "Itch double the priche for two."

Justin grinned. Taking advantage of Carry's glassy-eyed state, he paid Tess and instructed her to remove herself. With glee, she tucked her boon between her breasts and scurried off.

Justin clapped a hand on Carry's shoulder. "Carry, listen, I'm here to get—"

"Me! Please no. Too young for the old beyond. You were my friend, Justin. Tell 'em I'm not ready!"

"I'm not dead, you old sot. I didn't bloody well die."

Awareness flickered in Carry's eyes. He examined Justin with sudden sobriety. "Wha'd'y'mean, you didn't die?"

"It was a lie that I died."

Carry opened and closed his mouth like a fish, then he shifted his stance and studied the floor. A minute more and he looked up, eyes bright, and enveloped Justin in a bone-jarring hug. "Damn it to hell and back, Justin Devereux, you devil-dodging bastard, you're alive! Welcome back to the world, old man. By God, welcome back!"

Justin chuckled. "I might make the same welcome."

Carry grimaced. "I should call you out, you near scared me into my own grave, skulking like a specter from hell."

"Carry, did you think I'd gone to hell?" He laughed. "Almost, but an angel brought me back." He told his friend about Faith.

Before parting, they decided to meet that night with Marcus. Grant was rusticating. New baby, or some such, Carry had said.

Back at his house, no maid in sight, Justin visited his library where he'd known peace, the kind he craved for himself and his family. But the chaos in the hall reminded him that luxury was yet to be found, and would likely be hard-won.

He heard Mrs. Bolton speak with agitation. "But you didn't ... that is to say ... if we had been told ... hire a staff ... nothing ready ... the best we can." She was apologetic, fearful.

"Prepare our rooms, immediately," a brazen harpy said. "And have our dinner ready within the hour. Our servants, they follow, *demain*, tomorrow."

"See to it, man! We'll wait in the library."

Vincent! But it was too soon.

Justin sprang to the French doors and slipped into the garden, the latch closing as the library door opened. Fear of being taken again seized Justin, and he stood like a granite vine against sun-warmed brick, heart pounding, fists clenched. But within minutes, reason returned. He was no longer so ill as to be carried senseless to his doom. He was safe in London. Harris was near, as were any number of constables and magistrates.

He inhaled and released his breath. Upon the heels of relief came whimsy, and Justin imagined Vincent's face should he throw open the French doors and face him. If only he could.

In the library, Vincent and his wife bickered, the woman holding her own in the battle of wits.

"You're a heartless bitch, Aline," Vincent said. "I wish to God I had married a pure, unsullied maiden."

Justin almost hooted.

"Any maiden would be stupid to marry a lazy excuse for a man like you," the harpy hissed.

"And so you must be. Take yourself off, slut, you bore me. If not for your fortune, I would rid the world of your presence."

That started the woman laughing.

Justin was surprised. Even Vincent, rapacious as he was, usually remained more circumspect. Getting careless. About time.

"I demand respect. I'll brook no insolence from you or your servants. If they do not perform to satisfaction, they will be terminated."

Vincent laughed. "And how many have you discharged for their performance, *ma petite?* You tried them all, did you not?"

Someone got slapped. China shattered. Wood splintered.

Justin enjoyed himself prodigiously and wished to hell he could witness his brother's temper letting go, but it never did.

Instead, to his utter shock, he heard sounds of copulation, but when Vincent shouted *Catherine's* name, the fight began anew.

Justin took advantage of their distraction to get away. When he reached his stark room, he lay on the bed and pillowed his head in his hands, more shaken than he would like.

Vincent, here. With a wife as greedy and grasping as he.

Was she Vincent's ally or foe? Hard to tell. And was it luck or misfortune brought them together after all these months?

Twenty four hours after his first intrusion into Carry's home, Justin didn't have long to wait. He stood when he heard Marcus and Carry.

Carry threw the door open and allowed Marcus to enter first, prepared to be entertained.

Marcus stopped. "My God!" With a smile, he embraced Justin. "I knew you didn't stick your spoon in the wall." He looked at Carry. "Didn't I tell you Carry? Justin isn't dead, I said."

"No Marcus, you most certainly did not say. I wish to hell you had," Carry returned churlishly.

Justin caught Marcus up on his life, then he asked both men to help him prove Vincent's guilt.

The following afternoon, Justin waited in the garden.

"Muggeridge, Fitzalan, this is a surprise," he heard Vincent say. "What brings you here?"

"We're here to invite you to dine with us at Portman Square tomorrow evening," Carry said.

Vincent sounded marginally surprised and definitely delighted. Justin could even imagine his chest expanding.

Aline joined them then, and by the time Marcus and Carry left, they seemed well entrenched in Vincent's good graces. Justin was satisfied. Marcus and Carry would be there should Vincent's composure slip. They even planned to nudge it.

Vincent's pride was strong. Justin hoped there would come a

moment when he would not be able to keep from bragging about his success. As a matter of fact, Justin was counting on it.

Did they think he was stupid? Vincent slouched in a deep parlor chair, as he watched the Crown's public room through the barely-open door of the establishment's best private parlor.

A comely tavern wench snuffed a brace of candles proclaiming morning. His quarry, Marcus, Carry, and a third man, had been laughing and whispering all night.

He had been stalking Justin's friends for days and had seen nothing amiss ... until tonight ... until the third, the stranger. He saw only his back, and once his profile. The man's hair was gray at the temples. But there was something disturbingly familiar, yet elusive, about him.

Vincent was unnerved. Marcus and Carry had befriended him too readily, and he wanted to know why. After all, they'd been Justin's friends forever.

He was skittish too about what Hemsted had accidentally revealed. Justin's nurse had borne a child. The child of Justin Reddington, if the wench was to be believed, if *Hemsted* was to be believed, though the details had been nearly impossible to get.

Had their cousin, Justin Reddington, returned from America, after all these years? And why did the dratted man's name have to be Justin? It had puzzled him as a child. It *alarmed* him now.

By all that was righteous, his brother *had* to have died. He'd been given enough poison to fell an ox. Vincent started with awareness. Where had that come from? Why did he expect a dead man to walk into the room?

He lifted his tankard and took a long, deep draft, wiping his mouth on his sleeve. Sometimes he feared he was losing his grip on reality.

Was it so impossible that Justin's friends should come offering hands in friendship? Except they'd come right after he'd got the news about Justin's nurse and her unexpected bundle. Damn it was irksome, this unending night of clandestine merriment and secrets, for all the world as if they were poking fun at *him*.

Vincent shifted in his chair and pretended to sleep. But he couldn't still his shaking hands ... and that made him angry. Furious. Mad enough to want to hit something, or someone.

When renewed laughter came from the trio, Vincent clenched his fists. If he didn't get a glimpse at that man's face soon, he'd go look. By God he would.

Vincent knew he was nearly out of control, and he tried to think rationally. Marcus and Carry could be in earnest in their offer of friendship. He could be mistaken in his distrust.

Perhaps Reddington had gone to Killashandra, had lustily taken the wench—any man would—and they'd been forced to marry.

It could have happened. Perhaps.

God knew he'd lusted after her. He couldn't bloody well blame Reddington. He only wished he'd got there first.

In the public room, Carry pointed his fork and chewed thoughtfully. "Talks his way out every time," he said, lifting his empty tankard, slamming it down and going on. "Too careful, no matter how corned, salted and pickled he is. Fell on his face before he uttered your name Thursday, and even then, he only wept over his dear brother going to his just reward."

Justin raised his tankard. "To brother's just rewards."

"I think he's primed and set to bury it," Carry said. "We need to find a way to catch him out. Deliberate when he talks, y'know, like a man speaks to his wife when he's been to his bit of fluff."

Justin smiled inwardly. *He* would never look at another woman again. Just thinking about Faith made his heart ache for the way they'd parted. He wanted to go home to her, tell her he was sorry, make passionate love—"

"Are you hearing anything I'm telling you, man? He's got that look again, Carry. Never thought I'd see the day. Justin Devereux, moon-eyed. Makes a man sink into a decline, it does."

Marcus motioned to the tavern wench to refill his tankard, and he watched her with speculation till she left. "I'm so grateful to have Jade to moon over. What's Faith like?"

Justin grinned. "I'm caught. Guess you can tell." He chuckled. "Her eyes are like emeralds, but with more facets. Ebony hair like spun silk. And when I touch her, she's all warm and willing." He cleared his throat and shrugged.

"Poppycock," Carry said. "Lust, pure and simple."

Justin laughed. "You're a cynic. I was too."

"You should envy him, Carry," Marcus said. "Justin traveled a bloody long road, damn near died, but he's got something a lot of men dream of. You should find a wife that'd make you all calf eyed."

Carry straightened and gave a low whistle. "Tell me I'm not dreaming."

Justin turned. "Bloody hell!" He went to greet Carry's apparition.

"Justin." Faith stepped into his arms. "You're safe."

"What the hell are you doing here?"

"Shut up and kiss me."

That took the bluster out of him, and he kissed his wife until his son let out a wail from between them.

"Figures she's yours," Justin heard Carry mutter as he took Brian from Faith. "I should think you'd be used to coming between us," he whispered, kissing Brian's brow. He turned to Carry. "You're not dreaming."

Faith caressed his face, his arm, his chest. "You're all right. I was so frightened." She unfastened her cape and loosened Brian's blanket. "Vincent is on his way to London."

"No he's not. He's here. We're living in the same house."

Marcus prodded them, a hand at their backs. "Come along old boy; you too my dear. Making a spectacle of yourselves. Not good when in hiding. Bespoke a small parlor. Right this way."

Vincent extracted his handkerchief from his waistcoat and mopped his brow. He took a great gulp of air to lessen the vise around his chest, but the constriction worsened.

It took ten minutes to breathe easy. Still, his hands shook.

The palsied trembling had begun the moment Miss Faith Wickham had called the familiar man, Justin, and stepped into his strong, healthy embrace. And he wasn't Justin Reddington, either.

The bastard lived. Lives!

But not for long. Vincent took another calming breath and a large draught of ale and began to feel in control again.

For a while, he considered possible moves, and, eventually, he smiled. Now that he knew his enemy, he could plan his strategy.

This time, he would not fail.

CHAPTER SEVENTEEN

THE DOOR TO the small private parlor shut. "Thanks Marcus," Justin said, handing Brian over. "Hold your godson a minute."

"But ... but, but...."

A wiggle, a smile, and the tip of his cravat in a tiny mouth, stole the stuttering bluster right out of Marcus Gordon Fitzalan.

When Justin was certain Brian was secure in his friend's arms, he took Faith into his own. "Remind me to beat you when we get home." He stole her response with a kiss meant to make up for every harsh word and moment apart. "Faith, I'm sorry for the things I said, the way I left you. If I could go back and—"

She put her fingers to his lips. "It's finished."

He nipped her earlobe. "God, how I missed you."

"Your friends will be embarrassed," Faith said pulling away.

Carry shook his head, denying embarrassment and fixed her in his delighted gaze. "Faith, did Justin say you have a sister?"

"Later, Carry," Justin said. "How did you get here, Faith?"

"Squire Kennedy's coach and coachman. Jem came, too, and since Vincent doesn't know him, he's at your house looking for Harris. "Vincent ordered me here to meet with him. He said if I didn't come, he'd take Beth away from me, and I was so—"

"Bastard. He thinks I'm dead and he's still got me by the—"

"Justin!" Carry startled Brian with his shout.

Justin nodded his thanks and turned back to Faith. "What were you saying, Love, before I interrupted?"

Faith fingered a silver button on his waistcoat, paying close attention to the way it fit into, and slid out of its green silk frog. "Well, you needed warning, and you left upset, and I was sorry, and I missed you." She sighed, her eyes glistening.

Justin was so glad she was here, his knees went weak. She was his, and *no one* would separate them. To prove it, he slid his hands down her back and pulled her close, until Carry's cough brought him back to his surroundings.

When Justin looked up, his friends faced the wall cooing over Brian. "Thanks again. You can turn around now." He hugged Faith one last time and set her away from him. "Tell me, my would-be savior, where did you intend to stay?"

"At my uncle's in Cheapside. Come with us. I'm frightened Vincent will see you and...." Tears filled her eyes.

"My brother does not care about his servants. He doesn't even *see* them. I'm safe, but you're not. I want that coach to turn around and take you back to Arundel."

"But what about Beth and Vincent's threat?"

Vincent's reign as master of our fates is over. He has no say in Beth's life. It's time to put a stop to all of it, now.

Brian cried in earnest, and Justin had only to look at Faith to know it was time for his son's feeding. He led her to the hearth and turned a chair away from the company.

When Faith put Brian to her breast, his son's fury became ecstasy. And with the lusty suckling, he and Faith shared a knowing look. He kissed her, then his son's plump cheek. "Beth's with your mother?"

She nodded. "She misses you. She lost you once and she's frightened. I had to promise, more than once, that you'd return soon, and I don't want to break that promise.

"You won't." He returned to his friends. Marcus examined the ceiling and Carry seemed mesmerized by his boots, just because they shared a room with a nursing woman? But Justin decided to wait to tease them later.

Carry nodded toward the hearth. "Can't send her back today. Probably exhausted. Come to my place. Big house. Two of you." He cleared his throat. "Spend some … er … time with y'wife. Room for the babe and all."

"I'm staying there, too," Marcus said.

"Thanks Carry. They'll be safe there, with the two of you, and I'll feel better."

Carry nodded. "Settled."

A few minutes later, Faith returned, patting the baby's back, his warm little face against her neck.

"That was quick," Justin said.

"His schedule is off. He wasn't hungry, simply in need of comfort." Her look said she too wanted comforting. He put his arm around her. "We'll stay at Carry's tonight. Marcus'll get Jem and Harris. All right Marcus?"

His fellow scoundrel nodded. "Happy to." He cracked open the door to the common room and snapped it shut again. "Bloody goddamn blighter! Vincent just walked in the front door."

Justin tightened his hold on Faith. "What the hell's he doing here?"

"I don't like it," Carry said. "Never knew Vincent to slum it. You think this is where he and Catherine used to—" He paled. "Sorry, Justin, Faith. Fools babble and all that."

"It's all right Carry. See where he is now, will you?"

He looked again. "Getting propositioned by the wench that fair dipped her—" He coughed. "On his way up the stairs now."

"Good." Justin pulled Faith's hood over her head. "Here, hold the baby under your cloak." He fastened the pistachio cape. "Time for you to go." He kissed her quick and hard. "Carry, get them out of here. I'll meet you at your house."

"Come *with* us," Faith pleaded.

"No. If Vincent saw us together, he'd recognize me and it'd be finished, to our detriment. Much as I want to be with you, you're safer without me. Carry, leave first to make sure all's clear. When I tell you, Faith, you march right out that door. Be calm and keep your head down. Marcus will be watching."

"Now's the time," Carry said and left.

Justin kissed Faith quickly and pushed her. "Go. Now!"

She looked back once, hugged Brian close, and went.

Marcus watched a moment, shut the door and smiled. "They're clear. I'll go check the stairs, then it's our turn."

"I don't give a bloody damn what happens to me, I just want Faith and Brian safe."

"They will be." He checked the common room again. "Wait, the wench Vincent followed up the stairs is back out there. Stay here. I'll see if I can find out where Vincent is."

Justin paced with the same frustration as when he'd paced in his chair the night Faith dined with Vincent. As then, reminding himself that an ill-timed appearance could jeopardize everyone he loved, he groaned and swore. If anything happened to them....

Marcus rushed in. "Vincent went out the back door about the time Faith went out the front."

"NO!" Justin ran.

Outside ... chaos.

Imagining carriages and cliffs all over again, Justin pushed his way through a chattering throng in the keeping room. He ignored two men being unbound in the center of them and barreled through to the street. Empty. He spun on his heels, sick, adrift.

When Carry shouted his name, dread sizzled through him.

Stepping from the crush, Carry, hands bound, accelerated Justin's fear. "Faith? Brian?" The horror in Carry's eyes pierced Justin with stark reality, alarming and calming at once. He was no good to them if he was frantic. He released Carry's lapels, his hands shaking so much, he could barely untie the rope.

Carry apologized, chafed his wrists, apologized again.

He must mistake raw fear for fury, yet Justin hadn't the time to sidestep. "Tell me."

"Put 'er in the coach, gave directions, and just like that, the coachman here...." He indicated a wounded stranger. "Fell at my feet." He shook his head in apology. "Got hit from behind."

Justin swallowed the anguish clogging his throat. "Find Faith's brother and see him safe, will you? Marcus, come with me." He grabbed Carry's arm. "You did your best."

Faith regarded Vincent across from her as the speeding coach whisked them away. She knew not where they traveled, but it was far away from Justin. Perhaps forever.

Cold eyes, bruised and sunken by depravity, examined her with such bone-deep perusal, instinct warned her to mask her panic.

Though she could not measure Vincent's state of mind at this moment, she knew she and Brian were in the gravest danger, and as if he sensed it, her babe stirred and whimpered. She must be strong for his sake, and for Beth and Justin.

Justin had already traveled a long, dark road from death, to claim her once; surely he could find her now, among the living.

Brian's whimpers progressed to a disenchanted wail.

Vincent's steel gray eyes impaled her. "Feed him. I want to watch."

Faith was unable to check her shudder. "He's not hungry."

His smile profane, Vincent's laugh iced her heart. "I would

have liked to watch, too, while you took your pleasure of a dying man to conceive his son. Too bad my brother was too ill to ... ah ... participate. Was it your ride killed him?" His obscenity incited him to raucous laughter. He laughed so long that for the first time in her life, Faith considered, nay wanted—despite her healing instincts and with full cognizance of the sin—to do murder.

As Brian's fussing dueled with Vincent's mirth, she began to suspect that she might conquer Vincent's power if she denied it. And since starving her son would be like affirming it, she attempted to feed him under cover of her cape.

Vincent caught her movement, his sudden silence and hot eyes sending prickles through her. "Take off your cloak," he ordered.

The prickles froze in her veins and expanded painfully.

Vincent leaned forward, and the instant Faith lowered her eyes to conceal her terror, he snatched her son from her arms. Her involuntary scream startled Brian, making him cry in earnest. But when she reached for him, Vincent pretended to drop him.

The more Faith begged, the hotter Vincent's look.

When she lunged for Brian, Vincent's boot to her stomach cut her breath.

With a foul grin, barely holding Brian under his little arms, Vincent raised her son, until his head touched the carriage roof.

Brian not only stopped crying, he wiggled and cooed, enjoying the ride. That seemed to startle and unsettle Vincent, and as if he couldn't bear such joy, he silenced it by releasing one of Brian's arms, dangling and frightening him.

Faith screamed and screamed.

"Bare your breast!" he shouted. "Bare it and prepare to feed him, else I drop him. Do it now!"

Faith scrabbled to untie her cloak, her hands shaking so hard, she could barely unbutton her bodice. When it was undone, her face aflame, Faith lowered the fabric to expose herself. She would do anything—Anything!—to protect her child.

The icy air on her breast became her enemy—if she did not know by the feel of it, she would know by the look in Vincent's eyes exactly when her nipple budded, and she shuddered.

Seeming calmed by the sight, Vincent lowered and cradled her son, smoothing a slanted brow, fingering a dark, baby curl, before giving him back.

Once she had him, for a wild, crazy second, Faith considered throwing open the coach door and jumping. But Brian sought her breast so fast, she forced herself to allow the physical connection to wash over and calm her, closing her eyes to thank God for Brian safe in her arms again.

He suckled greedily as always. How could she have thought to do this quietly, even under cover of her cloak? He made such lusty little sounds when he nursed.

"If I had not been certain of Justin's miraculous resurrection before seeing your child, I am now." Vincent's words opened her eyes and pulled her attention to himself once again. "However did you manage it?" he asked reaching toward her—to touch her breast, she feared. And she prayed for the strength to do what must be done for her son. "Your plan was brilliant," she said in a rush.

As she'd hoped, her words stopped him.

"How was I brilliant?" He sat back against his seat in anticipation of her answer.

"The poison," she said. "Disguised as medicine, and someone to administer it while you were in France. Very clever."

Vincent's smile turned to a scowl. "Then why didn't it work?"

"Because every time I was late giving Justin his medicine—"

"Miss Wickham!" he shouted, sitting forward. "I told you my brother's health would be in jeopardy, his very life at risk, should you dose him even a few minutes late." He shook his head with what appeared to be genuine sorrow and deep disappointment. "I believed

I could trust you. How late were you?"

"As much as half an hour, but—"

"Young lady, were I mean spirited, I should turn you off without a recommendation for such irresponsible care. My brother's welfare is uppermost in my mind."

Vincent's rebuke frightened Faith more than his shouting, and her heart tripped in her breast. Had the man played the grieving brother so long that he was lost in the pretense?

"I ... I apologize, your Grace," she said, playing servant to his master. "I assure you it will not happen again."

He folded his arms and sat back. "See that it does not!"

Faith's doubt was gone. Vincent no longer straddled the edge of sanity, but had left it far behind.

Brian fell asleep pressed to her breast, her milk running freely, soaking her dress. She wanted to move him but feared any motion or sound, a whimper even, might shift the delicate balance of Vincent's mind. Instead, she sat unmoving, watching the unpredictable man who held them in his power.

When Vincent finally slept, his mouth hung open and spittle collected in droplets at the corners.

Faith thought again about jumping. She wondered if the coachman was aware of the abduction, if he might be of help, but she doubted it.

She gazed about the velvet-cushioned cab of the well-appointed vehicle. Nothing sharp to do for a blade, nothing rope-like for choking. Faith shuddered at her mind's gruesome turn.

Keep Brian safe, her good sense said. Keep yourself safe, too, it reminded her, so she could care for him. Be sensible. Take no chances.

Justin will come. He will come.

When Vincent's snores filled the cab, Faith shifted Brian and closed her bodice. She brought the hem of her cloak up, folded it and placed it, like padding, between her wet dress and him.

She remained awake and on guard.

It was full evening when they stopped. She shifted Brian and he took to whimpering again.

Her captor woke confused, disoriented. Faith wondered if his sanity had shifted again. The coachman opened the door and Vincent stepped out. "Ah. We are here," he said as he raised his hand to help her alight.

She ignored it, stepped down and away from him.

His scowl told her he was the hate-filled Vincent once more.

Mrs. Tucker opened the door, and despite the circumstances, Faith felt a sense of homecoming. As if to prove it, the housekeeper enfolded her in a hug. Then with genuine surprise, she noticed Brian, examined his face, and began to cry.

"Yes," Faith said. "He's Justin's, Mrs. Tucker. I was carrying him when we left."

Vincent's ashen face contorted with rage. "Enough! Where is my wife?"

"In her bed, I expect," Mrs. Tucker said with a disdainful sniff.

"Gather your things. You're dismissed. Be gone within the quarter hour or your family will be turned off their farm."

The housekeeper's face lost color. "But, your Grace, my mother is ill, and we've been Killashandra tenants for generations."

"Squander many more minutes and you'll not be tomorrow."

The woman left in tears, and with her, Faith's hope for an ally in the house.

Vincent took Faith's arm in a bruising grip, propelled her upstairs, and barged into Justin's father's bedroom, where a gilded, silk-canopied bed on a raised dais centered the room. A set of steps led up to it, and two naked ... "Hemsted!"

As Vincent charged the bed, Faith slipped from his grasp and backed slowly toward the door.

"Slut!" Vincent roared as he backhanded the woman across her garish, rouge-pot face.

Like a spitting cat, she hurled insults, her French flawless and rapid. A dispute escalated, drawing Vincent's full attention.

Faith hugged Brian and stepped closer to the door and freedom.

Hemsted jumped from the bed and came to her. "Are you all right? Did he hurt you? Where's Justin?"

Justin. Faith fought despair. If Vincent had his way, Justin would die.

Hemsted's expression said he understood and cared, and that nearly undid her. Nevertheless, she swallowed her urge to confide in him. She couldn't trust him, or anyone, anymore.

"You're not safe, I think. Come," he said, and as Vincent had done, he grasped her arm to haul her along. But she'd had enough of being dragged like yesterday's trash, and she stood her ground. He was Vincent's man, Justin had often reminded her, and it was time to remember that.

"Don't be a fool," Hemsted hissed below his breath, checking his ire. "I'm your only chance."

"You told him I'd borne a child," she accused.

He looked as if she'd struck him. "Faith, I never meant to—"

"Miss Wickham," Vincent called. "Is the blighter accosting you too?"

Hemsted sighed, seeming to understand he'd lost, and despite his unclothed state, he bowed with ludicrous formality and kissed her hand. Then he unhooked her cloak, removed it from her shoulders, and threw it over his own, fastening it to cover himself. "A friend in need," he said, self-mockingly, his face a study in regret. And he left the room.

The furious Frenchwoman marched up to Faith and raked her with disdain. "What did he say to you?" she demanded with suspicion.

"He ... he begged my pardon for the embarrassment."

The painted features softened. "Always the gentleman, my Max," she said with an indulgent smile.

Vincent approached. "Miss Wickham—or did you marry my brother? No matter. You shall be free of him soon enough. May I introduce my wife, Aline. She will spread her legs for anything with a lance." He gazed with disgust at his wife and indicated Faith with a nod of his head. "Lock her up with her brat till I decide what to do with her."

"Braying ass. Why should I?"

"Money, my dear, money. Ah, yes. I see that does indeed make a difference. With you, it's greed, followed closely by vengeance and lust. Or does lust head the list, my pet?"

Vincent mocked the hatred on his wife's *visage* with a laugh. "I bid you good day, Faith. I may call you that, may I not? After all, we will soon become *very* well acquainted."

He smiled. "As soon as I eliminate my *brother*, that is."

CHAPTER EIGHTEEN

WHEN JUSTIN AND Marcus arrived at Killashandra, a stable boy told them the master had arrived with a woman and a babe. Heart hammering for knowing Faith was near, yet far from safety, Justin entered the empty kitchen, Marcus behind him, to take the back stairs.

As they reached the foyer, Hemsted came running downstairs—naked, but for Faith's billowing pistachio cape. "Justin. Thank God you're here. I just left Faith in the gold bedroom; she refused to—" Hemsted hit the floor with a thud.

Satisfaction filled Justin as he flexed his hand and examined the unconscious form. "Truss him up and lock him in the linen cupboard," Justin said. "Top of the stairs to the left. Key's on a hook inside. Take the cape and let the bastard freeze."

Marcus grinned and dragged him by his feet, Hemsted's head hitting each step, until Justin stopped him. "By his shoulders, Marc." And Marcus reluctantly obeyed.

"See if Faith is upstairs, but let me deal with Vincent. Keep Faith and Brian safe for me, will you, one way or another? Beth too. There aren't many people I'd trust with that."

Marcus nodded soberly as he dragged the man of affairs away.

Justin went to the library, Vincent's favorite haunt and as expected, Vincent was there. As they faced each other, for the first time since the cliff in Bognor, Justin's fury was savage, and dangerous, for it nearly robbed him of caution.

From his seat behind the desk, Vincent smiled and raised a pistol—a 17th century, multi-shot German cavalry pistol that Justin had purchased in France. "Odd how one's past returns to take a bite of one's backside," Justin said. Then he remembered his father's matched pair of smoothbore dueling pistols, loaded and waiting in a drawer on the balcony above.

This blend of fury and fear for loved ones was dangerous, as he suspected. If he were thinking clearly, he would have fetched the pistols before stepping into Vincent's net.

"Took you longer than I expected," Vincent said. "Sit down."

Justin sat, Vincent's confidence an unpleasant surprise. All right, he could play the game. "This is the last time you come near my wife or one of my children, Vincent."

"*One* of your wives you mean?" Vincent said, chuckling.

"I have proof you fed me poison as medicine."

Vincent's smile widened. "I never fed you a drop."

Justin sighed. "Enough. Already I tire of this. Do what you will with me, but leave my family alone. Just indulge me in this last, if you will. Did you plan to throw Catherine over the cliff, or was your decision made on the instant?"

Vincent examined the pistol. "Catherine was a good mistress. And I had planned to keep her as such."

"Your grief is staggering," Justin bit off, trying to curb his rage, to keep his cards close, when he wanted to jump the desk and strangle his brother, the bloody gun be damned.

Only fear of abandoning Faith and his children to Vincent's mercy stood between him and any number of irrational, vindictive deeds. That he and Vincent might be more alike than he wished to admit was a notion Justin thrust aside for later perusal.

Despite all, he must remain calm. The way to wrest control was to make one's foe relinquish it. "You know, Vincent," he said, smile genuine, for he could predict a reaction. "With regards to Catherine, I always wondered why you were content with used goods—second-hand, so to speak—especially mine."

On target, Vincent's fury came. "The bitch went crazy. When I aimed that gun at your back, she grabbed my arm and sent the shot wide, damn her soul. Still, it served its purpose, though not as well as a bullet would have. It spooked the horses that carried you over the cliff. I thought she'd tear me open with her claws, crying your name and screaming for all she was worth."

Cat had cared? She'd even tried to save him? That was jarring.

"You didn't realize, did you?" Vincent's tone showed grief. "I lived my whole life with people who loved you more. I simply did not need another." He shrugged. "So I sent her after you."

What was the matter with him, feeling sorry for the man who tried to kill him? The man who murdered Catherine and abducted Faith and their son. He had to remain level-headed and strong. "You must have been beside yourself when I survived."

Vincent narrowed his eyes and raised his chin.

Justin cheered inwardly. "How did you feel when you realized I had risen from the dead, so to speak?"

Vincent shot to his feet. His chair teetered and fell, echoing in the vaulted chamber. He steadied his aim and growled.

"As if that were not enough," Justin said chuckling, throwing fuel on the fire of Vincent's agitation. "Not only did I survive your poison, I married the nurse you hired to give it to me."

Nostrils flaring, Vincent wrapped both hands around the gun's grip and stepped closer.

Standing would affirm Vincent's advantage, so Justin remained sitting, pretending a calm that was so far from fact as to be laughable, but if Vincent stepped a fraction closer....

"And my son," Justin said, stretching, crossing his ankles. "What think you of my son?" Fear for his boy pounded in his brain, but Justin silenced it. "A right proper heir, is he not?"

"Stop!" Vincent shouted. "Stop pretending you have it all, you bastard. I do. I have your wife and your precious heir. All you have is Beth." Vincent's laugh, as if he'd amused himself, alerted Justin to a shift. "You have Beth, did I say?" Vincent chuckled. "You never questioned her paternity, did you?"

Justin attempted to mask his shock. Failed.

"I see from your look, you did not. I suspect you guess the truth now, then." He nodded. "Yes. I am Beth's father."

Stunned out of mind, Justin forced a smile—weak at best, he feared. Still he persevered. "Did you call *me* a bastard?"

Vincent revealed renewed agitation, giving Justin heart. "We both know you are the bastard, not I."

Vincent's gun hand lowered. "How long have you known?"

"Twenty years or so. You?"

A sneer contorted Vincent's mask. "On my sixteenth birthday, from that balcony, I heard your father call our mother a slut, naming me her worst mistake. She said I was one of many, her worst, marrying him." Pain weighted Vincent's laugh. "I wasn't even high on the mistake list, no nor on any other. The old man called me a bastard and I stood like stone, praying she would correct him. But she never did."

A breath, a shake of his head, and Vincent seemed to awaken. "The birthday must have been hard on the old man." He smiled wryly. "You've known longer than I, yet you treated me the same, until I put a stop to it. I didn't want or need your pity."

"No, just my title and my money. So much for sentiment."

"Sentiment is for women like Faith." The light in Vincent's eyes foretold another thrust. Justin braced himself. "Hemsted proposed marriage to Faith in Arundel. Did you know that?"

Despite steeling himself, Justin was robbed of breath.

"I see from that tic in your cheek, brother, that our little nurse was … keeping secrets, shall we say?"

By not telling him about Hemsted's proposal, Faith had in effect, lied to him. How far did her deception extend? Ah, Faith. Faith. Could no woman be trusted?

"Today, Justin, your wife betrayed you again. Do you know what she has been doing this past hour or more?"

He pictured Hemsted, Faith's cape billowing behind, and shut the image away. "Trying to get away from you, I expect."

Cunning lit Vincent's eyes. "Fornicating with Hemsted. Found them myself in your father's bed. A woman of passion, your wife. Her sounds of satisfaction do tend to inflame the senses."

Justin's insides clenched. His fists ached to connect with bone … Hemsted's, Vincent's. Hemsted's words, 'I left Faith in the gold bedroom,' became a haunting chant.

Undeniable proof of Vincent's claim. And yet. And yet....

Then everything fell into place. He was being dosed with poison again, venomous poisonous words. Who better to administer this new toxin than the man who knew his every reason to mistrust? Their mother's bastard, Catherine's lover. What viler poison than to name Faith unfaithful? The very words were a paradox. Justin laughed. As certain as he was that Catherine betrayed him, was he certain Faith did not, could not.

Faith had delivered him from hell. She had borne his abuse. For the love of God, she had given him life. His. Beth's. Their son's. Justin grinned.

Setting his jaw, Vincent tried to collect his tattered confidence. That he searched for his next thrust was obvious. "Why do you think Faith told Hemsted of your marriage? She knew my man would tell me. She wanted me to remove you as an obstacle between them. Max is crazy for wanting her. And she feels the same. Neither of them can get enough of—"

A shriek, piercing, shrill, drew their gazes to the library balcony. "You lie, you wretched excuse for a man. Max loves me!" Aline screamed.

Vincent barked a laugh. "Love you? Who could?"

Justin had never heard him speak more coldly. He saw his chance to disarm Vincent the same moment Aline raised her own weapon. And Justin's heart sank, for in those hands, his father's dueling pistols would be as deadly as a loose cannon.

"Stupid bitch," Vincent said, just loud enough to narrow his wife's eyes and bring a deadly smile to her lips.

She took aim. The gun exploded.

Justin leapt to push Vincent aside and broke his fall instead. Shocked he lowered his brother to the floor and watched blood seep through the azure waistcoat, the grotesque stain spreading. In the silence, amid the metallic odor of blood, Justin tried to grasp the situation. Was the game finally over?

He caught a movement, looked up, and knew it was not.

The game would continue. New players, new rules.

He had forgotten her, his widowed sister-in-law, the coarse woman he did not know and did not like. And he supposed he should not have been surprised when she aimed the second of the pistols at him. Fate. Destiny. A bite in the backside.

Aline nodded as if she read him. "I will kill you both and make it look like you killed each other. And after I inherit your money, I will go away with my Max."

"Don't be ridiculous, Aline," Faith said stepping onto the balcony from the upper hall, stopping Justin's heart. "I stand to inherit, not you. I am Justin's wife, after all."

"Faith, don't!" Justin shouted, the sight of Aline re-directing her aim toward Faith nearly felling him.

With Faith up there, a gun at her heart, and him down here, how could he save her? How? Slowly, he began to rise.

"Get down!" Aline shouted. "Or I will shoot her."

Justin complied instantly.

"Stay," Aline ordered. "I warn you."

He nodded, not certain she caught the move. Faith spoke to her in a soothing tone, but Justin could not discern her words for the fear pounding in his head. He closed his eyes, swallowed. Dear God, he prayed. I love her so much.

Something touched his hand. He looked down. Another shock. Unexpected. Cutting him to his marrow.

With obvious and painful difficulty, Vincent pushed the German pistol into Justin's palm. Oh, no. Oh, God.

He hated this man. Hated him. Yet a shot of love, the good times passing swiftly through his mind, made Justin both furious and grateful. The result: pain, swift, crippling.

Vincent's expression just now must mirror the boy standing like stone, waiting for the word bastard to be rejected. Imploring, anxious, desperate.

Tears blurred Justin's vision. He tried to speak, but Vincent cautioned silence with wide eyes.

"Max does not love you, Aline," Faith said so loudly Justin knew she intended him to hear. "He loves me."

Justin turned back to the balcony, the weapon he now held hidden between him and Vincent. He tried slowly to rise and Aline caught the action. "An inch higher and I kill her."

Justin heard the deadly click. He knelt again, panicked as when he saw that carriage by the cliff. Powerless. He caressed the gun, but he was too near the floor and Aline too far back on the balcony—and too close to Faith—for him to dare a shot.

"Max is taking *me* away with him," Faith declared.

"You're lying," Aline spat. "Max made love to me all last night."

Her tone was smug, her head raised with pride.

"I just saw Max," Faith said. "And he told me ..." She smiled. "*Showed* me he wanted me. If you had satisfied him, why would he still want me?" Faith inched closer to the jealous woman putting herself in further peril.

Justin needed to turn their attention, to move them apart. "Damn it, Faith, Aline, stop it!"

They ignored him. "Max begs *my* favor," Aline said, voice shrill, defensive, her mind as fragile as her husband's.

"I'll fight for him," Faith said. "He is a magnificent lover and the father of my son."

With the statement, something in Justin expanded. Faith's words set him free. He could trust her every bit as much as he loved her. As much as she loved him. If she had not proved it in so many other ways, she did so now—deliberately baiting an irrational woman to save him—but God, oh God, she frightened him to death.

Faith was as scared as she hoped she appeared bold, but if Aline lost her temper, she'd lose concentration and, maybe, make a mistake. "Max does not want you, Aline."

"He does want me," Aline preened. "And he will follow me back to France, because I am a duchess."

Faith tried a trilling laugh, and though badly done, it was good enough to unsettle the woman. "You're not a duchess. Your husband was never the duke. Vincent stole Justin's title and planned his murder, but he failed. Your husband died a pauper."

Aline hurled a string of guttersnipe invectives in her husband's general direction. "I'm glad the wretch is dead. He could do nothing right. I would kill him again, could I do so."

Hemsted's cat, his shadow, crawled through an open window beyond Aline's vision. Faith looked away, examined the room and took her time to glance back. Lord, how she wanted Hemsted to be there. She schooled herself not to react if she saw him. When she finally did—hunched on the parapet outside the window—hope surged. But he moved out of sight and she couldn't believe it. She'd placed her hope in him and he'd abandoned her.

Aline repeated something Faith had failed to catch, touching the gun to her shoulder.

Looking into the lower library, Faith told Justin with her eyes and her heart that she loved him. And with his, he said the same. "For eternity," she said aloud, and he nodded.

"Aline, where are you?" Hemsted called and entered below, stopping to take in the sight of Justin by Vincent's body.

At Aline's gasp, he looked up. "Darling," he said. "Are you all right?"

Faith was confused. He couldn't be surprised; he'd heard them from the ledge. Did he love Aline? They'd been in bed together. His words were in accord with that evidence, and yet they seemed foreign, unreal.

"See if my wretch of a husband is dead, Max," Aline said then bring the other one up here.

"Aline, the wire to lower the chandelier is coiled up there," he said. "In a case on the side wall. Truss her up."

Aline smiled and urged Faith toward the side wall.

She must have been beautiful once, Faith thought, might still be, but for the over-application of powder, rouge and jewels.

Hemsted hesitated when he saw Vincent lived, and when he saw the gun in Justin's hand, he looked him full in the face.

Justin couldn't use the gun on him. Aline would kill Faith in a wink if her Max was harmed. And another thing, something about Hemsted had disturbed Justin since meeting him, and his unease wasn't based on jealousy, either.

Hemsted attempted to take the gun from him. Justin grasped it tight. Hemsted begged for Justin's trust in an intangible, but undeniable, way and tugged again. Bloody hell.

Faith already trusted this man. And Justin trusted Faith. Was it not time to trust her instincts too? He fought the turnabout a moment longer—it was difficult to let an old habit die—then he let go of the gun.

Hemsted slipped it into his pocket and indicated Justin should stay.

Justin did.

Hemsted climbed the circular stairs.

And why, Justin wondered, did he remain? Because he feared for Faith? Because he trusted Hemsted? Or for both reasons?

Faith's heart beat with hope, despite her bindings, when Hemsted reached the balcony. "Aline, Vincent lives," he said.

The woman sucked in her breath and with dispatch turned and spent her second and last shot in Vincent's prone body.

Faith heard Justin shout, "No," and thinking he'd been hit too, she fought for consciousness.

Aline dropped the dueling pistol and stepped into Hemsted's arms. He kissed her with deliberate passion and the Frenchwoman sighed.

Faith struggled from the wire and backed nearly to the door when Aline shrieked, then she saw Hemsted's gun. Knowledge that he was her enemy flashed across her face. "Treacherous jackal! You want *her*?" She laughed. "Too late." She aimed at Faith, but Hemsted stepped between them and took the shot.

Aline and Justin met in the center of the stairs—her going down and him running up—and Aline fired again.

Faith screamed as Justin staggered. He reached out and caught Aline's necklace, and amid a shower of jewels, the two tumbled to the floor. Aline's painted features contorted in shock, her eyes dripping black tears, she lay like a discarded marionette, her neck bent at a ghastly angle.

Justin's lifeless body lay beside her.

CHAPTER NINETEEN

THE GUNSHOT THAT grazed Justin's shoulder pained him less than his head, which, when it hit the floor, had knocked him unconscious.

Her lap his cradle, Faith wept and thanked God in turn.

Justin was too dazed to speak, but he echoed her prayers in his heart. When he gathered strength, he shifted their positions and took her into his arms, though he couldn't clutch her as tight as he wished.

When they'd salved their shattered nerves with contact long enough, Justin looked toward the top of the stairs. "Hemsted?"

"Oh, Lord," Faith said. She shot from his embrace and made for the stairs. "He took the bullet meant for me."

Justin almost blacked out again. He hadn't realized how close he'd come to losing her.

Faith knelt by Hemsted, his boyish smile a relief, and examined him. His right thigh was drenched with blood.

He cleared his throat and almost chuckled. "She aimed low when she saw it was me she'd shoot. I thank my Maker for her bad aim."

Faith's face flamed.

Justin—despite his lack of color for climbing the stairs—chuckled. "I take it she missed."

"Believe so," Hemsted replied.

"Let's see," Faith said, unbuttoning his breaches.

And both men shouted, "No!"

Despite them, Faith bound Hemsted's wound and got him to the settee where he could lie down. Binding her husband's shoulder came next. Then she checked Aline. "Her neck is broken," Faith said, and Justin nodded.

Last, Faith approached Vincent—the man who tried to kill him, then to help him. Emotions battering him, Justin followed her, never expecting to find Vincent watching them.

Justin knelt beside Faith as she fumbled to untie Vincent's cravat and tear open his shirt. Her hands quickly covered in blood, she tried to stop the flow from the largest of Vincent's wounds by pressing folded fabric against it.

Hemsted sat up. "I'm sorry, Justin. But he tried to kill you. And to save Faith, I had to make Aline spend that bullet."

Both Vincent's wounds were deadly, Justin knew, and he would tell Hemsted that later, when Vincent could no longer hear. "To save Faith's life," he repeated, stunned anew by the unthinkable. "Have I thanked you yet?"

Hemsted shook his head. "It isn't necessary. I saved her as much for myself." He smiled at Justin's frown. "You know what I mean. She's yours, I know. I guess I've always known it."

Questions came to Justin then. But they would have to wait.

"Don't try, m'dear," Vincent said as Faith ministered to him. He looked at Justin. "Wish I could change things."

Justin touched his shoulder. "You did. Tonight."

Vincent nodded imperceptibly. "Glad it's over." He nearly closed his eyes, then he opened them wide with panic and grabbed Justin's sleeve with more strength than Justin would have guessed possible.

"Beth—"

"Is mine," Justin said. "She's *mine*."

Vincent relaxed, tears in his eyes. "Yes."

He looked at Faith. "Knew when I saw you." He swallowed with difficulty, grasped Justin's hand. "Meant for you. Gave you a proper heir."

Justin nodded, his brother's face blurring, fading with his life.

Vincent's grip relaxed and he found the peace he sought at last.

Hemsted lay back on the settee as if he could hold himself up no longer, and Faith stepped into her husband's arms.

"Where's Brian?" Justin asked after a few minutes.

"Carry has him," Marcus answered, stepping into the room. He practically growled when he saw Hemsted. "Everything under control?" he asked.

Justin nodded. "Where the devil have you been?"

Marcus looked back at Hemsted, indicating him with a nod. "The rogue knocked me out, took my clothes, and locked me in the closet." He looked down at himself. "Found these in the gold bedroom." He smiled. "Carry's locked in there still—the gold bedroom that is, not the closet—bouncing that bawling tiger of yours. Can't feed 'em, I believe. Faith locked him in first, after he tried to rescue her. I locked him in second. He's not too happy with either of us."

Faith shrugged. "I was afraid you'd need me, Justin." She was playing with that silver button again.

"I'll beat you later," he said against her hair. He wasn't going to let her go for a month when this was finished.

"Why's he loose?" Marcus asked with an aggrieved look at Hemsted. "And what's he doing cozying up, I'd like to know?"

Eyebrows raised in silent question, Justin turned to Hemsted, that nagging discomfort returning. "Why do I feel as if I know you?"

"I knew you were Justin Devereux the minute Faith said you

were Justin Reddington."

"The devil you say!"

Hemsted smiled.

Justin recovered his equilibrium, though he was still perplexed. "What makes you think I'm not Justin Reddington?"

The charming man of affairs inclined his head. "Justin Reddington, at your service."

Justin barely heard Faith's gasp or Marcus's oath. He was too shaken. He'd both gained and lost a brother tonight.

"I came back to search for my identity," his newfound brother said. "Becoming Vincent's man of affairs fell in with my need to search for the truth here at Killashandra. I can tell from your look, Justin, that you already know we're half brothers."

Justin went and extended his hand. "Welcome home, Justin."

Reddington shook it. "Welcome back to the living, Justin."

"Justin and Justin," Faith said. "I'll never know which is which."

Reddington grinned. Her husband growled.

At midnight, Harris arrived with the magistrate and Aline and Vincent's bodies were taken away. "I want to bury them in the family vault," Justin said, and Faith agreed.

Justin, Marcus and Reddington watched a disgruntled Carry, a babe sucking on his cravat, return Brian to his mother.

Marcus and Carry left for London.

"Reddington, make Killashandra yours for as long as you want it. We'll find you a place of your own, eventually, get you named in the will and all that. For tonight, you can have the gold bedroom."

The new brothers shared their first hearty laugh. Harris went to fetch Mrs. Tucker to come and care for her new master.

Justin roused the coachman to take him, Brian, and Faith to Arundel. Brian slept in Faith's arms while Justin told her he couldn't live without her, and she promised he wouldn't have to.

Two people had died; a respectful silence was suitable. Still they couldn't help celebrate life with a kiss or a touch. Justin was safe and free for the first time since they had met, but Faith suspected the realization had not come to him yet. They even slept for a while, lulled by the coach's rhythm.

When they arrived, the black of night had turned to the smoky haze of morning. They went right to Beth and kissed her. She opened her eyes, smiled, said, "Poppy, Mama," and went back to sleep. Then they stood in each other's arms, savoring their new freedom to live and love for a lifetime..

"You surprised me tonight," Faith said.

"No doubt," Justin replied. "Which time?"

"You have such a jealous streak, I expected you to charge the stairs in fury when I said Hemsted was Brian's father so I could disarm Aline, or push her over the railing."

"Humph. Remind me not to cross you."

"I was frightened for your life!"

He closed his eyes and held her close. "As I was for yours."

She stepped back. "Why *didn't* you run up the stairs in a jealous rage?"

"Because I trust you."

THE END

An excerpt from

Holy Scoundrel

KNAVE OF HEARTS, BOOK FOUR

PROLOGUE

The Zebulon Fishkill Academy for Unruly Boys, 1805

BLIGHTED KNAVE!" OLD Fishface said as he tossed Gabriel Kendrick by the scruff of his neck into the heating stewpot of rotting hay, sweaty animals, and ripe manure. The Academy stable.

"Muck out a stall," the heartless schoolmaster told one of the younger dormitory discards, "and find yourself a place to sleep, like *these* scoundrels did. Simply keep the animals clean, groomed, and fed, and you might fare half as well."

Gabe regarded the blighters who came before him—the unruliest of the unruly—spines straight, proud despite their punishments, and he raised his chin as high as theirs.

"This one," Fishface said, pointing his way, "is here at the whim of an aristocrat. A charity case. Lady Bountiful does not want the vicar's son sniffing around *her* girl."

So much for the pretense of respectability, Gabe thought.

"Lord or pauper matters not to me," Fishface added, slapping his big belly, "as long as tuition is paid. These are your quarters, the lot of you. Make the best of it."

Their jailer-schoolmaster slammed the door and left them to their own devices.

"He set to kick us out of school?" Gabe asked his new inmates.

Justin Devereux, a future duke, chuckled. "'Course not. He wants the money we bring in. If he had his way, he'd keep us forever. We grow up and break out is how we leave *this* place."

"Except for Daventry here," Gabe said. "The *Lady* who . . . *sponsors* me is springing him. He's the spare to her heir."

Nick Daventry laughed. "Being *nearly* an heir is, I vow, the longest prison sentence a man can get."

Gabe eyed Justin Devereux. "You do know that your brother Vincent, *your* father's spare, got you kicked in here with a vile lie, do you not?"

Justin gave a half nod. "Since *Vincent* was not firstborn, then yes, he usually *is* my problem."

Andover, in line to be a Marquess, stepped toward him. "Kendrick? Be ye knave or scoundrel?"

Gabe thought about that. "Bit a' both, I'd say. Knave of hearts, maybe. But Fishface is right to worry about me and the girl with the title. I won't give her up." *As if her mother would let him near Lacey after this.*

"Guess we're all of a piece," Andover said. "Each a knave of hearts and scoundrels all."

Marcus Fitzalan slapped Gabriel on the back. "We have to make our time here count. Form a bond; be there for each other when needed. Swear a lifetime oath."

Andover nodded. "So for now, *and* after we go our separate ways, we show our scoundrel faces to the world but we send for each other in times of trouble, whatever life hands us?"

"I like that," Gabriel said, a vicar's son determined to match the strength of an aristocrat. "I might not be rich, but I'm strong. I can hold up my end. Whatever you say."

"Till the end of our days," Fitzalan cautioned. "We've bonded in our rebellion, and that's the strongest of friendships forged."

Gabriel smiled.

So knaves and scoundrels, lords and paupers alike, they sealed a lifetime oath, each raising a tin cup of brackish water.

And a fine pact they made of it.

CHAPTER ONE

Arundel, The South Downs, West Sussex

England, Summer 1828

L ACEY ASHTON, UNNOTICED in the midnight shadows, fixed her hungry gaze upon Gabriel Kendrick, the most formidable of the ghosts she had come home to face.

Dwarfing his surroundings, Gabriel bent to keep his head from an intimate encounter with a raw-oak barn beam while protecting the newborn lamb in his keeping, a smile in his eyes, if not on his face . . . until he saw her. Gabriel the indomitable—named for the bright angel when he should have been named for the dark—stood frozen in vulnerability.

A heartbeat, no more, and the scoundrel narrowed his eyes, stepped forward, stretched to his full staggering height, and squared his shoulders to a stunning span. Lucifer, sighting prey, spreading charred wings.

His chiseled features, graven in shadow, sharpened to unforgiving angles as his dark-fire gaze seared her.

Lacey stepped back. In that moment, despite her resolve, she wanted nothing more than to turn tail and run . . . except that she could not seem to move.

Here stood the father of her child, while between them stood the lie she'd told to deny it—saving him and tormenting him in one horrific stroke.

A horse snuffled and shuffled in its stall, freeing the scent of hay musk into the grip of silence, injecting reality into unreality, replacing the past with the present, and allowing her finally to draw breath.

As forbidding as her nemesis appeared in lantern light, dressed entirely in black, the tiny white lamb tucked into his frock coat humanized him, the contrast bringing his cleric's collar into conspicuous and bright relief.

A vicar's trappings, a scoundrel's soul, and no one seemed to know, save her.

He no longer fit the image of the young man she had carried in her heart. His features, familiar despite the firmness of his jaw, had been lined and bronzed by time and parish responsibilities to a mature and patrician air. His leonine mane, still an overlong tumble of sooty waves, thick and lush, bore strokes of gray at the temples. No phantasm here, but the bane of her existence in the flesh, more daunting, more vitally masculine. More a threat to her sanity than ever.

As if he could read her, Gabriel shifted his stance, on guard, watchful, yet before her eyes, a hard-won humility replaced his arrogance.

He did not do humble well, and his attempt jarred her.

He'd always been proud, even when they were children—he, the indigent son of a vicar who squandered parish funds; she, the daughter of a duke. But now, their roles had been reversed, and the duke's daughter stood, impoverished, disowned, before the boy who'd adored her, then hated her, with all his heart, face to face for the first time in five years. "Gabriel," she said, wishing her voice did not tremble and her body did not remember.

For his part, Gabe foolishly wondered if the sum and substance of all his dreams, good and bad, could hear the sound of his cold stone heart knocking against his ribs, bruising him to his core. "Lace," he said, her name emerging raw and raspy.

Mortified at his self-betrayal, he cleared his throat to try again, but a shadow fell between them, cutting the anguish of the moment.

Gabe focused on the newcomer. Yves "Ivy" St. Cyr stood there beaming, his little red dog at his heels. Ivy, whose puppet wagon they'd once chased giggling down High Street. The happy vagabond grasped Gabe's hand and pumped it, making him feel the dolt for failing to extend it. "Ivy," Gabe said, relieved his voice worked again.

The puppet master beamed. "I see you found the surprise I brought you."

Found it? He could not take his eyes from it.

"YES, GABRIEL," Lacey said. "I have come home."

As was her habit and his curse, she answered his unspoken thought. Whether her words eased or deepened his anxiety, he could not decide, but he hoped fervently that his shock and yearning were not as plainly writ on his brow for her to read.

"She's staying with me for now," Ivy said. "Helping with my puppet shows until she finds a place here in Arundel to live. There's *plenty* of room in my wagon."

Gabe worked to comprehend Ivy's words and form a coherent response, while the horrible gladness burgeoning inside him begged release to the point it constricted his chest and stole his breath. He found concentration necessary to fill his lungs.

"You'll stay at Rectory Cottage," he said. "Both of you. More room than in that gypsy wagon." Gabe raised a hand while Ivy prepared a token protest.

Gabe shook his head. "No argument, now." He had always suspected that Ivy enjoyed making people as well as puppets dance, though with the best of intentions. He'd probably kept Lace as up to date on his life and failings as Ivy kept him apprised of Lacey's unholy exile. So of course the puppeteer offered no argument to having a roof over his head and a hearth to warm himself. But Ivy did grin and wink at Lacey. "Took pity on my old bones, he did."

And there, Gabe thought, did they not know each other almost too well?

As Lace had once commanded, Gabe bowed before her. "My lady." Instantly, Gabe saw that his insolent use of a title was a hurtful reminder of her status before her fall from grace, and for that reason, it pierced him as well. "I apologize," he said. "That was . . . unforgivable."

"Yes, it was."

She tried, and failed, to mask her distress.

Gabe watched, his heart racing as she turned to their friend. "Ivy," she said, "I can't stay. I'll sleep in the wagon while I look for— No, I'll take the morning coach back to Sussex. Staying won't do."

Panic rushed him. Handing Ivy the lamb, Gabe placed the flat of his hand against Lacey's back to stop her retreat, turn her, and propel her toward the vicarage before she objected further.

Her familiar heat warmed his palm and spiraled like smoke from a chimney to surround his icy heart, causing a painful, thumping nudge in the center of his chest.

He retrieved his hand and fisted it in self-preservation as he looked about him for an answer to his dilemma.

The vicarage kitchen, friendly, welcoming, pleased him absurdly, seeing it as he was through Lacey's eyes. But she stepped from his reach. "I won't stay. I won't."

He could not let her go. Not again. Just thinking about the possibility wounded him. Like a knife had sliced him open, the thought of losing her again near left him bleeding.

To save himself, he turned and bent on his haunches to stoke the fire in the grate, chase the damp, and warm the undersized lamb.

Ivy's pup, a German Dachshund, placed her front paws against his thigh seeking attention, its tail beating an amiable tattoo, yet Gabe could concentrate on nothing save Lacey.

Lace home, here, in his house, where he'd pictured her a hundred times. A thousand.

His Lacey. As beautiful as ever. More beautiful. His.

No, not his. Never again his. That was past.

He was a proper vicar now, staid, unemotional, his passion a vice overcome. Long-buried. Dead. Except that it was not, he had just tonight discovered.

Gabe turned to the sound of a throat being cleared, almost surprised to find Ivy standing there, exhausted, a sleepy lamb in his arms.

"It's late; I'll prepare your rooms," Gabe said, rising from the hearth. "MacKenzie's asleep."

The lamb bleated and Gabe reached to stroke the downy-soft head against Ivy's arm.

"She's hungry, the wee thing," Lace said.

"I was planning to fix a bottle." Gabe felt stupid, overlarge, oafish beside Lace, and remembered a time that hadn't mattered.

"Did she lose her mother?" Lace asked.

Gabe relieved Ivy of his burden, feeling more comfortable with the lamb in his arms like a shield, he thought fleetingly, but against what? "She's a twin," he said, "and a runt to boot. Her mother rejected her." He stroked the fragile neck and the mite closed its eyes in ecstasy.

Obviously pierced by the memory of a mother's rejection, Lacey nevertheless watched, transfixed, as if he, *and only he*, could soothe her as well.

Hope flared in him. He saw . . . yearning . . . in her blue-green eyes. The kind that had once made him lower her to the grass and—

The fire snapped, shooting sparks into the air, breaking the taut thread of tension between them.

They both stepped back, set free by the sound.

Lace looked anywhere but at him. "I'll fix her a bottle."

"I'll get you a bottle." They spoke together, stopped together.

He gave a half-nod and set the lamb on its wobbly legs. Then he proceeded to take everything from the scullery that Lace would need to feed the mite.

Not sure what more he could say without exposing old wounds, Gabe nodded and headed out to get their bags. The click, click, click of puppy paws on the slate floor behind him assured him that Ivy and his dog followed.

ONCE GABRIEL quit the room, Lacey nearly swooned from the effort she'd expended pretending indifference while jolted out of mind.

She glanced about her at the kitchen that had been a haven for half her life. Twenty years ago, Gabriel's mother had taught her to make jam tarts and sew her first stitch by this very hearth.

Here, tonight, she came face to face with the stormy, soul-deep longing that led to her downfall—memories she could not classify; she had not come to terms with them after five years. In her mind, they were not wicked, though not quite righteous, either. Nevertheless, she'd brought upon her family the ultimate disgrace.

After the birth, and death, of her fatherless child, Ivy had taken her from here, where she grew up, to the Peacehaven Home for Downtrodden Women, in Newhaven on the Sussex Coast.

There, she'd tried to hide. But she'd been brought back to life with a vengeance and with love, first by Jade, and then her girls—women really, who had suffered at the hands of their men. Eventually, Jade's Marcus, too, had helped bring her back.

At Peacehaven, she'd regained her self-respect, grown strong, confident, assertive. She'd discovered, and finally accepted, that she must face her past before she could hope for a future.

This morning she'd set boldly forth, carrying heart-flags of purpose and determination, eager to brave the world she'd left behind . . . and ended trembling in a vicarage kitchen, fragile as the lamb butting her leg.

Despite herself, Lacey smiled at its antics. "What makes you think I have what you need? Do I look like your mama? Oh." Lace placed a hand on her aching chest. The self-inflicted wound, unexpected and sharp, the more so in this place where she had brought a fatherless, stillborn babe into the world.

Determined to calm herself before Gabriel returned, she poured milk into a pan to warm as she rinsed a lambing bottle and nipple. She reminded herself that her purpose in returning stood at hand— her little cousin, Gabriel's stepdaughter, asleep upstairs, the child she would save . . . as soon as she saved herself.

So near, yet so far. So possible, yet not. Only Gabriel stood between her and success, between joy and despair.

Some things *never* changed.

Lacey sat on the floor near the hearth and coaxed the lamb into her lap by tugging gently as it followed its grip on the nipple.

She was home. To face her ghosts. An entire village of them, specters who'd condemned her and turned their backs on her, called her wanton, and rightly so—Gabriel at their head, she sometimes suspected.

While his flock considered him a saint, they'd called her a sinner. About the latter, they were correct. About the former—

Gabriel himself—however, they were mistaken. He was human, all too human. Flawed. No one knew that better than she.

Oddly enough, she believed she'd forgiven him a long time ago. 'Twas herself she could not seem to pardon.

Gabriel returned to the kitchen after bringing Ivy and their bags upstairs, and Lacey tried to appear composed as she sat before the fire, the greedy newborn in her lap suckling lustily.

Gabriel stopped beside her, hands behind his back, a paradox of a scoundrel, bigger than life, deadly handsome, stirring her just by looking at her.

As if he realized it, he stepped away, fixing his gaze on the old oak table with its slab of a top and legs big as tree trunks. Then he sat, confused for a moment as to what to do with his beefy hands, which he placed finally on his thighs.

"Where's Ivy?" she asked, her dratted voice a wobbling croak.

"Fell asleep while I was showing him his room, the pup beside him. I took off his shoes and threw a blanket over them. Is he getting old, our Ivy?"

"The pup's name is Tweenie; she's his shadow. And he's not as old as he is stubborn. He insisted on driving through, all the way from Newhaven. I'm sorry we arrived so late; we made a late start. I'm glad we didn't awaken you."

To her dismay, Gabriel rose and dropped down beside her to stroke the drowsing lamb's lanolin-soft wool.

Too close. Oh, God, he was too close. "The Duke of Ainsley and the Marquess of Andover, who occasionally visit Marcus, also send their best. They said you were a holy scoundrel in school."

As if she hadn't spoken, the mite roused at Gabriel's attention and suckled again as if it hadn't eaten in a week, until it was pulling loudly on air bubbles.

Lacey tried to wrest the empty bottle from the lamb's grip, and as she did, Gabriel's big brown hand stroked too far and grazed her breast.

The two of them froze at the contact, gazes locked, a primitive, unnamed energy rising hot and thick between them—an intangible yet undeniable force, savage.

Lacey's heart raced, her nipples budded, her womanhood flowered. To keep from crying out at her body's betrayal, she bit her lip and tasted blood.

No wonder Jade's eagerness for Marcus, Abigail's for Marc's brother, Garrett. Love had surrounded her, not just lust. Not like this hot rush between her and Gabriel.

GABE'S BREATH left him. He struggled for air. A burning desire flared in him, molten and heavy. He'd controlled passion for years, the more so with his wife, Clara's, staunch approval after their sorry wedding night. But a minute in Lacey's company and passion, long-dead, reared up wild and alive.

Trapped. By weakness.

Strength lay in denying passion—a hard-won lesson for him. But around Lacey, lust overcame determination, and strength became a wisp of smoke where once had burned a zealot's fire.

Lacey. Lace. Home. His Lace.

No, and again, no.

She used to make him call her *Lady* Lacey when he wanted to call her Lace, like the rest of her friends did, except for the day he'd come home a new-minted parson, when he'd finally called her . . . his.

Why did he still feel like that worthless boy with the torn shirt and dirty nails? Why, when his clothes were new and his home comfortable and clean, elegant even? Why, when the gray dress Lace wore, which must once have been blue, had been mended and pressed to a pauper's shine?

Trapped. By passion. By Lacey. Gabe wanted to swear, to rage. He wanted to pull her into his arms and kiss her until she gave as good as she got. As only Lacey could.

If it were not for the fact that he wasn't the only man to know—

Gabe rose to his feet and crossed the kitchen to get as far away from her, from captivation, as possible.

He wasn't certain he could bear to be near her without taking her into his arms, any more than he could bear the constant reminder of her betrayal and his foolishness.

"I'm looking forward to spending time with my cousin," she said, her nervous rush of tumbling words pulling Gabe from pain and shivering him to his bones. He gazed at her across the room, hoping he would see no greater significance than her words betrayed. "My daughter," he said, desperate, for some strange reason, to stake his claim.

Lacey rose, lifting the lamb in her arms. "Your stepdaughter," she corrected. "I hope she hasn't forgotten her real father."

Gabe approached her then. He'd face any and all demons, real or imagined, for Bridget. "Her father died before she was born. Her mother and I married before Bridget turned two. I am the only father she knows."

"I am her cousin, kin by blood."

"Blood, as we know, does *not* always tell."

Lacey stepped back beneath the pain of his verbal blow.

As unexpected to him as to her, his barb had been born of instinct and self-preservation, but as always, her pain became his. He might just take to bleeding on her behalf, and then how foolish would he look?

Frustrated over his callous behavior, over how brutish he must appear to her, he reclaimed the lamb with more force than he intended, yet he could not seem to compose himself. He wished to the devil he didn't bloody well care how he appeared or how Lace felt. "I'll show you to your room."

Preoccupied by his demons, Gabe made for the stairs, then he realized he'd committed the unforgivable and gone before her. He should have allowed a lady to precede him as he would the lowliest in rank . . . except that Lacey was no longer a lady, he hated to remember.

Neither was he a gentleman, she had often reminded him.

He stopped to let her pass.

Holy Scoundrel is available for purchase at all major retailers.

AWARDS AND ACCOLADES:

Captive Scoundrel

1997 From the Heart Award Winner as KEEPING
FAITH, Georgia Romance Writers

1996 A Romance Writers of West Texas Author Award

ABOUT ANNETTE BLAIR

A NEW YORK TIMES bestselling author for Penguin Books, Annette Blair left her job as a Development Director and Journalism Advisor at a private New England prep school to become a full time writer. At forty books and counting, she added cozy mysteries and bewitching romantic comedies to her award-winning historical romances. Now she's stepped into the amazing world of self-publishing.

CONTACT ANNETTE

To receive updates when Annette releases a
new book, sign up for her mailing list at:

www.AnnetteBlair.com

Twitter: @AnnetteBlair

Facebook.com/AnnetteBlairFans

Made in the USA
Columbia, SC
24 February 2023

12948040R00146